Praise for

Éclair and Present Danger

"Laura Bradford has done it again. *Éclair and Present Danger* is filled with interesting, realistic characters and a plot that will keep you turning pages all the way to the sweet reveal at the end. This scrumptious new series is not to be missed."
—Paige Shelton, *New York Times* bestselling author

"A tasty, twisty tale full of felonies and flavor! Laura Bradford cooks up a delightful cast of characters led by clever amateur sleuth and dessert rescuer Winnie Johnson. The plot is delicious and moves at a swift pace, keeping the reader guessing while frantically turning the pages as Winnie tries to solve the murder of an old friend and makes sure that his killer gets his just desserts."
—Jenn McKinlay, *New York Times* bestselling author

"The wonderful whodunit is a must-read that will not allow you to put it down. I wish I could give it more than 5 stars."
—Open Book Society

Dial M
for Mousse

Laura Bradford

BERKLEY PRIME CRIME
New York

BERKLEY PRIME CRIME
Published by Berkley
An imprint of Penguin Random House LLC
375 Hudson Street, New York, New York 10014

Copyright © 2018 by Laura Bradford
Penguin Random House supports copyright. Copyright fuels creativity, encourages
diverse voices, promotes free speech, and creates a vibrant culture. Thank you for buying
an authorized edition of this book and for complying with copyright laws by not
reproducing, scanning, or distributing any part of it in any form without permission.
You are supporting writers and allowing Penguin Random House to continue to
publish books for every reader.

BERKLEY is a registered trademark and BERKLEY PRIME CRIME and the B colophon
are trademarks of Penguin Random House LLC.

ISBN: 9780425281253

First Edition: January 2018

Printed in the United States of America
1   3   5   7   9   10   8   6   4   2

Cover art by Brandon Dorman
Cover design by Judith Lagerman
Book design by Laura K. Corless.

To the many angels-on-earth who have appeared in my life when I've needed them most.

Acknowledgments

Every time I get to sit at the computer and spend a little time with Winnie and the gang, I smile. I hope, if you're here again, too, that it's because they do the same for you. But as much as I love the characters in my fictional worlds, I love the characters in my real world even more—people who make my world brighter in all sorts of ways.

With that in mind, I'd like to thank Kayla Caputo, who answered my endless questions about magic in a way that I could understand. A thank-you also goes out to my dessert-naming brainstorm buddies, Lisa Kelley, Lynn Deardorff, and Eileen Pearce—even if the silly things we came up with didn't make it into this book, they still made me laugh.

I'd also like to thank my editor, Michelle Vega, and my agent, Jessica Faust. This book marks the publication of my thirty-first book, a milestone I'm proud of for many reasons.

And, last by not least, I'd like to thank you—my readers. Whether you're just now finding me through the Emergency Dessert Squad Mysteries, or you've been a fan of my work (such as my Amish Mysteries) for a while, the fact that you're here—with this book in your hand—matters to me. I have lots more coming down the pike, so be sure to visit my website for more information: laurabradford.com.

Chapter 1

Winnie Johnson knew it wasn't polite to stare. She'd been taught that little life lesson when she was no more than three. But when you made your living baking, and your latest creation earned an elevated lip–nostril combination from one of your closest friends, it was hard to look away. "I try to tell myself it will get better—that the next go-round will surely be better than the one before, but it never happens. And I'm not the only one who feels this way, dear. Parker does, as well." Bridget O'Keefe set her plate on the wicker table beside her favorite rocking chair and raised her eyes to the porch ceiling. "Maybe it really is time to start thinking about heading south to that fancy-schmancy retirement community Louise Rickter moved to last year. I talked to her on the phone just the other day and she's convinced the warmer weather would do far more for my aching joints than any of my overpriced doctors do."

Winnie sucked in her breath so hard and so fast, Lovey

lifted her head from her slumber atop Bridget's lap and hissed. "How long have you been feeling this way? And why on earth didn't you tell me sooner?"

"I don't want to burden you with my ever-growing list of health problems, dear." Rocking forward on her chair, the eighty-year-old thrust her elbow across the gap between their chairs. "Did I tell you that I may have ankylosing spondylitis? My elbow was absolutely throbbing throughout the night."

"I'm pretty sure ankylosing spondylitis has something to do with the spine, not the elbow." Winnie rose to her feet and made a beeline for the table and the barely touched strawberry shortcake she would have laid odds on in the edible-home-run department.

A bit too much vanilla, perhaps?

Maybe a smidge less sugar?

Bridget returned her hand to the brown and white tabby's head and slumped her broad shoulders against the back of the chair. "My spine *has* been a bit creaky lately. . ."

Grabbing hold of the plate, Winnie hoisted it up to eye level.

Consistency is good . . .

Color is spot-on . . .

The creak of the screen door on the other side of the porch registered in Winnie's head a split second before her best friend's giggle and the subsequent moan of appreciation from Winnie's downstairs neighbor.

"Winnie? Did you know Mr. Nelson has had a crush on me since the moment he first laid eyes on me behind the counter at Delectable Delights?" Renee Ballentine asked over the click of her stilettos against the wooden floor.

A host of replies covering a wide range of sarcasm

danced across Winnie's tongue, but in light of the more pressing matters on her plate (both figuratively and literally) she settled on an answer that required the least amount of syllables.

"Um, *duh* . . ."

The clicking built to a crescendo before ceasing completely beside Winnie. "Are you going to keep staring at that strawberry shortcake or are you going to let me give it a try?" Renee asked.

Slowly, Winnie lowered the plate back to the table in favor of a thorough once-over of the ample-figured woman who was single-handedly responsible for Mr. Nelson's growing clip-on bow tie collection. Bypassing the cleavage view no doubt being enjoyed by her housemate, Winnie focused, instead, on the emerald green eyes twinkling back at her without a care in the world.

"Man, you're good," she mumbled before crossing her arms in front of her own (and far less endowed) chest. "So how long, exactly, have you been lying to me, too, Renee?"

Renee ran her red-tipped fingers through her pixie-style haircut and then shook any disheveled strands of white-blond hair back into place with a flick of her head (and a hard swallow from Mr. Nelson). "Did someone forget to eat her pound of sugar today?"

Bracing her hands atop her hips, Winnie widened what she hoped was an accusatory look to include a bow tie–wearing Mr. Nelson and their ailment-infested next-door neighbor, Bridget. "Did any of you ever *think*, for even a *second*, that maybe, just maybe the reason Delectable Delights failed was because you pretended you liked my desserts? And maybe, if you'd told me this, I could have used Gertie's ambulance for something entirely different like . . ." She cast about for something, anything, to drive home her point, settling finally on the feline gearing up to hiss at her for what had to be the millionth time in little more than four months. "Like an emergency *dog* spa!"

In a flash, Bridget's hands were over Lovey's ears and Mr. Nelson was caning his way over to the table, his attention no longer on Renee. "What's going on, Winnie Girl?"

"This!" Again, she lifted Bridget's plate off the table, only this time, instead of inspecting it for clues, she brandished it between them. "How many times have you guys gushed over my latest creations, telling me they're the best thing ever?"

Sticking his finger in his ear, Mr. Nelson played with the volume on his hearing aid and then made a face at Renee. "The *volume* appears to be on . . ."

"It better be." Winnie flopped onto the chair in front of Mr. Nelson's chessboard. "Was anything *ever* good? My Don't-Be-Blue Berry Pie? My Worry No s'More Bar? My One Smart Cookie? My Hot Flash Fudge Sundae?"

She stopped, closed her eyes briefly, and then jerked upright on the chair, snapping her fingers at Renee. "I saw your eyes roll back in your head when you tried that Dump (Him) Cake you helped dream up! You were in heaven! There's no way you could fake that."

"Technically, I could," Renee mused as she clicked her way over to the porch railing. "But considering I lamented the effects of that cake on the scale the next morning, you know I didn't."

"And *you*!"—Winnie shifted her next snap to indicate a clearly baffled Mr. Nelson—"I've caught you eating your way through what was supposed to be a customer's pie more times than I can count! No one *made* you do that."

Bridget took a moment to address a wide-eyed Lovey. "This is why sleep is so important, little one. People who stay up all night, trying out recipes instead of sleeping, risk going mad. I've seen it before. With Hildegard Reeves. She lived on the other side of Silver Lake and routinely gave up sleep to crochet. Needless to say, dear old Hilde spent the last few years of her life under heavy sedation in the loony bin ward of Silver Lake General."

"Look at her!"—Renee pointed at Lovey—"It actually looks like she's nodding along with what Bridget is saying, doesn't it?"

"Wit Woes."

Winnie turned a wary eye on Mr. Nelson, his mouth full with Bridget's cast-off strawberry shortcake. *"Wit woes?"*

He swallowed. "It does—look like she's nodding, that is." He lifted the remaining shortcake to his thinning lips and winked at Winnie. "This is goo-od, Winnie Girl."

"Thirty minutes ago, I'd have believed you, Mr. Nelson. But now, not so much."

He stopped chewing and stared at her. "I may be a prankster, Winnie Girl, but I ain't no liar. Never have been, never will be."

"But Bridget said you two are always hoping my desserts get better, but they don't." There was no denying the hurt in her voice or the way Mr. Nelson nearly choked on whatever amount of shortcake still remained in his mouth.

"I said no such thing!" Bridget protested.

"Yes, you did! You said it as you were rejecting the very same strawberry shortcake Mr. Nelson is eating right now!"

Bridget's eyebrows dipped downward in confusion only to return to their normal resting place in short order. "I wasn't talking about *your desserts*, dear. I was talking about the summer folks. They seem to have multiplied in number and annoyingness this year."

Wiping the back of his weathered hand across his mouth, Mr. Nelson brushed away all lingering remnants of his shortcake. "I couldn't agree more."

"So you *haven't* been humoring me about my baking these last two years?" Winnie asked as her gaze darted between Mr. Nelson and Bridget before landing on her slack-jawed employee-turned-friend. "What? It was an honest mistake . . ."

Renee crossed to Bridget's rocker, lifted Lovey from the elderly woman's lap, and then turned the animal so they were eye to eye. "I know Winnie isn't your favorite person in the world, but I think it's best if we operate on the assumption that this most recent break in her sanity is a result of Jay being out of town."

"Rendezvousing with his famous ex-wife, no less," Bridget added.

"The famous ex-wife his daughter requested to see . . ." Mr. Nelson's hand came down on Winnie's shoulder and squeezed ever so gently. "Jay Morgan knows what he has in you, Winnie Girl. I'm as certain of that as I am that your strawberry shortcake just now was the best strawberry shortcake I think I've *ever* eaten."

Blinking against the sudden and equally unwelcome mist in her eyes, Winnie smiled up at him. "Thanks, Mr. Nelson. On both counts. And I'm sorry I accused you of lying about my desserts. I guess I jumped to conclusions."

"Nothing you can't fix with another one of them short-cakes." Mr. Nelson removed his hand from her shoulder and lowered himself onto the rocking chair next to Bridget's. "So what did I miss about the summer folks?"

Bridget stopped rocking and, in a move belying her age and her oft-reported ailing health, jumped to her feet. "They're back. Isn't that enough?"

Mr. Nelson nodded.

"Last night, after I picked Ty up at Bob's, we stopped at that ice cream stand out by the lake." Renee tucked Lovey into the crook of her arm and leaned back against the porch railing. "One of them was out there, too. Just sitting on the shoreline skipping rocks."

"One of *them*?" Winnie echoed.

"The summer people. Only this one was super good-looking."

Hope pulled Winnie forward in her chair. "Did you talk to him?"

The single mom who turned more heads than the promise of free candy, shrugged. "Ty was curious about what this guy was doing. So, he wandered over to the shoreline with a few rocks of his own and tried to make them skip, too. Mystery Hunk watched him a few times and then showed him how to do it right."

"*That* sounds promising. . ."

"If he'd actually said something, maybe. But he didn't." Renee exhaled dramatically, the sudden rush of air making Lovey's ear flick in response. "Ty, of course, didn't care. He learned how to skip a rock. But when everything I said to the guy—from *Wow, you're good at that*, to *Thanks for making my son smile*—was met with a single nod of his head or a quick hand to his chest, I have to assume he wasn't interested."

"Did he have *eyes*?" Mr. Nelson asked.

"Yup. Two. And they were a real pretty charcoal color."

Mr. Nelson surveyed the now-empty plate in front of him

7

and shrugged. "Musta been a blind, charcoal-eyed mute. Only thing that makes sense about that story."

"Winnie, have I told you how much I love this man?" Renee gushed.

Before Winnie could respond, or offer Mr. Nelson a cool drink of water to counteract his sudden panting, she heard her kitchen phone ring once through the open upstairs windows. Less than a second later, the sound morphed into a vibration inside her back pocket, and she reached for the device. A quick check of the screen revealed an unknown number.

"Hello?"

A brief hesitation gave way to a female voice. "Oh, I'm sorry, I was trying to reach the Emergency Dessert Squad. I must have misdialed—"

Winnie sat up tall. "No. You didn't misdial. This is the Emergency Dessert Squad. How can I help . . ." Her words petered off as the object of Mr. Nelson's affection set Lovey down on the porch and clapped her hands.

"You're saying it wrong," Renee whispered.

Oh. Right.

Winnie cleared her throat and began again. "You've reached the Emergency Dessert Squad, please state your emergency."

"This is Sally Dearfield out at Silver Lake Artists' Retreat. I'd like to place five separate orders to be delivered to our current residents around noon on Monday."

"We can do that." She saw a pen-topped notebook sliding across the table toward her free hand and mouthed a thank-you at Renee. "Have you had a chance to look at our list of rescue desserts?"

"I have, but it mentions on your website that you can also customize to the customer. Is that true?"

Winnie opened the notebook to the first blank page and readied the pen. "Of course. I'll just need a little information about each customer, as well as specifics on their ailment or problem. If you know a little bit about their taste in flavors, that's always helpful. Oh, and I'll need to know if there are any allergies I should work around."

"No allergies. As for the recipients, there is a poet, a magician, a mime, a comedian, and a puppeteer."

"And each of their issues?" she asked, even as the creative side of her brain began to mull over a slew of possible flavor combinations and the forms each could take. "I mean, the reason they need to be rescued?"

"The potential end to their careers, for starters."

Winnie stopped writing. "So you want these to be motivational in nature?"

"I'm hoping the prospect of being penniless and publicly mortified is all the motivation they really need. But a clever little rescue dessert for their respective craft certainly can't hurt. Especially if it's timed just right."

Chapter 2

Leaning back against the center island, Winnie took in the faces assembled around her kitchen table. Bridget, who'd claimed the head chair, was detailing, to no one in particular, the reason behind her most recent wince. Lovey was half licking, half watching from her nearby windowsill hammock. Mr. Nelson kept shifting in his seat in the hopes of securing the best view of Renee. And Renee, in turn, was sending a not-so-occasional glance in the direction of the dark-haired thirty-eight-year-old seated at the far end of the table, seemingly oblivious to all but the last piece of apple pie on his plate.

"I tell you, Winnie, you should have a show on television." Greg Stevens forked up the pie's remains and lifted it to his lips, stopping just shy of inhaling it the way he had every other bite to that point. "There's no way the stuff on that dessert channel is as good as your stuff. No way, no how."

Winnie savored the momentary surge of pleasure that

always accompanied such praise and then shrugged it away as her more modest side dictated. "Thanks, Greg."

"No. Thank *you*." Greg, aka Master Sergeant Hottie, as he was known throughout Silver Lake, swallowed the last bite and pushed the plate into the center of the table, eliciting what sounded like a moan of pleasure from Renee as he did. "So what's up? Why did you call us here on a Sunday afternoon?"

"So you can brainstorm a few dessert names with me."

Renee took one last longing look at Greg's toned upper arms and slowly brought her focus onto Winnie. "Is this about that call you took out on the porch yesterday? The one from the artists' retreat?"

"It is."

"You have quite an extensive menu as it is, dear," Bridget reminded.

"For now, I suppose. But Sally Dearfield, the woman I spoke to, wasn't terribly specific about what she wanted beyond, perhaps, a motivational twist." Winnie plucked the printout from the center of the island and gave it a little wave. "However, she did e-mail me some information about each of the recipients along with the name of the respective cottage he or she is staying in for delivery purposes."

Pulling the page close, she began to read aloud. "First, there's Colin Norton. He's a poet." She looked over at the table and the four pairs of eyes trained on hers. "So I'm thinking something with a deadline. Or maybe a nod to writer's block."

"You could do something with a block of fudge, perhaps," Bridget suggested.

"That's certainly something we can play with." Winnie returned her attention to the paper and the next name on the list. "Then there's Todd Ritter. He's a magician."

11

Renee clapped her hands. "Tricks! Rabbits! Poof!"

"Whoa, whoa, whoa . . . Let me tell you about everyone else before we start throwing around ideas, okay?" Winnie moved on to the third line. "And then we've got George Watkins."

"George Hawkins? I know a George Hawkins." Mr. Nelson ran his crooked fingers along his stubbled jawline before bringing his hand down to the table with a *thump*. "But George ain't got any teeth on account of pickin' one too many fights at the VFW hall over the years."

Winnie stifled the urge to laugh, and instead tapped her finger to her ear and waited. Then, when Mr. Nelson had adjusted the volume on his hearing aid, she repeated the name. "This man's name is George *Watkins*, Mr. Nelson. He's a mime."

"A mime?" Greg echoed. "Seriously?"

"That's what it says in Sally's e-mail."

"I think it would be mighty difficult to be involved with a mime," Bridget mused.

Mr. Nelson practically choked on his laugh. "See, now I think a mime would be a perfect mate for you, Bridget. After all, it's not like anyone can ever get a word in edgewise around you, anyway."

"Oh snap!"

Bridget shifted her glare from Mr. Nelson to Renee and back.

Uh-oh.

"Moving right along . . ." Winnie dropped her gaze back down to the paper and the final two names on the e-mailed list. "There's Abby Thompson, a puppeteer, and Ned Masterson, a comedian."

Greg pushed back his chair, rose to his feet, and wandered over to Lovey's windowsill hammock. "Can you do something with a funny bone for the comedian, maybe?" He scratched Lovey behind the ears and then moved on to the area on both sides of the cat's spine. "You know, maybe tie it in to a break somehow?"

"Hmmmm . . ." Winnie carried the paper over to the table and swapped it for her idea book and its accompanying pen. "Maybe what we should do is brainstorm words for each artist. Perhaps one of those words will lead us to the right dessert."

Opening the notebook to the first clean page she could find, she brought the focus back to Colin Norton, the poet. "So what words come to mind when you think of a poet?"

"Rhyming!" Renee offered.

Bridget nodded. "Short!"

"How about haiku?" Greg gave Lovey one last scratch between the ears and then stretched his arms above his head. "Man, I was so bad at those in school. I spent way too much time clapping out syllables rather than actually trying to write anything coherent."

"Wait. What about meter?" Bridget suggested.

"And the writer's block idea you mentioned earlier—don't forget that." Renee reached across the table, plucked the pen and notebook from Winnie's hand, and took over writing duties. "Anyone have any dessert ideas we can springboard off *short*, *rhyming*, *haiku*, *meter*, or *writer's block*?"

"We could do Go Away, Writer's Block of Fudge or . . ." Winnie stood, walked two feet, and spun around. "I know! I could make a s'more-flavored fudge and we could call it—"

"No s'More Writer's Block of Fudge!" Greg and Bridget said in unison.

Winnie laughed and then pointed at Renee and the notebook. "Put that one down for now. It's certainly a strong contender for our resident poet, Colin Norton."

"Who's next?" Bridget asked.

Winnie consulted the e-mail and then made her way back to the table. "Todd Ritter. Our magician. So go ahead, start shouting out words . . ."

"Tricks!" Renee shouted. "Rabbits!"

"Top hat!"

Winnie nodded at Greg and then smiled at her house-mate. "Mr. Nelson? Any thoughts from you?"

"Now you see 'em, now you don't."

Bridget exhaled her frustration loud enough for everyone to hear. "And how on earth is Winnie supposed to work *that* into a dessert, Parker?"

"If she can work a rabbit into a dessert, she can work a sleight of hand into a dessert, too." Mr. Nelson stuck his finger in his ear and looked up at Winnie. "You think, with the way technology is explodin', that maybe these hearing-aid folks could finally come up with a way to let people like me block out specific voices?"

Winnie started to laugh but stopped as the man's words hit their mark. "Wait—sleight of hand! That's it!"

Resting the pen atop the notebook, Renee cocked her head in such a way as to afford a quick view of Mr. Nelson, Bridget, and Greg all at the same time. "Brace yourselves, everyone. Winnie is about to blow."

"No. No. This is great. I can make Sleight of Hand Pies! And I can fill them with all sorts of different things—apples, cherries, blueberry, lemon, whatever. The possibilities are endless, quite frankly."

"I called it, didn't I?" Renee mused as she retrieved her pen and began to write.

Greg joined Winnie over by the island. "You could also do something with hand pies for the mime, you know."

"Yes, let's move on to the mime." A quick check of the printout refreshed her memory on the name—George Watkins. "Mime . . . mime . . . Anyone?"

"Waves hands!" Renee suggested.

Bridget wrapped her fingers around her empty coffee mug and pulled it against her chest. "Quiet. Silent."

"Hold on a minute, Winnie Girl. Greg makes a good point. If you're making hand pies for the magician fella, why can't you make some extras and give them to the mime?" Mr. Nelson pulled his ball cap off and scratched the top of his head. "And if you decided to make some of them snickerdoodle pies like you made me for my birthday last year, I'd be willing to take any leftovers off your hands."

"Ever the philanthropist," Bridget mumbled.

Greg pointed at the refrigerator and, at Winnie's nod, helped himself to a can of soda. "I think you should save anything snickerdoodle-related for the comedian. It fits better."

"The comedian?" Renee looked up from the notebook and blinked (doelike) in Greg's general direction. "Why?"

"You know . . . the snickers part."

Winnie did a little jig where she stood. "Yes! Yes! When in Doubt, Go for Snicker-Doodles! Or . . . maybe . . . It's All About the Giggles and the Snicker-Doodles . . . or—"

"Your Jokes Make Me Snicker-Doodle," Greg said as he lifted the soda can to his lips and took another sip.

"That's it! Perfect!" Winnie pointed to Renee. "Write that one down exactly the way Greg said it."

Renee started to write but looked up at Winnie instead. "So you want me to put that under the comedian instead of the mime?"

"Yup." Winnie stopped jigging long enough to consult her printout and the last name on the list. "The snicker-doodles are for Ned Masterson."

"Ned Masterson?"

"That's the comedian's name."

"Oh. Okay." Renee jotted the dessert name down and then shifted back in her seat, robbing Mr. Nelson of his carefully arranged cleavage view. "But now we still don't have anything for the mime."

"Let's put him on hold for a little while and move on to the puppeteer." Again, Winnie checked the printout. "Abby Thompson."

"Marionettes!"

Renee pointed her pen at Bridget and added, "Strings! Paper bags! Socks!"

Strings . . .

Running her finger down the list, Winnie paused next to Abby's name.

No allergies . . .

Prefers low sugar . . .

"I know. I'll go with string cheese—quartered and rolled in a variety of things like hazelnut, peanut butter, jimmies, nuts, or whatever, and we can call it, World on a String-Cheese Treats or Never Let 'Em See the String-Cheese Treats."

Greg lowered his soda can in favor of a hearty laugh that echoed around the kitchen. "I like Never Let 'Em See the String-Cheese Treats. Too funny."

"You think?"

"Definitely."

Mr. Nelson snapped his fingers and gestured toward the notebook in front of Renee. "Might want to lean forward again and write that one down, pretty lady."

It was Winnie's turn to laugh as Renee folded herself back over the notebook and into Mr. Nelson's preferred sight range. A glance at Greg netted a visual match to her own amusement.

"So are you done with us, Winnie?"

She turned her focus toward the not-so-amused Bridget. "I am. But you guys were all amazing. I couldn't have come up with these names without you."

Renee dropped her pen onto the notebook and rose to her feet. "That's not true and we all know it. But this was still fun. Gave me something to do while Ty is with Bob for the day."

"Trust me, everyone's input was invaluable. Always is."

Pulling his cane out from its holding spot beneath the table, Mr. Nelson mirrored Renee's movement toward the door and then paused to glance back at Winnie. "When you're deciding on your fillings for those hand pies, remember to stay away from blackberries. You don't need any more dead bodies on your hands, Winnie Girl. It's not good for business."

Chapter 3

Winnie slowed the Dessert Squad to a stop at the traffic light and shifted her focus from the road to the passenger seat. "I have to say, it's a little weird having someone other than just Lovey sitting up here in the cab with me."

"Trust me, it's weird for me, too." Renee pulled her hand off Lovey's back and gave her fingernails a thorough once-over. "Usually when you head out on a call, I clean up the kitchen and then man the phones while either watching television or the goings-on out on the street."

Winnie's answering laugh yielded a sleepy hiss from Lovey. "You say that like Serenity Lane is a hot bevy of entertainment."

"Because it is!" Renee stopping fawning over her latest choice in nail color and widened her eyes on Winnie. "I used to think your neighbor Cornelia Wright was so focused on walking that little sheltie of hers that she simply wasn't aware of Harold Jenkins following along behind her on his electric scooter thingy. But not only is she *aware* he's back there, I think she's actually throwing out the bread crumbs for him to follow."

The light changed from red to green and Winnie moved her foot to the gas pedal. "I'm pretty sure Cornelia isn't the bread-baking type."

"Ha. Ha." Renee brought her hand back down to Lovey and ran it along the feline's back. "Seriously though. What woman wears a pencil skirt and heels to walk her dog? And who stops to check their lipstick while walking said dog?"

"*You* would," Winnie pointed out, grinning. "*If* you had a dog, of course."

"If I knew Master Sergeant Hottie was following me— yes. And therein lies my point."

It made sense. It really did. Still, though, Winnie wasn't entirely convinced Renee's summation was correct. Cornelia Wright seemed perfectly content with her beloved little dog, Con-Man. And really, Harold Jenkins? The man wore flannel twenty-four/seven . . .

Shaking her head, she made herself focus on the task at hand. Or, rather, tasks. "Okay, so what's the next direction? I know we head around the lake, but beyond that, I'm not a hundred percent sure."

"Take the road that skirts the northern edge of the lake to the first gravel lane *after* the public-access parking lot. It should be on our left." Renee lowered the passenger side window halfway and lifted her chin to its answering summer breeze. "So did you talk to Mr. Wonderful at all this weekend? Has he seen her yet?"

More than anything, Winnie wanted to pretend she didn't know who or what Renee was talking about. But she couldn't. Besides, maybe Renee could offer a fresh take she, herself, had been unable to see thus far.

"Jay called briefly last night as I was getting ready for bed," said Winnie.

"And?"

"He and Caroline arrived at the hotel around five o'clock our time."

"And?"

"The flight went okay from what I could tell. Caroline was in the room with him so I'm not sure if I was getting the whole story or a watered-down version."

Renee sighed. "Of course it wouldn't even enter the little diva's brain to give you two a few minutes alone, right? Or perhaps it *did* and that's *why* she stayed put."

"Anyway, not more than five minutes into our conversation, Didi texted Jay to tell him she was in a limo outside the hotel's front door. So he had to get off and, you know, deal with all of *that*."

"It still bothers me that eleven years have gone by since that sorry excuse for a mother walked out on Caroline and now, suddenly, Caroline feels this urgent need to reconnect with her? I mean, c'mon." Renee scrunched her perfectly proportioned nose at the brown and white tabby purring peacefully in her lap. "Something smells pretty bad in all of this, doesn't it, Lovey?"

Winnie passed the lake on her side of the car and then turned left. Renee's words were not much different from the ones that had been playing in her own head as Jay had ended the call the previous night. Still, she needed to step back. To entertain all aspects. "I—I think it makes sense. High school isn't for sissies—we both know this. And while Jay is an amazing dad, I'm sure there are things Caroline would rather bounce off her mom."

"Didi Evans stopped being that kid's mom the day she walked out of her life," Renee argued. "Why Caroline can't see that blows my mind. Then again, why she'd want to mess with her dad's happiness blows my mind even more."

Renee was right. Caroline's timing was most definitely suspect. Especially when it came on the heels of Jay really stepping up his game where his and Winnie's relationship was concerned.

"Maybe you're right," Winnie conceded. "Maybe there *is* something less than innocent behind Caroline's sudden longing to see her mother. But even if there is, it shouldn't have any bearing on my relationship with Jay."

At Renee's prolonged silence, she checked the rearview mirror and then slowed the Dessert Squad to a near crawl. "What aren't you saying, Renee?"

"Just the kind of things newly divorced women tend to think in situations like this, which, translated, means nothing you should worry your dessert-naming brain over." Renee waved her hand in the space between them and then pointed toward a sizable gap in the trees just beyond the public access parking lot. "See that over there? I think that's our turnoff."

Winnie followed the path indicated by Renee's finger and slowly piloted the ambulance onto the gravel lane. Part of her wanted to know what her newly divorced friend was thinking on the subject of Jay, but the part of her that loved what she did for a living knew it was time to focus on the day's rescues. Like her emergency Dessert Squad, Silver Lake Artists' Retreat was a fairly new enterprise in town.

If Sally was pleased with Winnie's assorted dessert rescues, it could spell more business in the future . . .

"Are you ready for your first, second, third, fourth, and fifth rescues?" she asked as they bounced from one gravelly rut to another.

Renee released a cheerleader-esque squeal that perked Lovey's ears upright. "Yes! But what do I do? Do I push the gurney? Do you need me to hang the frosting bag on the IV pole?"

"Just follow behind Lovey, she'll show you what to do."

"Seriously?"

"You doubt me?" Winnie countered.

"No, but . . ."

Winnie slowed to a stop as they reached the first in a row of rustic cabins. "Okay . . . According to the number on the door right there, this is cabin number one. Who did Sally say was assigned to this one?"

"I'll tell you in one second." Renee smoothed Sally's e-mail across the portion of her lap not covered by Lovey and ran her finger past the details of each artist to the specifics on their accommodations. "It looks like this is Ned Masterson—the comedian."

"So Your Jokes Make Me Snicker-Doodles are up at bat." Winnie shifted the ambulance into park and smiled at her best friend and employee. "You ready?"

"You bet I am."

They were just heading out of the fourth cottage with Lovey in tow when Renee grabbed hold of Winnie's arm—hard.

"Whoa. Watch those talons, my friend. They're lethal."

Renee brought her lips to within exhale range of Winnie's ear. "It's him!"

Halting the gurney midway down the walkway, Winnie looked left and right. "Who?"

"The supercute guy from the lake the other night."

When she spotted nothing resembling a human, she widened her visual range to include the pathway that ran behind the cottages. Sure enough, a man Winnie judged to be in his midthirties was making his way toward the retreat's main building, his head dipped down, his hands jammed into the front pockets of his jeans. "You mean the rock skipper who never spoke?"

"Yes!" Renee shout-whispered. "Isn't he *gorgeous*?"

"I can't really tell. He's moving rather fast."

"Well, he *is*. His eyes are almost a charcoal gray and his hair has this playful little swoop in the front." Renee followed him with her gaze until he was completely out of sight and then turned back to Winnie and sighed. "I swear, it took everything I had not to walk over to him and run my hands through his hair that night."

"I bet *that* would have gotten him talking . . ." Winnie smacked her hand over her mouth only to let it slide down to her chest as she began to laugh. "Oh my gosh, this is too funny."

Renee's slightly overwaxed left eyebrow arched upward. "What is?"

"You described him the other day as tall, dark, and brooding. But he wasn't brooding at all."

"How do you know?" Renee asked, bringing her hands to her hips. "You weren't there."

"But he's *here*. At the artists' retreat. And if I'm right, we caught him as he was leaving the back door of cabin number five."

"So?"

She pulled Sally's e-mail from inside the packet and turned it so Renee could see the name residing just below her fingertip. "That's George Watkins. He's the mime."

"Noooo."

"Oh yes. In fact, I'd bet"—Winnie waved the paper at the shelf beneath the gurney—"Lovey, here on it."

Hisss . . .

"But why didn't he talk at the lake?" Renee protested. "He wasn't performing."

Winnie stuck her tongue out at her bequeathed cat and then continued pushing the gurney toward the Dessert Squad parked at the end of the sidewalk. "I guess he was just practicing. Like I do every time I experiment with a new combination of flavors."

Renee's shoulders drooped. "So he's not going to be in his cabin for his rescue, either?"

When Winnie reached the ambulance she pushed the gurney around to the back and opened the gate. "You heard what Sally said when I called her from outside the comedian's place. Just set the dessert inside on the table and move on."

"But what's the fun in that?" Slowly, Renee headed down the walkway toward Winnie, her stilettos making soft clicking sounds against the concrete. "She could call a regular bakery for that."

"Bite your tongue."

"Well, she could . . ."

Winnie waved off her friend's argument and, instead, focused on placing the plate of assorted hand pies where the plate of string cheese treats had most recently been. "Look, if Sally specified a delivery time and then opted to call a meeting for her recipients in another location at the exact same time, that's her choice. You heard me offer to make all five of the deliveries to the main building. But she declined."

Renee lifted her hands into the air. "I know, I know. It just doesn't make any sense."

"I guess the meeting wasn't as short as she seemed to think it would be." Winnie reached into the warming container and extracted the bag of white chocolate drizzle. "Here, can you hang this on the IV pole and follow me up to the last cabin?"

"But why? We already know he's not there. Why not just drizzle the stuff on the pies now?"

"Because that's not how we do things. Besides, your hot mime could get to the main building only to find out the meeting is already over. He could walk back here in like two seconds." She shut the back gate and looked down at Lovey. "You ready for round five, Your Highness?"

Hisss. . . .

"I'll take that as a yes, you nasty thing." Winnie motioned for Renee and the IV pole to follow her onto the walkway. "Do you think this cat is *ever* going to wrap her pointy-eared head around the fact that I'm her new owner?"

"When you asked me that the first dozen times or so after Gertie willed her to you, I was certain she would. But now? I'm not so sure."

"Great."

"An adversarial relationship doesn't necessarily have to be tragic." Renee and the pole moved into place alongside Winnie and the gurney. "Just so long as you both keep your proverbial and not-so-proverbial claws to yourself, it'll be okay. Besides, Lovey has Bridget, Mr. Nelson, and me to give her affection."

Laura Bradford

Winnie stopped the gurney. "To give *Lovey* affection? Are you kidding me?"

"Suck it up, my friend," Renee said. "Suck. It. Up."

She looked from Renee to Lovey and back again and then resumed her trek up to the front door of the mime's cabin, the soles of her paramedic shoes no longer silent against the walkway. "I'm not asking for her to lick my face. I'm not asking her to rescue me from a burning building. I'm simply asking that she stops hissing at me every time I so much as look at her. Is that really that much to ask when I'm the one who provides her food, her shelter, and her unending supply of cat toys?"

"Apparently, yes."

When they reached the door, Winnie straightened up, pushed away her angst with a deep cleansing breath, and knocked.

"Why are you knocking?" Renee asked. "We already know he's not in there."

"Maybe, while you were dashing any hope I had for my relationship with Lovey, he came back." When there was no answer to a second and third knock, Winnie opened the front door as Sally had instructed. "Then again, maybe he didn't."

Winnie reached up, disengaged the IV tube from the bag of melted white chocolate, and drizzled its contents across the top of each and every hand pie. When she was done, she nudged her chin in the direction of the plate. "So what do you think? Does it look good?"

"It looks fabulous." Renee lifted the plate of hand pies off the gurney and carried it through the short hallway to the galley-style kitchen.

"Don't forget our business card."

"Got it, boss." Three slow inhales later, Renee was back and pulling the door closed behind them. "He's not even *in* there and the place smells like masculine awesomeness."

Winnie couldn't help but laugh as Renee took two steps toward the ambulance only to stop and look back longingly at George Watkins's cabin. "This guy really left an impression on you, huh?"

"He was amazing with Ty. So patient. So encouraging."

"But you said he didn't speak."

"His smile and his head nods said it all." Renee wheeled the pole down the walkway, collapsed it down to a third of its normal size, and tucked it in the back of the ambulance as Winnie prepared the gurney.

"We *could* stop by the main building on the way out if you'd like. You know, just to tell Sally the deliveries have all been made . . ."

Renee ran around the side of the ambulance and examined her reflection in the passenger side window. Two flicks of her hair later, she was yanking the door open and calling for Lovey to pick up the pace.

"So I take it you like that idea?" At Renee's emphatic nod, Winnie slid the gurney into its holding spot in the back, locked and closed the tailgate, and ventured around to the driver's-side door. Once she was settled behind the steering wheel, she pointed at the cat already seated in her friend's lap. "This time, Lovey, you stay put. It's one thing to stow away on the bottom of the gurney where most people don't notice you, and quite another to just stroll right into a meeting."

Hissss . . .

"Do you see? This cat is out of control."

"Try talking to her in a slightly nicer tone of voice." Renee leaned forward, planted a kiss between Lovey's ears, and was rewarded for her efforts with a distinct purr. "It's not rocket science, Winnie. It's really not."

Winnie opened her mouth to protest—to reference all the olive branches she'd offered to the ungrateful beast—but let it go as she piloted the Dessert Squad into the visitor parking spot outside the retreat center's main building. "Okay. Moving on. Are you ready to meet your hand-flapping hunk?"

The question wasn't meant to be rhetorical, but when Renee's answer came in the form of the blonde bombshell's rapid exit from the car, it had clearly been interpreted as one.

Well, alrighty, then . . .

Winnie slid out of the ambulance and met Renee en route to the door. On the way, she shoved her hand inside the inner pocket of her EDS jacket and extracted a business card. "Might as well leave this with Sally so she's got it at her fingertips when the next group of artists comes in, don't you think?"

Shrugging, Renee pulled open the door and stepped inside, her emerald green eyes dancing with excitement. "You do realize I have a new mission in life, yes?"

"Oh?" Winnie maneuvered around her friend and led the way down the hallway toward the murmur of voices coming from an open room on the left. They passed a small but well-stocked library and an even smaller business center complete with two computers and a single printer. "And what, exactly, is this new mission—"

The collective gasp that greeted their arrival in the meeting room doorway had Winnie hooking her thumb over her shoulder and bumping into Renee. "I—I'm sorry, I wasn't trying to interrupt—"

"Winnie! Look!"

She followed Renee's red-tipped finger down to the floor

and the sixty-something woman lying facedown at their feet. Before she could process the scene, the man Renee had pointed out to her not more than twenty minutes earlier flopped onto the ground and stared unseeingly up at the ceiling, his hands splayed atop his throat.

Seconds later, the lone standing female in the group staggered against the wall, her hand moving inside the puppet clutched to her chest. "You mean it's—it's . . . over?"

"Anyone got a fork?" quipped a balding man on the far side of the circle. "That could probably tell us for sure."

Another man, this one wearing a top hat, waved a closed fist above the body and—*poof!*—opened his fingers to produce a fork. "Voilà!"

"What's going on in here?" Winnie demanded as her gaze traveled back down to the lifeless body.

"If I may quote the words of fellow poet Mary Elizabeth Frye: 'Do not stand at my grave and weep; / I am not there. I do not sleep. / I am a thousand winds that blow. / I am the diamond glints on snow.'" A tall man with a thick crop of dark blond hair met Winnie's eyes and guided them back toward the ground with his finger. "Or, in the words of the unread masses, Sally Dearfield is dead."

Chapter 4

Winnie followed Lovey onto the front porch and collapsed into the rocking chair next to Mr. Nelson and his one-man chess game. "Well, *that* didn't go the way I'd hoped."

Pulling his hand from the white bishop, the seventy-five-year-old former navy man consulted his watch. "What took you so long, Winnie Girl? I expected you home hours ago."

"Where should I start . . ." She tipped her chin upward and stared at the porch ceiling they'd treated to a fresh coat of paint not more than three weeks earlier. "Wait. I know. It was a disaster—a complete and utter disaster."

A flash of movement out of the corner of her eye brought her housemate's chessboard back into her sight line in time to see the black rook removed from the board in a burst of celebration. "Aha! Gotcha!"

She swung her attention toward the Dessert Squad and did her best to focus on the bright colors of the logo rather than the memory of Sally Dearfield's face as Greg and his EMT, Chuck, confirmed what Winnie, Renee, and the five assembled artists had already known.

"Winnie Girl?"

Swallowing against the lump she felt forming in the base of her throat, she made herself look at Mr. Nelson once again, the smile she wanted to have for him nowhere to be found.

"Did something go wrong with your rescues?" he asked as he abandoned his game play in favor of Winnie. "You don't look too good."

"Sally Dearfield is dead."

He stared at her over the rim of his glasses and then removed them from his face completely. "You put blackberries in some of those hand pies, didn't you?"

"No. But even if I had, she dropped dead in the main building. My desserts were waiting for the artists in their respective cabins."

With a quick snap of his fingers, he summoned Lovey onto his lap. "Is that what all those sirens were 'bout two hours ago? Sounded like New York City for a few minutes."

"Greg and his crew responded in the eventuality Sally was still alive—but she wasn't. The cops, of course, came, and a little while later, so did the chief."

"Russ Vanwinkle was out there, too?"

She drew back, confused. "Russ who?"

"The butcher out at Silver Lake Market."

"Noooo. Why would he be there?"

Mr. Nelson ran his hand down Lovey's back. "Because he's the only one who knows quality beef."

"Quality beef—" And then she knew. Mr. Nelson's hearing aid was either too low or in need of a battery. She tapped her ear and waited for him to make the necessary adjustment. When he did, she took the conversation back to the veer-off spot. "*Chief* Rankin was out at the scene."

"The chief there for any particular reason?" Mr. Nelson asked without missing a beat.

"Because there was a dead body, I imagine."

Mr. Nelson pulled his hand off Lovey and leaned forward. "Do you think there was some hanky-panky involved?"

The lump was back. Only this time, it tasted a lot like bile. She swallowed it back down and willed herself to breathe. "I don't know."

"Was she alone when they found her?" he asked.

"All five of the artists in residence at the retreat center this week were with her when it happened."

He resumed his petting of Lovey but kept his eyes rooted to Winnie's. "What do you think happened?"

"I don't know. I guess maybe she had a heart attack or something." Pulling her mousy brown ponytail in front of her shoulder, she played with the ends while she mentally revisited the moment she and Renee walked into the building—the murmur of voices morphing into a collective gasp as they stopped inside the . . .

She sat up tall. "Wait a minute! That gasp!"

"Winnie Girl?"

Rising to her feet, she paced her way around the porch—from the rocker, to the front railing, to the side railing, and back to the rocker, only to do it all over again. Granted, she was probably a little traumatized from everything that had happened that afternoon, but her memory had always been one of her strong suits. There was no reason to think that had failed her now.

"Mr. Nelson? I think they gasped for our benefit."

"*Our* benefit?"

"Mine and Renee's."

A familiar flush of color creeped into his cheeks, prompting her to stop midway through her third lap to wave it away lest she lose him to his favorite fantasy world. "Not now, Mr. Nelson. This is serious."

He cleared his throat and gave her his best concentration face. "I'm listening."

"Just now, thinking back over the scene . . . There was a shattered teacup next to Sally's body that Greg postulated broke as a result of Sally's falling." Winnie resumed her pacing, her feet suddenly propelled by more than just her legs. "But we didn't hear anything shattering! And they gasped when we stepped into the doorway—as if Sally had just collapsed at that moment! But she couldn't have. If she had, we'd have heard the cup shattering!"

Lovey eyed Winnie suspiciously from her spot on Mr. Nelson's lap—a lap that was now inching forward on the chair, thanks to Winnie's words. "You think one of them artists killed her?"

Was it possible?

Was that why they all seemed so cavalier about Sally's death?

"Winnie Girl?"

She reached the front railing and turned to face her friend, the horror of finding another dead body bowing to the sudden certainty of her answer. "I'd bet the Dessert Squad on it."

She was just putting away the last of the ingredients from her early-morning baking session when Renee strode into Winnie's apartment with a large brown bag and a drink carrier in her hands. "Ty is having dinner at Bob's, so I'm having dinner here . . . with you. Don't worry, though, I stopped at Luigi's on the way here and picked up a meat-filled ravioli for me, chicken farfalle for you, and a little tiny scoop of pureed meat for Lovey."

Winnie closed the cabinet above the sink, rehung the dishcloth on its hook, and crossed to the table and the intriguing aromas emanating from the now open to-go bag. "Oh. Wow. You have no idea how good that sounds right now."

"So you don't have other plans?"

"Nope." Retracing her steps, she returned to the cabinets to secure two plates and the necessary silverware for their meal. "Now that everything is cleaned up from this morning's deliveries, I have no other plans."

"Hey, I'm sorry I didn't come back here with you after everything that happened but—"

"There was no way of knowing our deliveries would end with a dead body and having to wait on Chief Rankin to ask us questions." Winnie set the plates and silverware on the table and sank onto the bench seat as Renee reached into the bag, pulled out each of their meals, and then claimed the spot on the opposite side of the table. "Which brings me to the fact that I've been unable to think of anything else since I got home."

Renee opened the plastic lid on her ravioli and scooped a generous helping onto her plate, her green eyes bouncing between the food and Winnie. "You and me, both."

"Can I ask you something?" Winnie said, pausing her fingers atop her still-sealed meal.

"Shoot."

"What's your gut say about what happened at the retreat house today?"

"You mean besides the fact it's the first time I've seen a dead body up close and personal?" Renee forked up a ravioli and popped it into her mouth.

Winnie opened her own meal and took a moment to breathe in the medley of scents before transferring some food onto her own plate. "I'm talking, specifically, about what you think might have happened to Sally."

"I don't know. Maybe a heart attack? She was packing quite a few extra pounds around her middle, if you noticed." Piercing another ravioli onto her plate, Renee inspected it closely and then popped it into her mouth, too. "Not that I should talk, of course. Ever since Bob traded me in for a younger model, the numbers on the scale have been creeping upward—a pound here, a pound there."

"Oh, please. You look fabulous twenty-four/seven, Renee." Winnie took a bite of her farfalle and then chased it down with a quick sip of soda. "I spoke to Greg by phone about an hour ago, and he said the medical examiner is pretty certain Sally didn't die of natural causes."

Renee stopped chewing. "Meaning?"

"They detected a bitter almond smell on her body."

"So? She ate some almonds before she dropped. Does that really matter?"

"A bitter almond smell is often an indicator of cyanide poisoning." Winnie ate a few more bites and then pushed her plate forward. "Pieces of the shattered teacup have tested positive for it as well."

"Why would she put cyanide in her tea . . ." The question disappeared between them as Renee's eyes widened. "Wait. Are you saying what I think you're saying?"

Winnie spotted another piece of farfalle that looked particularly tempting and ate it quickly. "If you think I'm say-

Laura Bradford

ing Sally was very likely murdered, then yes, I'm saying what you think I'm saying."

"But why? And by whom?"

"I can't answer the why. But as for who might have done the deed . . . I'm thinking it was one of the people in that room when we found her."

Renee sucked in a breath and, in the process, made herself choke on a ravioli. A sip of water and a few coughing fits later, she was ready to speak. "Do you think it was my hot mime?"

"*Your* hot mime?"

"I saw him first."

"I'm not trying to claim him, Renee, I'm just asking about your choice of pronouns, is all." Winnie swiveled to the side, threw her leg over the bench, and carried the small container of pureed meat over to Lovey's bowl. "Lovey! Renee brought you a treat."

A slight jingle from her bedroom grew louder until the brown and white tabby was peering around the corner of the kitchen. When Lovey spotted the addition to her bowl, she pranced all the way into the room as Winnie straightened and returned to the table and her still wide-eyed friend.

"Winnie, you can't leave me hanging like this . . ."

"I don't know if it was your hot mime or not, Renee. It could have been him, or it could have been one of the other four. *That* part, I haven't figured out yet." She grabbed hold of her to-go container and gave it a little shake. "Do you want to take the rest of this home for you and Ty for tomorrow?"

At Renee's nod, she deposited it back in the bag and carried her plate over to the sink. "But I *will*. One way or the other."

"You will what?"

Winnie considered washing the dish right then and there, but opted instead to rejoin Renee at the table. "Figure out which one of them killed her."

"Uh, don't you think maybe you should let Rankin do that? It is, after all, um, sort of *his job* . . ."

"And, hopefully, he'll do it. But you and I both know there's only so much you can accomplish when you only show up at the office for an hour here and an hour there."

Renee closed up her ravioli container and added it to the bag, her eyebrows furrowed. "Last I checked, we were still trying to grow EDS's business."

"And we are."

"So, don't you think that's a better place to expend your energy?"

"I do. And I will. Figuring out who killed Sally and why doesn't have to affect that." She pointed at Renee's plate and, at the woman's nod, added it to the sink. "I have a couple of hand pies left from this morning. Do you want one?"

Renee leaned around the edge of her bench, clicked her tongue behind her teeth, and summoned Lovey to her side. "What do you have?"

"Apple, blueberry, and strawberry."

"I'll take the apple." Renee lifted Lovey onto her lap and, using her long nails, scratched the cat behind the ears while simultaneously sizing up Winnie. "I guess the part I don't get is why it matters. I mean, don't get me wrong, it's horrible that woman is dead—doubly so if she was murdered. But you didn't even really know her, did you?"

Winnie placed a plump apple hand pie on a dessert plate, added a fork, and passed it across the table to Renee. "The only conversation I ever had with the woman was when she placed the order and when we called her outside the first cabin to find out how she wanted us to handle a no-show."

Setting Lovey on the bench beside her, Renee took a bite of the apple hand pie and released a moan of pleasure. "So, so good." After a few more bites, she met Winnie's gaze once again. "Then I repeat, why does it matter?"

"Because we were played this morning, Renee, and it ticks me off."

"Played?"

Winnie recounted what she'd figured out while talking to Mr. Nelson earlier that afternoon and then leaned against the center island while Renee digested her words. Sure enough, the hand pie was abandoned for a fist smack atop the table. "You know what? You're right! I didn't hear a cup shatter . . . and I didn't hear any sort of thump, either. If she'd collapsed as we reached the door, we should have heard both!"

"My sentiments ex—" A series of vibrations against her skin stole the rest of her sentence and sent her reaching into her back pocket for her phone. A quick check of the caller ID screen brought an instant flutter to her chest. "It's Jay!"

Renee grinned. "Go on, I'll wait."

Lifting the phone to her ear, Winnie took a deep breath and wandered around the corner and into her bedroom. "Hi."

"Hey, Winnie. How are you?"

"Missing you." The second the words were out, she wished she hadn't sounded quite so fervent, but then again, why hide how she felt? "So how's it going with Caroline and her mother?"

"Surprisingly well. Dinner was great last night, and breakfast at Didi's house was pretty darn delicious."

She tightened her hold on the phone and swallowed. "Y-you went with them?"

"Didi insisted. And in hindsight, it was probably smart. Anyway, so what's been happening on your end?" he asked through the sudden roar of insecurity in her ears. "Did you have any deliveries today?"

"I did. Five, actually."

"Five? That's great!"

She made herself focus on the enthusiasm in his voice rather than the road her imagination was trying to take where he, his daughter, and his ex-wife were concerned.

Let it go.

This trip is about Caroline . . .

Dropping onto the edge of her bed, she made herself smile as she often did when she was uncertain. It was a trick she'd been taught when she was a little girl—a trick that worked and netted her the first in a long line of elderly friends. "All five deliveries were actually to the same place, but each was a different rescue for a different person."

When he didn't respond, she continued. "You know that artists' retreat across the lake from your place? There's a group out there right now—a poet, a magician, a mime, a puppeteer, and a comedian. I did a rescue for each one of them, only they weren't actually in their respective cabins when I got there so it ended up being more of a standard delivery than a true rescue."

"Uh-huh."

Uh-huh?

"Anyway, Renee went with me this time on account of the fact we were making all five deliveries in one main trip. At first I wasn't sure how Lovey was going to handle having someone in the passenger seat, but since it was Renee and not me . . . she saw it as an opportunity to get some lap time."

"Yeah, uh-huh."

"Jay?" she asked, her voice hesitant even to her own ears. "Is . . . is everything okay?"

"Huh, what?"

"You seem kind of distracted. Is everything okay?"

"No, no, it's fine. Didi just walked in the door and I guess I got a little sidetracked for a minute. So tell me again what you were saying?"

The roar was back, smile be damned. "What was the last thing you heard me say?"

"You said you had five deliveries today—which, by the way, is really fantastic, Winnie. How'd everyone hear about you?"

She took a deep breath and started again. "It was five deliveries to one place, actually. You know that artists' retreat across the lake from your place?"

A giggle in the background was followed by the sound of Jay's answering laugh.

"Jay?" she asked after a moment. "Are you still there?"

"Yeah, yeah, I'm still here. Sorry about that. I—"

Winnie stood and began the slow trek across her tiny bedroom toward her kitchen and the friend she'd left behind to take this call. "You know what? It sounds like now isn't such a great time to talk so I'll let you go. If you get some private time later on, give me a call, okay?"

"Yeah, you know what, that's probably best. I'll give you a call when things are a little less hectic here."

She could have sworn she said good-bye but she wasn't really certain of anything except the heaviness in her chest as she slipped the phone back into her pocket and stepped into the kitchen once again. "Sorry about that, Renee."

"No problemo, Winnie. So how is it going with the Hollywood Hag? And did you tell him about the body we saw?"

"No, I—he only had a few seconds to talk. I'll tell him

next time." Bypassing the table completely, Winnie made her way over to her baking cabinet and began pulling out every ingredient she could find.

"You want to bake something *now*?"

"I *need* to bake something now."

Chapter 5

Winnie was on her second cup of coffee when she heard Renee's giggle at the bottom of the stairs. "Better late than never."

She glanced at the kitchen clock and then down at the floor as Lovey pranced her way over to the sun spot in the middle of the living room.

"I felt that flick on my leg, Little Miss."

Lovey responded by flopping onto her side and preening her nether regions with reckless abandon.

"Must you always do that right there? In the middle of everything?" Winnie implored. "Have you no shame?"

The public bath ceased long enough for Lovey to narrow her sudden displeasure on Winnie.

Hissss . . .

"Oh, I'm sorry. My mistake." She rolled her eyes to the ceiling before fixing them, again, on the tabby who hiked her leg still higher on her shoulder. "Continue on with your beauty regimen, Your Highness."

"Talking to yourself again?"

Winnie turned toward the door and the voluptuous blonde peering back at her with pure amusement. "You're late."

"Mr. Nelson wanted to show me something." Renee tossed her purse onto the kitchen table and flopped down at the same spot she'd inhabited during dinner the previous evening.

Holding up her hands in surrender, Winnie squeezed her eyes shut. "I. Don't. Want. To. Know."

Renee resurrected her downstairs giggle and added a playful snort. "Since when do you think along those lines?"

"Have you *seen* the way Mr. Nelson looks at you? And how many bow ties he now owns because of you?"

"He was wearing a red one today." Renee set her elbow on the table and dropped her chin into her hand. "Why can't he be thirty years younger? I mean, really? Is that so much to ask?"

"If asking Lovey to refrain from licking her private parts in the middle of my living room is too much to ask, shaving thirty years off Mr. Nelson's life is probably a bit unlikely, as well."

Renee dropped her hand and her head onto the table and sighed. "It figures . . ." Then, like a parched man making his way through the desert, Renee lifted her chin just enough to afford a view of Winnie's face. "So what did you end up making last night? And can I have some?"

"I started out making thumbprint cookies because I had a rather strong urge to press and push something, but when I was done, I decided to make cannoli and mousse, too."

"Cannoli, mousse, and thumbprint cookies—those'll both work."

"I can let you have the cookies and mousse." Winnie crossed to the refrigerator, opened the door, and gestured at the covered plate on the middle shelf. "The cannoli, though, are accounted for."

Renee looked around only to shift her focus back to Winnie. "By . . ."

"Colin Norton, I think."

"You *think*?" Renee repeated. "And who on God's green earth is Colin Norton and why does that name sound familiar?"

"The poet from the artists' retreat."

"He didn't like his No s'More Writer's Block of Fudge?"

Winnie transferred the cannoli plate to the center island and shrugged. "I don't know. I haven't spoken to him."

"So who ordered the cannoli, then?"

"I did." Winnie looked down at the cookies and resisted the urge to pat her own back. "I'm thinking they're probably a bit traumatized with everything that happened yesterday, so I'm going to make a follow-up delivery to Colin. If I don't get what I want from him, I'll deliver the thumbprint cookies to one of the other ones."

Renee placed her hands over the table. "You're not making any sense, Winnie."

"It's like I said last night, over dinner. I think one of those people killed Sally and used our presence as a way to make it seem as if her death was a shock." She looked around for the rescue bag and, with the help of Renee's pointed finger, located it on the smaller, portable island that served as extra work space for larger rescue orders. "I don't like being used by anyone, least of all a murderer."

"So you've taken it upon yourself to order a rescue for a man you've never met?"

"That's right." She added fresh napkins, plates, and plastic utensils to the recovery bag and then zipped it closed. "And, technically speaking, we did sort of meet him yesterday."

"Over top of Sally's dead body."

"Semantics."

Renee wandered around the table to stand beside Winnie. "Dare I ask why you chose cannoli?"

"Because, as the saying goes, You Cannoli Run but You Can't Hide . . ."

The giggle and the snort were back for a second and far louder encore. "You are a real piece of work."

Winnie hiked the strap of the rescue bag over her shoulder, balanced the cannoli plate inside the bend in her opposite arm, and made her way over to the hook that held the keys to the ambulance. "It's my job."

"And you don't think that name is going to, um . . . I don't know . . . maybe raise suspicion when you hand it to this Norton guy?"

Winnie snapped her fingers toward the living room and watched as Lovey lowered her leg and came running over to the door. "That's just the behind-the-scenes name. For Colin Norton, it's simply going to be referred to as Cannoli Imagine What You're Going Through."

At Renee's gaped mouth, Winnie added, "I talked to Greg last night before I went to bed. He told me he was pretty sure the five people in that room are going to be required to stay in town until the investigation into Sally Dearfield's death is completed."

"So Chief Rankin *is* going to investigate."

"In his own way, I suppose." Winnie opened the door for Lovey and followed the cat down the stairs to the front door.

"I'll be back. You can help yourself to a few thumbprint cookies if you want—just excuse the ones that went all the way through to the plate. I was still working through a little bit of frustration at that point."

"You're a nut. You know that, right?"

"I'll have to take your word on that." Winnie stopped at the bottom of the stairs and waved up at her friend. "If an order comes in, you know where to find me."

They were on the main road on the way to the lake when she finally relaxed her hold on the steering wheel. "So what do you think, Lovey? Think we'll learn something from the resident poet that will crack this case wide open?"

Lovey looked at her and blinked.

Progress . . .

"Hey, I'm sorry I was a little cranky with you last night after Renee went home." Winnie tried to focus on the road and the lake they were approaching on her left, but try as she did, her thoughts kept circling back to the reason her first batch of cookies had been virtually mutilated by her overzealous thumb. An image of Jay's ex-wife had kept appearing in the middle of each and every tablespoon of dough she rounded onto the baking pan. "I mean, I knew he wasn't going to be able to escape this little trip out to California without having *some* dealings with her . . . but dinner? And breakfast? And getting sidetracked from *our* phone call by her showing up again?"

She fixed her gaze on Lovey for a split second and released the sigh she'd been holding back all morning. "I don't want to lose him, Lovey. He's . . . perfect for me."

And it was true.

In fact, until the moment she walked into Jay Morgan's office to make her first-ever dessert rescue, she'd been perfectly content with the notion of a life made up of baking and elderly friends. But the six-foot classically handsome college professor changed that with little more than a smile and a genuine desire to get to know her and the people and things that mattered to her most.

Yes, his sixteen-year-old-daughter, Caroline, had done her best to cause problems for them, but somehow, someway, the teenager's best efforts had failed to cause any sort of rift between them.

So far, anyway . . .

"She's been without her mom for eleven years, Lovey. *Eleven years.* Why the sudden need to reconnect now? With a woman who traded her for fame and fortune and never looked back?" Winnie mused only to settle on an answer that was as plain as the little pink nose on Lovey's face. "Because she *wanted* it to cause problems for me and Jay . . ."

At the sound of Jay's name, Lovey's ears noticeably perked.

"I know," she whispered. "I miss him, too."

She turned left just beyond the lake and then lost herself in mental images of the first man who'd ever made her dream about something other than chocolate, puff pastries, and how to combine the two in deliciously innovative ways. Yes, she still dreamed her way through the kitchen, but now it was a tour often interrupted by flashes of light brown hair with a sprinkling of gray around the temples . . . a strong chin . . . blue-green eyes . . . an infectious smile . . . and the memory of a warm hand cupping her cheek . . .

Shaking her head, she made herself focus on the road in front of them and the turnoff that was little more than two car lengths away. There would be time to think about Jay later. After she delivered the cannoli to the first of five suspects in her mind's notepad.

"Okay, Lovey, here's how this is going to go." She slowed to a near crawl as pavement gave way to gravel beneath the ambulance's tires. "You're going to be a little difficult about getting back under the gurney when the rescue is complete. You don't have to totally disappear, just be a little cagey. That way I can make small talk that segues into some out-and-out question asking, okay?"

A quick glance at Lovey yielded another blink.

"Just know that if you let me down, you're getting nothing but dry food tonight. Got it?"

Hisss . . .

"So much for progress." She steered around a rut in the middle of the driveway and slowed to a stop in front of the first cabin. With a turn of her wrist, she cut the engine and then deposited the keys into the inside pocket of the rescue jacket she'd donned before backing onto Serenity Lane. "Okay, let's do this."

Less than five minutes later, she rolled the cannoli-topped gurney to a stop at Colin Norton's front door and knocked, once, twice. But instead of the sound of footsteps, she heard a window lifting to her right.

"Hello?"

She stepped back in an effort to see the window and was rewarded for her efforts with a visual of the man who'd announced Sally's demise via a poem by Mary Elizabeth Frye. "Mr. Norton?"

"Yes?"

"I have a delivery for you."

"I didn't order anything."

48

"I know that." She left the gurney and sidestepped her way over to the window. "I ordered it for you."

"But I don't know you."

"Technically, that's true. But I delivered one of my rescue desserts to you yesterday."

The man's rounded face pressed forward against the screen. "The s'more-flavored fudge? That was from you?"

"It was."

"The title you gave it was very, very clever . . . although writer's block is not something I've ever had to contend with." His brown eyes slid down her uniform and then turned right toward the front stoop. "So? What did you bring me this time?"

"Cannoli." She cleared her throat and hit the silent reset button on her answer. "Or, rather, Cannoli Imagine What You're Going Through."

"Cannoli Imagine What I'm Going Through?" he echoed.

"That's right."

"Meaning?"

"With what happened here yesterday . . . with Sally Dearfield." When he showed no reaction, she continued. "It had to be such a traumatic experience to watch someone drop dead like that in front of you."

Unless that was your plan . . .

He leaned forward until she was fairly certain he was going to break the screen and then stepped back. "Cannoli, you say?"

She nodded.

"I'll meet you at the front door." Reaching upward, he braced his hands on the inside edge of the window and slammed it closed with a thump.

Chapter 6

Engaging the foot brake on the inside of the gurney's back right wheel, Winnie straightened her uniform coat and turned to face the man who'd followed her down the hallway and into the tiny kitchen. "As I said outside, I Cannoli Imagine What You're Going Through in light of yesterday, and I hope that, if nothing else, this lightens your burden a little."

A hint of pure glee lit Colin's dark brown eyes just before he leaned around Winnie and helped himself to a cannoli. "Oh wow. This looks delicious . . ." He took a bite and moaned almost immediately. "I thought the fudge was good, but this—this is divine."

"That's music to my ears." She balanced the rescue bag on the edge of the gurney and worked its zipper around to the back. When the contents were exposed, she grabbed a napkin and a plate and offered both to the man. "Or should I say poetry instead of music?"

He stopped, swallowed his second bite of cannoli, and studied her across the piece that remained in his hand. "Victor Hugo said, 'Music expresses that which cannot be put into words and that which cannot remain silent.' But it was Gustave Flaubert who said, 'There is not a particle of life which does not bear poetry within it.' So I leave it up to you"—he dropped his gaze to her name tag—"*Ms. Johnson*, to decide which would be more apropos."

"Call me Winnie." She removed the remaining plates, napkins, and plastic utensils she included with each rescue and set them on the small dinette table in the corner. "Did you always dream of being a poet?"

"From the moment I wrote my first haiku in second grade." He wiped his hands on his napkin and stood erect, like a soldier. "No two are alike, making a blanket of white, snow is so pretty."

She stopped midway back to the gurney and began to count in her head. "Five syllables, seven syllables, five syllables . . . Very nice!"

"That was my first dalliance with poetry, and I haven't looked back since."

Retrieving the cannoli plate from the gurney, Winnie instead deposited it onto the tiny kitchenette table, her ever-growing smile accompanying her every step. "That's kind of how it was with baking for me. I made my first-ever batch of cookies when I was five years old. Something about putting all those ingredients together to create something completely different was fascinating to me. Add in the reactions I got to what I'd made and, well, I was sold. And, just like you with poetry, I haven't looked back, either."

"Then it seems we have something in common."

"You mean besides what we saw yesterday." She made a

show of zipping the rescue bag closed and placing it on the makeshift shelf below the gurney's mattress.

"Saw?" he echoed only to swat the question from the air with a flick of his wrist. "Right. You mentioned Dearfield's death. I'd almost forgotten."

She forced a nervous giggle from her lips. "I *wish* I could forget. But the last thing I expected to see when I stopped to speak to Sally was her dead body."

"Yes, that had to be rather unfortunate."

Unfortunate? Really?

"Anyway, I must get back to my work." Colin gestured toward the gurney and then the door. "Can I help you to your—"

"What's that like?" she asked quickly. "To be able to capture a moment in time and then write about it in such a way that the person reading your work can feel as if they are right there with you, living that same moment?"

"It's a gift."

"An *awe-inspiring* gift." She peeked into a tiny parlor with a single armchair, a matching ottoman, a basket of magazines, and a desk. Strewn across the desk were letters—some out of their envelopes, others still inside. "Is that fan mail?"

He followed the path forged by her index finger, his throat moving with a hard swallow. "Why, yes . . . yes it is!"

"But you just got here."

"I . . . I bring them with me." He elevated his chin with an inhale. "For . . . inspiration. Now, I'd be happy to walk you out to your car if you'd like."

Seizing the opportunity afforded by the man's momentary distraction, she employed the tip of her shoe to nudge Lovey off the makeshift shelf between the gurney's wheels and onto the ground. When the cat obliged, she feigned surprise. "*Lovey?* What on earth are you doing here?"

Colin spun around, his gaze following Winnie's down to the floor and the bored-looking feline now sitting in the middle of the kitchen. "That's a cat!"

"I know, and I'm so sorry. She must have gotten into the car when I wasn't looking. She's a bit of a pill like that."

Lovey lifted her chin, flattened her ears, and stared straight at Winnie.

Hisss . . .

The anxiousness Colin had shown regarding Winnie's departure disappeared and he crouched down to the ground, extending his hand toward Lovey as he did. "Come on over here, pretty lady."

Sure enough, Lovey pranced over to Colin, the purr of her personal motorboat impossible to miss in the otherwise silent room. "'The cat went here and there / And the moon spun round like a top, / And the nearest kin of the moon, / The creeping cat, looked up.'"

You mean *traitorous* cat, she thought before addressing Colin once again. "Wow, that's lovely. Did you write that?"

A noticeable pause gave way to a slight shake of his head. "No. No. That was written by William Butler Yeats—a man many consider to be an important contributor to twentieth-century literature. What I just quoted was merely the beginning of his poem, entitled 'The Cat and the Moon.'"

She stifled the urge to yawn and, instead, widened her eyes in rapt interest. "It's beautiful. I would imagine it must be nearly impossible to write with everything going on right now."

"I can always write," he countered.

"I guess that makes sense. I do some of my best baking when I'm surrounded by craziness." Then, hoping against hope to hit on something that could assist in her quest to find Sally's killer, Winnie continued. "So what poetic masterpiece are those letters going to inspire you to write today?"

"*Letters?*" he hissed, not unlike Lovey.

She swept his attention back toward the desk. "Your fan mail."

"Oh. Right." His shoulders eased in time with an exhale he rushed to cover. "I was going back and forth between a piece about a mountain and another about a mask, but now that the audition is no longer at play, I will turn my efforts toward submitting both for publication, instead."

"Audition?" she prodded. "Audition for what?"

Slowly, his eyes came back into view as his hands slipped down his face. "That's why we all came to this horrible little place. To show the decision makers what we can do."

Afraid to move, afraid to breathe, she kept her voice modulated. "Decision makers?"

"The ones tasked with selecting next year's *Do You Have What It Takes?* cast."

She drew back. "The reality talent show?"

He nodded.

"They're casting here? In Silver Lake? I—I didn't know that."

His jaw tightened. "That's because they're not."

"I don't understand."

He clamped his mouth closed, inflated his cheeks, and then released the air they held along with a groan of angry frustration. "'Heav'n has no rage, like love to hatred turn'd / Nor hell a fury, like a woman scorn'd.'"

Feeling him slip away, she did her best to reel him back in. "I'm familiar with that second part. What poem is that from?"

"It's not from a poem, Ms. Johnson. It's a line from a play written by William Congreve in the late sixteen hundreds."

She could hear her heart thumping in her chest and knew it was a sign she'd stumbled onto something. Whether it was a something that was wise to explore when no one other than Renee knew where she was, though, was a little less clear. Still, another question or two couldn't hurt, right?

"She must have done something really awful, huh?"

Colin pulled his hands from a second pass through his thick hair. "She?"

"Sally Dearfield." When Colin said nothing, she pushed a little further. "She is who you were referencing with that line from the play, isn't she?"

The second the words were out, she knew she'd pushed too far. Suddenly, the almost trancelike state that had kept him talking off and on over the last few minutes was gone, and in its place was a man who knew exactly where he was and exactly whom he didn't want to be talking to.

"It's time for you to go, Ms. Johnson. So please collect your cat and your paraphernalia and get out."

Aware of a chill making its way down her spine, Winnie snapped her fingers at Lovey. "Okay, Lovey, it's time to go home."

Lovey took one look at Winnie and darted into the small sitting area off the kitchen, the tip of her tail the only thing visible as she moved between the love seat and its matching ottoman.

"Lovey, come here right now!"

A single yellow eye peeked around the legs of the lone end table and—*winked*?

Winnie felt her mouth go slack as her thoughts traveled back to the car ride and the conversation that had brought them to that very cabin . . .

Okay, Lovey, here's how this is going to go. You're going to be a little difficult about getting back under the gurney when the rescue is complete. You don't have to totally disappear, just be a little cagey. That way I can make small talk that segues into some out-and-out question asking, okay?

With the help of the nearest wall, Winnie steadied herself against a reality she simply couldn't ignore.

Lovey was following directions—*Winnie's* directions.

Granted, her timing was miserable, but at least she was—

A sharp and fast elbow in her side cut short her proud parenting moment and she recoiled in pain as Colin strode into the room, grabbed Lovey by the back of her neck, and tossed her at Winnie. "Here. Now go."

Chapter 7

Winnie pulled onto Silver Lake Boulevard and tapped the Speaker button on her phone. "Hello? This is Winnie."

"Imagine my surprise when, in the middle of the morning staff meeting, Frank makes mention that you—my next-door neighbor and supposed friend—are the one who called in the dead body out at the artists' retreat *yesterday*." A quick sniff was followed by a sigh that could be described only as highly agitated. "But don't fret, dear. At least you shared that little tidbit of information with . . . *Parker*."

Uh-oh.

Winnie considered various damage control options but before she could settle on one, Bridget continued, the agitation in her voice morphing into something that sounded a lot more like hurt. "I realize you don't have the same affection for me that you do for Parker, but is it really too much to ask that you think of me every once in a while, dear?"

Laura Bradford

"I think of you all the time, Bridget," Winnie protested.
"Oh?"

Uh-oh. Times two.

"I suppose that's why the pain and suffering that held me prisoner in my home yesterday warranted a phone call, as well as a personal visit to see if I needed anything." A well-placed pause was quickly followed by, "Or am I remembering that incorrectly, dear? I do tend to slip into delirium when I'm too weak to get out of bed and properly hydrate."

"Bridget, I'm sorry. I told Parker because he was sitting on the porch when I got home. And when we were all done talking, I pretty much locked myself away in my apartment for the rest of the night."

"You could have invited me over to have takeout from Luigi's with you and Renee . . ."

She started to question how Bridget knew Renee had stopped by with dinner but let it go as the view of her driveway from the woman's front window filled in the momentary blanks in her brain. "I didn't know she was coming, Bridget. She just showed up in my apartment with dinner."

"What did she bring?"
"Bring?"
"For dinner."

"Oh. Wow. I don't really remember—wait. Yes, I do. She brought a ravioli for herself and a farfalle for me."

"Were there leftovers?"

"Yes, but she brought them home for Ty." Winnie turned left at the next four-way intersection. "So are you feeling better today?"

"Yes. I rebounded from death's door shortly before dawn."

Winnie nibbled back the laugh she knew would seal her

fate with the woman, and instead gave what she hoped were appropriate clucking noises. "Was it your sciatic nerve again?"

"No, that was *Sunday* evening, dear."

"A flu?"

"No."

"Cold?"

"Since when has a cold incapacitated me, dear?"

Last week? The week before that?

Before she could speak, Bridget got back to her original point. "No, dear, I had something much more severe. So severe, in fact, the doctor is unsure of its name."

"I'm so sorry, Bridget. I hope Dr. Whitman can identify what it was."

"As do I, dear. I'd hate to see anyone else suffer the way that I did last night."

Winnie made a left onto Main Street and found herself instinctively glancing in the direction of the storefront that had once played host to her own bakery, Delectable Delights. At the time, faced with rent she could no longer cover, she'd been certain her lifelong dream had met its demise. But now, looking back, she couldn't help but see that moment in time as merely the end to one life chapter and a springboard into the next.

After all, if she hadn't been forced to close the bakery, she wouldn't have started the Emergency Dessert Squad. And if she hadn't started the Emergency Dessert Squad, she might not have met Jay.

Then again, she could think of one person who probably wished she hadn't . . .

"Winnie, dear? Are you still there?"

Shaking her thoughts back into the moment, she slowed

for a pedestrian and then continued down Main Street. "Hey, I'm half a block from your office. Any chance you might like to do lunch?"

Movement from the passenger seat pulled her gaze off the road just long enough to find Lovey staring at her, wide-eyed.

"Oh, wait. I can't do that. Lovey is with me."

"Bessie, our receptionist, loves cats," Bridget insisted. "Lovey can stay with her while we eat."

"Are you sure?"

"Of course. I'll have her walk down to the main lobby with me now and she can take her while we go off to lunch."

"Don't you want to check with her first in case she doesn't want a cat hanging around?" Winnie asked.

"Bessie will be fine. I'll bring her back dessert from wherever we go to lunch."

There was no denying the excitement in Bridget's voice over the notion of being asked to lunch and, for a moment, Winnie felt a wave of self-imposed guilt wash over her from head to toe. She'd been so busy the last few weeks with the Dessert Squad and Jay that she hadn't really stopped to assess how little time she'd spent with the elderly woman.

Her life was richer because of Mr. Nelson and Bridget. They'd been her biggest cheerleaders since she'd moved to Silver Lake and, more specifically, Serenity Lane. She owed them the same in return, regardless of how busy her life got.

"I'm pulling up now and . . ." The words fell away as she spied Bridget's stout frame and crop of snow-white hair already standing in the lobby door. Beside her stood a bean-pole of a woman with curly red hair and horn-rimmed glasses. "Okay, I see you."

Swinging wide, Winnie claimed the first open parking

spot she could find and then turned toward her regal passenger. "Be a good girl for a little while and I'll get you home as soon as possible, okay?"

Lovey's answering hiss morphed into a purr as Bridget opened her door and extracted her from the seat with a series of soft coos. "You're going to have a wonderful time with my friend Bessie, aren't you, sweet girl?"

"Hi, Bessie." Winnie stepped onto the pavement and smiled across the top of the Dessert Squad at Bridget's coworker. "Are you sure this is okay? Bridget and I could always do this another—"

"Nonsense! It's perfectly fine, isn't it, Bessie?"

Bessie looked from Lovey to Winnie and back again, shifting her nonexistent weight from one foot to the other as she did. "I—"

Bridget whispered something in Lovey's ear and then handed the animal off to Bessie. "If you find yourself starting to sneeze, just open that window between editorial and advertising and take a few deep breaths. We'll be back after a while. Winnie and I have a lot of catching up to do."

"Wait. Bessie is allergic to cats?" Winnie asked.

Hooking her hand inside Winnie's upper arm, Bridget tugged her toward the sidewalk that lined their side of Main Street. "If we don't dawdle, we'll be back before the hives start."

Winnie set the remains of her sandwich back on her plate and helped herself to a chip from the basket in the middle of the table. "Now that I've gotten you up to speed on my part in finding Sally Dearfield, is it okay if I ask *you* a question?"

"Of course, dear." Bridget set down her soup spoon and smiled at Winnie. "Is this about your man troubles?"

"Man troubles? What man troubles?"

"Renee pulled up a picture of Jay's ex-wife on her phone the other day and I can only imagine how worried you must be."

"I—I'm not worried," Winnie protested.

Liar, liar, pants on fire . . .

"Good. Because Jay is a smart man. He knows that sincerity is more important in the long run than beauty . . ." Bridget dabbed at her lips with her napkin and then leaned across the table in Winnie's direction. "So just hang in there a little longer and be glad there's almost an entire country between them most of the time."

Bookending her face with her own hands, Winnie closed her eyes just long enough to take a deep, fortifying breath. "Actually, I just wanted to ask whether you'd heard anything about one of those TV reality shows possibly casting out at Silver Lake Artists' Retreat later this week . . ."

"A reality show? Casting in Silver Lake?"

Winnie helped herself to another chip. "Well, I think it fell through for some reason, but did you hear about it *before* it fell through?"

"If it had been a plan to begin with, I would have known. Shows like that want the media to know." Bridget shoved her empty soup bowl off to the side with her left hand and thumped the spot where it had been with her right. "What do you know that I don't, Winnie?"

"Nothing, really."

"You must know *something* to be asking these kinds of questions."

Winnie took one last chip and then pushed the basket

just out of reach. "When I was out at the Silver Lake Artists'
Retreat this morning talking to Colin Norton, he—"

"I thought you said you made your deliveries to the resort
yesterday," Bridget mused. "Which is why you were there
to witness the moment Sally Dearfield hit the ground."

"I did, although the second part of your statement isn't
entirely accurate."

Bridget's chin dipped to afford a crystal clear view of
Winnie atop the upper rim of her reading glasses. "Winnie,
dear, you told me just a few moments ago that you were there."

"To see her dead body, yes. But I suspect it hit the ground
before Renee and I stepped into that room."

"Meaning?"

"Meaning I think one of the people in that room put the
cyanide in Sally's teacup and—"

Bridget's gasp was so loud it not only drowned out the
rest of Winnie's sentence, it also drew the attention of more
than a few of their fellow diners. "Did you just say *cyanide*?"
she half hissed, half whispered.

Nodding, Winnie held her finger to her lips. "Greg said
there was a strong smell of bitter almonds in her mouth when
he tried to resuscitate her."

"But that would mean she was . . . *murdered*." Bridget
leaned forward, studied Winnie closely, and then plucked a
notebook from her purse and flipped it open. "Tonight, when
we have more time, I'll chastise you for keeping this from
me earlier in this conversation. For now though, I'll take
your apologies in the form of details."

"Look, I only know this from a conversation I had with
Greg. I'm thinking, if you haven't gotten wind of it at the
paper, it's not official yet. So please, don't use me as your
source."

Bridget narrowed her best stink eye on Winnie. "What kind of reporter do you think I am?"

"I'm sorry. I just don't want to get Greg in trouble."

"This isn't my first rodeo, Winnie."

"First rodeo?" she repeated, laughing. "Where did you get that expression?"

"The coffeehouse. It's where all the young people hang out." Bridget uncapped her pen and pointed it at Winnie. "So you didn't see Sally hit the ground?"

"No. But everyone in the room gasped as if it had just happened when Renee and I stepped into the doorway."

"I don't understand . . ."

"Her teacup was shattered on the ground next to her body. Abby Thompson, one of the artists in the room at the time, told Chief Rankin that Sally dropped it when she fell. But Renee and I never heard it fall despite the time it took for us to get into the building, locate the room they were all in, and get to it."

A flash of understanding registered in Bridget's dark eyes just before the tip of her pen started moving across the open notebook page. "So the gasp was for your benefit."

"Looking back, it sure seems that way." Swayed by the pull of the chip basket, Winnie helped herself to one more.

Bridget asked a few more questions, wrote down Winnie's answers, and then popped her head up once again. "Do you have a guess on who might have done it?"

Winnie leaned back in her chair and let her gaze travel across Bridget's shoulder to the window and the sidewalk beyond. "Not yet."

"Not *yet*? What does that mean, dear?"

"They *used* me, Bridget. They used me *and* Renee to paint a very different picture of reality. I'm not okay with that."

"But if the gasp was for your benefit and there were five people in that room when you arrived, how can you narrow it down to just one? Wouldn't it seem as if they were *all* involved?"

It was a point she hadn't necessarily pondered, but that didn't mean it didn't hold merit. "Maybe. It's certainly something to consider. But I definitely got the sense Colin had a real distaste for Sally."

"Do you know when this group of artists arrived?" Bridget asked.

Winnie paused at the question. "Sally didn't say. But I got the impression they hadn't been there long. So maybe two or three days at most?"

"So she was around them for two or three days at most before someone *killed* her? That doesn't make much sense."

Bridget was right. It didn't. Sure, a person could get under your skin after a few days. Heck, some people could do that in a matter of hours. But was three days of an annoying personality enough to make someone kill you? Probably not.

"Maybe the killer knew her before this week." Winnie sat up tall as her brain caught up with her own supposition. "Wait! When Colin made mention of this reality show audition that wasn't, I got the sense that's *why* he came here."

"Maybe she made it up to get bodies in the cabins," Bridget suggested. "Bodies are money, I imagine."

"Maybe. But in the next breath, he referred to Sally via that quote about hell having no fury like a woman scorned." She took a moment with that memory and then looked across the table at her elderly friend. "None of this makes any sense."

Bridget tapped her pen against her chin and then shot it into the air. "It does if Sally lured them here out of anger."

"Anger?"

"Think about the quote, dear. 'Hell hath no fury like a woman scorned.' If this Colin fellow was referencing Sally as the woman scorned, she was angry."

Dropping her head into her hands, Winnie batted Bridget's words around in her thoughts. Was Sally a bitter woman? Hell-bent on being nasty for the sake of being nasty? Or was it something far more specific to this particular group of—

She smacked her hand to her mouth as Sally's voice took center stage in her head.

I'm hoping the prospect of being penniless and publicly mortified is all the motivation they really need. But a clever little rescue dessert for their respective craft certainly can't hurt. Especially if it's timed just right.

"She was out to get them, Bridget!" Then, realizing she was speaking far too loud for their surroundings, she leaned across the table and lowered her voice to a whisper. "Now I just need to figure out why."

Bridget pinned Winnie over the top of her glasses. "How do you propose doing that?"

"That's a good question," she said. "And certainly one I need to work through. But for starters, I think we need to figure out what, if anything, these five artists have in common."

"We?"

Winnie answered her friend's questioning eyes with a teasing shrug. "I'm sorry, Bridget. That was awfully presumptuous of me to assume that with all your health issues you—"

"I'm in!"

Chapter 8

Winnie was back on Main Street and heading home when Lovey and the seat she was sitting on began to vibrate. Reaching past the now-irritated cat, she hit the Speaker button. "Does this mean you have something for me?"

"Hmmm. I'm feeling a bit used at this moment."

She returned the grin she heard in her caller's voice with one of her own and raised it with a laugh. "I'm sorry, Greg. You're right. How are you this fine day?"

Greg Stevens, aka Master Sergeant Hottie, cleared his throat, mumbled something unintelligible, and then followed it up with a loud click on his end of the line. "Okay, that's better."

"What's better?"

"I stepped out of the break room so I could have a little much-needed privacy."

At the next traffic light she turned right. "I take it it's been a quiet shift at the ambulance district?"

"I've been trapped in the break room with Chuck and Stan since we got back from the retreat house yesterday afternoon. I'm ready to strangle one, if not both of them."

"Considering that would result in a call and, therefore, something to do, maybe that's not such a bad idea," she quipped, turning left at the second four-way stop.

"Unless, of course, I'm successful from the start."

"You got called *yesterday* for a dead body . . ."

"True." Greg exhaled into the phone and followed it up with the kind of chuckle capable of weakening knees all across Silver Lake. "Anyway, I thought you might like to hear the word on the street. Or, to be more accurate, the recent e-mail chatter from the ME's office."

She piloted the Dessert Squad onto Serenity Lane and instantly slowed to a crawl out of respect to her neighbors. "Tell me."

"I was right. Cyanide was detected in and around the victim's cup, and the preliminary tox report pretty much seals it up."

"Wow. So it's really true," she murmured. "Sally Dearfield was murdered."

"No doubt about that one. And whoever did it, wasn't worried about being shy."

"Shy?"

"About the amount of cyanide they used."

"Ahhh . . ." She pulled into her driveway, shifted the vintage ambulance into park, and turned off the engine. "I imagine Chief Rankin knows about this?"

"I'm sure he does, though it doesn't appear he's in any

hurry to finger a suspect, from what I can see at this exact moment."

Pushing the door open, Winnie slid out of the vehicle and snapped for Lovey to follow. "Why do you say that?"

"Because I'm standing here in the bay, looking out at the sidewalk, and the chief is sitting on one of the benches outside, talking to one of his hunting buddies. And, by the looks of it, I'm guessing they're swapping their best jokes."

"I wish I could say I'm surprised but, alas, I cannot." A visual inspection of the section of porch she could see from the driveway yielded an empty chair in front of Mr. Nelson's chessboard. A glance at her watch filled in the gaps—Mr. Nelson, like virtually every other resident of Serenity Lane with the exception of Bridget, was taking a post-lunch nap. The snores that greeted her approach via the open first-floor windows simply served as confirmation. "I know you could probably get in trouble for telling me this stuff, Greg, but thanks for knowing I needed to hear it. I've thought of little else since it happened."

A series of beeps in the background accompanied her through the front door and up the stairs to her apartment. When they subsided, Greg's voice took over. "A call just came in. I'll catch up with you another time, okay?"

"Absolutely." She opened the door at the top of the stairs and then stepped to the side to allow Lovey the uninhibited entry the feline preferred. Still, the moment Winnie stepped inside behind the cat, she was greeted with a quick hiss. "Oh, and Greg?"

"Yeah?"

"Thank you."

"My pleasure." And then he was gone, his quick shout

to his coworkers the last thing she heard before their call officially ended.

"So, do you think Jay is *aware* of the fact that Greg is waiting in the wings, hoping he'll screw up?" Renee dropped to the ground to greet Lovey with a head scratch but kept her own cat-green eyes trained on Winnie. "Because he is waiting, you know."

Winnie set the rescue bag on the center island and pulled her shoulder out from beneath its strap. "Would you stop with that, please? Greg is my friend. You know this. I know this. And, believe it or not, *he* knows this."

"I also know that's not the way he wants it . . ." With a flick of her hand, Renee guided Winnie's attention to the order pad on the kitchen table. "An order came in not more than three minutes before you two walked through that door."

"Okay, tell me the details . . ."

Renee gave Lovey one last scratch and then stood. "First up, she was hoping for five o'clock."

"Done. And the reason for the rescue?"

"It's for this girl's teammate. Seems she accidently kicked said teammate after soccer practice yesterday. Seems they were horsing around and that's when the kick went down. Anyway, this girl is apparently pretty bruised up now and our customer feels bad." Crossing to the order pad, Renee glanced down at it quickly. "I asked if she had any thoughts on the kind of dessert this teammate might like, and she said cookies."

"Cookies," Winnie repeated en route to the sink. "Any allergies?"

"Nope."

"Any specific flavors mentioned?"

"Nope."

"Black-and-Blue Cookies it is, then."

Renee's laugh reached her above the sound of the faucet. "Black-and-Blue Cookies? Is that some sort of variation on black-*and-white* cookies?"

"Yep." She rinsed the hand soap off her hands, dried them with a paper towel, and then headed straight for the baking cabinet. "Hey, by any chance did Bridget call here in the past ten minutes or so?"

Renee headed for the drawer of pans and extracted two. "Actually, she did. I tried to make a little small talk with her but she just wanted—"

"The names of the artists currently at the retreat. Yeah, I know." Winnie stockpiled the ingredients she needed into her arms and carried them over to the island. "You did give them to her, right?"

"Of course I did! That woman frightens me." Setting the pans on the countertop beside the stove, Renee prepared them with a quick hit of cooking spray and then joined Winnie and her assembled ingredients at the island. "Is something going on?"

She measured out the flour and dumped it in the bowl. "It's been confirmed. Sally Dearfield was murdered."

Renee pulled her hand off the sugar container and gave Winnie a once-over. "Are you serious?"

"Technically, it hasn't been made public yet, but Greg let me know on the down-low."

"Wow. I've never witnessed a murder before." Renee verified the amount of sugar needed for the cookies and added it to the bowl.

"You didn't witness this one, either."

Moving on to the brown sugar and the amount indicated

71

by Winnie's index finger, Renee shrugged. "Close enough. I mean, we saw her dead body, didn't we? And you just said she was murdered."

"Cyanide has a way of doing that, yes. But the key factor in all of this is the fact that the gasp came well after her body hit the ground. That's odd, don't you think?"

"I do. But unless they were all in on it, wouldn't someone have said something about who did it? I mean, as stinky as I was at playing Clue as a kid, never in all the times I *did* play, did Colonel Mustard, Miss Scarlet, Professor Plum, and Mrs. Peafeather commit the crime together. I mean, the wrench wasn't that big, you know?"

"Um, I'm pretty sure it was Mrs. Peacock but that's okay. I get your point." And she did. But the cookies she was expected to deliver in a matter of hours needed to be her focus at that moment. Grabbing the electric mixer, she plugged its cord into the outlet and turned it on, the volume of her voice instinctively rising. "Anyway, Bridget is going to see if she can put together a little background information on the five artists currently staying at the retreat."

"You mean the suspects?" Renee stopped, nibbled on her lower lip for a moment, and then released it along with a sigh. "If you really love me, Winnie, don't tell me if Colonel Mustard ends up being the hunk from the lake the other night, okay?"

Winnie shut off the mixer and carried the beaters over to the sink. "If he does, I'll tell you *because* I love you."

"Blah, blah, blah." Reaching around Winnie, Renee plucked one of the beaters from her hand, ran a finger down the first of its four blades, and stuck the collected cookie dough into her mouth. "I know . . . I know . . . Raw eggs."

"You're incorrigible, you know that?"

"On account of the fact you tell me that at some point every day, yeah, I know that." Renee moved on to the second blade. "So what are you trying to find out about them?"

"Anything and everything. Where they're from, details about their careers, marital status, et cetera."

"Okay . . ." Renee looked at the remaining dough-covered blades and then tossed the beater into the sink beside its mate. "Next time I do that, smack me, okay? I don't need any more calories."

"Said the girl who insisted I add *taste tester* to her official job description," Winnie said, her tone deadpan.

Renee laughed. "Said the girl who actually added it."

Working fast, Winnie placed a dozen balls of dough onto the first cookie sheet, another dozen onto the second cookie sheet, and then placed them both inside the preheated oven. "Okay, so where were we? Oh yeah, I remember . . . When Sally called on Saturday to place her order, she said something that made me think she may have had a history with these particular artists. I may be wrong, but if I'm not, and it played a part in her death, I think it's worth a look."

"It probably wouldn't do me any good to take this moment to point out that you're a baker, not a cop, eh?"

"Nope, because I know that." Winnie set the timer on the stove and returned to the island and the next round of waiting ingredients. "I also know I've got to get this icing made and these cookies finished before five. So, if it's okay, I'd really rather table any further discussion on this particular subject until tomorrow."

"That's a big ten-four."

She eyed her friend. "A *big ten-four*?"

"Yeah." Renee dried her freshly washed hands with the hand towel and then wandered back over to the island. "It means I hear you . . . I got it . . . I'm picking up what you're putting down. You know, that sort of thing."

"I know what ten-four means, Renee. I also know that's police talk, not EMT talk."

"No comment."

Chapter 9

"One, two, three, four—and here we are." Winnie pulled alongside the curb in front of the two-story tan-colored house Renee had noted on the bottom of the rescue order and took a moment to compare the number on the mailbox with the number on her sheet. "Okay, Your Highness, it's cookie time!"

Rising up onto all four paws, Lovey unfurled her tongue with a yawn and then cast an irritated eye on Winnie. "Yes. I know. I promised you tuna this morning and I've yet to deliver. But in case you haven't noticed, the day has been a bit of a whirlwind."

Hissss . . .

"Ahhh yes, good chat. Good chat." She opened her door, waited for Lovey to jump out, and then made her way around the back of the ambulance for the cookie-topped stretcher, the IV icing bag and pole, and her rescue bag. When everything was ready, Lovey took her position beneath the stretcher and Winnie wheeled it up the front walkway to the doorbell.

Seconds turned to minutes before the mahogany door finally opened to reveal a dark-haired teenager wearing an athletic top and shorts and sporting an angry bruise on her leg.

"Vanessa Wilder?"

The girl's brown eyes widened. "Yes?"

"My name is Winnie—"

"I know who you are."

She couldn't help but grin. "I'm here to rescue you from your"—Winnie pointed at the teen's leg—"bruised leg."

Vanessa looked past Winnie to first the ambulance and then the cookie-topped (and Lovey-bottomed) stretcher. "Are you serious?"

Stepping back, she placed her hands on the stretcher and wheeled it into position between them. "These Black-and-Blue Cookies are Cindy Monoco's way of saying she's sorry for the bad kick."

Surprise turned to amusement via a quick squeal. "I can't believe she did this! How. Cool." Then, holding her index finger up in the air, she backed up. "Wait right here, okay? I have to take a selfie with this! Everyone is going to be so jealous!"

Five minutes later, Vanessa was back, phone in hand, hair freshly brushed, and mascara applied. Spinning around, she threw out her hand, hoisted the device into the air, and snapped three pictures of herself with the stretcher and, based on the angle of the shot, Winnie, too.

When Winnie was sure the photo session was over, she grabbed hold of the IV icing tube and added a little swirl of white chocolate to the top of each cookie before offering one to Vanessa. "You've been rescued."

The squeal was back, this time at such a high pitch, Lovey poked her head out from her hideaway spot. If Vanessa noticed, though, she gave no indication. Instead, the girl plucked a cookie off the plate and bit into it, her big brown eyes rapidly disappearing behind ridiculously long lashes. "Oh. Wow. Caroline is crazy."

Winnie drew back. "Excuse me?"

Vanessa studied the cookie in her hand and then took another bite, nodding as she did. "Caroline Morgan. Professor Morgan's daughter."

Winnie's hand found the edge of the stretcher. "No, I know that. You know her?"

"We've known each other since, like, sixth grade or something." Vanessa took another bite of her cookie and leaned into the open doorjamb. "So I never knew her mom. Caroline says her mom is Didi Evans, can you believe it? I mean, please—Didi Evans? Yeah, right. I've read tons of press on Didi since Caroline said that, and not once has Didi ever mentioned a kid. Kinda pathetic, don't you think?"

"There's no kinda about it." Winnie felt the weight of the girl's stare at the woodenness of her answer, but before she could truly come to Caroline's defense, Vanessa giggled.

"So the feeling is mutual, then, huh?"

"Feeling?" Winnie echoed, confused.

"Meaning, you don't like Caroline, either."

"No, I was referring to her—" She stopped as the implication behind Vanessa's words took front and center in her head.

Either?

She pulled her hand back against the stinging words. "I—I . . ."

"Seems to me you're pretty cool, actually. I mean, these cookies are pretty freaking amazing and your cat is adorbs."

In need of a moment to process everything, Winnie looked down at Lovey. But it didn't help. Vanessa simply prattled on and on.

"Let's face it. We both know this whole story about her famous mom is a crock—you said it yourself a minute ago—"

Winnie snapped her head up. "I didn't say that!"

"Yes, you did. I just said the whole pretend story about her"—Vanessa wiggled her now cookie-free fingers in air-quote fashion—"*famous* mom was kinda pathetic and you said there was no *kinda* about it."

"I wasn't referring to the fact that you don't believe her. I was actually—"

"I mean, what? She's sixteen. Shouldn't she be trying to get a boyfriend of her own instead of heading off on some trip with her dad so she can try to"—again with the air quotes—"*get her parents back together.* I'm mean, c'mon, what is she . . . *six*?"

Winnie opened her mouth to speak but closed it as her hunch turned into reality in the blink of her now tear-filled eyes.

No.

Not now.

You're on a rescue . . .

Vanessa helped herself to another cookie and raised it in the air. "These are really, really good, by the way."

It was hard to talk around the lump making its way up her throat but still, Winnie managed. "I—I'm glad."

Reaching into the hidden pocket on the inside of her uniform top, she pulled out a card and handed it, along with the cookie plate, to Vanessa. "In case you or someone you know wants to rescue someone in the future. Past rescue desserts are listed on the website and we can always create something completely new, too."

Vanessa took the card, tossed it onto a table just inside the open doorway, and then wiggled the fingers of her non-plate-holding hand at Lovey while addressing Winnie. "Is he part of all your rescues?"

"It's a *she*, actually, and yes . . . she is."

"Cool." The chirp of Vanessa's phone sent the teenager back into the house with her Black-and-Blue Cookies and little more than a nod at Winnie.

"I guess we're done," Winnie mumbled in Lovey's direction before grabbing hold of the stretcher and pushing it back down the walkway. When they reached the curb, she loaded the assorted gear into the back of the ambulance, deposited herself and her feline companion into the cab, and headed down the street in search of the first opportunity to turn around. "So much for making progress with Caroline back in April, huh, Lovey?"

Lovey blinked.

"I try, Lovey, I really do. Heck, you've seen the stuff I've done—the treats I've dropped off for her, the invites I've extended to her, the . . ." She shook off the rest of the sentence and replaced the ensuing silence with a sigh. "It doesn't matter, does it? I'm always going to be the interloper, aren't I?"

She slid a quick glance in the direction of the passenger seat to find Lovey curled up into a ball, sleeping.

"Lot of help you are."

But really, it didn't matter. Even if Lovey were awake (and could actually talk), there was nothing to be disputed. Facts were facts. Caroline despised Winnie. And considering she'd done nothing to earn that distinction short of catching Jay's eye, there wasn't anything she could do to fix it, either.

"Except call it quits with Jay." She felt her shoulders slump as the words left her mouth. "Oh, Lovey, why? Why, after having zero interest in a relationship for more years than you've been alive, do I suddenly have to fall head over heels for someone with a kid who wants nothing to do with me? I mean, really. What was I thinking?"

That Jay is kind . . .
That Jay is smart . . .
That Jay makes my knees weak . . .
That Jay makes me laugh . . .

Turn by turn she wound her way through one Silver Lake neighborhood after the other until she found herself on the road that led to the lake—a road that was as far from Serenity Lane as one could get while still being in the same town. Yet even with the realization that she'd driven farther than she'd intended, she stayed the course, the approaching six o'clock hour releasing her from the constraints of the workday.

If an evening rescue had come in, Renee would have called. And based on Ty's soccer schedule, she knew her friend had switched the Dessert Squad's main number to ring straight through to Winnie's phone before heading out the door to pick up her son and transport him to the appropriate field. The phone, like Lovey, however, remained silent.

It was moments like these when she wished the ambulance had a radio. If it did, she could roll down the window, turn up the volume, and sing along with whatever catchy tune happened to be playing at that moment. Since it didn't, she simply cracked the window enough to allow for a breeze and tried to focus on something other than Caroline.

Caroline . . .

"She'll come around, won't she, Lovey?"

Lifting her head ever so slightly, the brown and white tabby offered a sleepy hiss as her response.

"Who asked you?" Winnie shot back.

You did, dummy . . .

"Ugh. Ugh. *Uggghhh!*"

Desperate for a change of scenery, she turned into the public parking lot where she'd first met Caroline and parked under a grove of buckeye trees. The second the engine shut off, Lovey was on her feet, scoping out their surroundings.

"I need a moment to collect my thoughts, Your Highness. Can I count on you to stay put for five—maybe *ten* minutes, tops?"

Lovey elongated her upper body in her favorite regal pose and then darted out of the cab the moment Winnie opened the door.

"*Love-yyyy!*" She stamped her foot on the asphalt parking lot—once, twice. "You get back here right now or you can forget that whole tuna-for-dinner promise I made this morning!"

When it became apparent Lovey wasn't going to return, Winnie slammed the door and followed the cat across the parking lot and over to the picnic table with the best view of Silver Lake. Claiming a spot across from the belligerent animal, she looked down at her cell phone, squared her shoulders, and scrolled through her contacts until she reached Jay's number.

On one hand she knew she shouldn't call. Jay knew she wanted to talk and he had said he'd call back again when he had more time. Yet even with the nearly twenty-four hours that had passed since he'd made that unrealized pledge, she couldn't get around the fact that she simply needed to hear his voice.

Pressing the Call icon next to his name, she brought the phone to her ear and counted along with the rings—one, two, three, four, five . . .

The sixth and final ring faded away as his voice—the one she'd wanted to hear more than any other at that moment—filled the line.

"Hi, you've reached Jay Morgan. I'm unable to get to the phone right now, but if you leave your name and number, I'll get back to you as soon as possible."

She closed her eyes and waited for the inner calm she'd come to equate with the sound of his voice, but it didn't happen. Instead, all it did was stir up the same questions that had been lapping at the edges of her day.

Why wasn't he calling back?

Why was the trip that had been billed as time for Caroline to spend with her mom becoming time for Jay to spend with his ex?

Movement out of the corner of her eye snapped her attention off the phone and her mental woolgathering and redirected it toward the man seated on the edge of the embankment, skipping rocks across the surface of the lake, one after the other. She watched for a moment only to get her attention rerouted back to the phone via a single beep.

For a moment, she considered calling back and actually leaving a message this time, but in the end she let it go. Jay knew how to reach her when he was ready.

"*If* he's ready . . ."

The sensation of being watched brought her attention back to the man on the edge of the lake—a man no longer skipping rocks but, rather, looking at her with a mixture of curiosity and amusement.

"Don't mind me," she called. "I live with an antisocial cat."

Lovey jumped down from the picnic bench and meandered her way across the pebbled ground toward the man. As she approached, he reached out, prompting the tabby to run the rest of the way. Two seconds later, she was on his lap, curled up.

Amusement pushed his eyebrows upward just before he brought his hands to the base of his neck in theatrical surprise.

Hiking her leg over the bench, Winnie brought her feet onto the other side and stood. "Trust me, the cat you see at this moment, is not the cat I live with."

The man pulled his head back to inspect Lovey and then shrugged, a slight smile playing across his lips.

Winnie closed the gap between the picnic table and the man only to stop as she got close enough to see his face. "Wait! I think I know you. You're one of the artists staying out at the retreat place, aren't you?"

Stilling his hand atop Lovey's back, he looked up at Winnie, his charcoal-colored eyes wide.

He pointed at Winnie and then rubbed his stomach as his smile widened to full capacity.

And then she knew. He was George Watkins, the mime.

The one who'd been heading toward the main retreat building from his cabin as she and Renee were approaching with his rescue dessert. The one who'd captured Renee's attention for his patience with her son.

She stuck out her hand and watched it disappear inside his own. "I'm Winnie. Winnie Johnson." When he released her hand, she used it to gesture toward his lap. "And this is Lovey."

Lifting his hand to his forehead, he saluted the feline. When Lovey purred in response, he smiled again.

"She sure seems to like you."

He nodded and then pointed to the parking lot and Winnie's Emergency Dessert Squad.

"Yes, that's mine."

A second tummy rub was followed by a nod and a contented eye roll.

"So you enjoyed your dessert?"

The enthusiasm behind his nod warmed her from the inside out. "I'm glad. When Sally Dearfield called and . . ." She held on to the rest of her sentence for a moment as she noted the change in George's demeanor at the mere mention of the now-deceased woman. His eyes clouded over, his hands tightened into fists, and the smile he'd been so free with to that point, faltered.

When he became aware of her focus, however, his reaction changed to one of interest. She took that as her key to continue. "Anyway, when Sally asked me to tailor my desserts to your assorted crafts, I had to call in the troops for a little assistance."

His eyebrows quirked with a question.

"I can come up with a dessert for any occasion. But finding just the right name sometimes requires a brainstorming session with my friends. And I have to tell you, this particular session was punctuated with a whole lot of laughter." She redirected her attention toward the lake and the handful of small rowboats and kayaks that dotted its surface both near and far. "It's not every day I get to bake for a poet, a magician, a puppeteer, a comedian, and *a mime*."

When he showed no response, she bent down, picked up one of the rocks from his pile, and turned it over in her hands. "You met a member of my brainstorming crew here a few evenings ago. She was here with her son and you taught him how to skip rocks."

The smile was back along with what appeared to be a pleasant memory based on the slow nod of his head.

"I take it you grew up around water?" she asked.

He nodded, grabbed hold of a nearby stick, and drew what appeared to be a crude drawing of the United States in the dirt beside his leg. When he was done, he pointed his stick along the eastern border.

"You grew up in Maryland?"

He moved the stick up a little.

"Delaware?"

He moved it a tad north.

"New Jersey."

He smiled.

"I've never been." She let her eyes drift across the lake once again, the early evening sun shimmering across its surface like millions of sparkly diamonds. "So are your kids all master rock skippers, too?"

He lifted his left finger into the air and pointed at his empty ring finger.

"You're not married."

He shook his head.

"Ever married?"

Again, he shook his head.

"Renee will be thrilled to hear . . ." The sentence she hadn't meant to utter aloud faded into the late-evening air.

Uh-oh.

"That I ran into you!" She peeked at the man to gauge his reaction and then mentally patted herself on the back for her quick-thinking save. "Though, you've seen her again since you skipped rocks with her son."

His left eyebrow quirked.

Winnie took a breath and then plowed ahead, watching for any noticeable reaction to her words. "You may not have noticed, given what was going on at that exact moment, but she was right there next to me when we walked into that meeting room yesterday morning—when you were all standing around Sally Dearfield's body."

Something about the shift to his body propelled Lovey off his lap and next to Winnie's feet. Before she could truly process the man's response though, he frowned and pointed at the corner of his eye to suggest a tear.

Intrigued, she took a gamble and asked the first question that came to mind. "Did you know Sally? I mean, before you checked in to the retreat this weekend?"

He hesitated briefly before rising to his feet and tapping the face of his wristwatch.

"You have to go?" Winnie surmised.

A quick nod confirmed her guess as did his move toward the walking trail that would take him around the lake and, eventually, back to his cabin on the retreat center's grounds.

"Wait!"

He turned, his eyes hooded.

She floundered around for something, anything, to say while simultaneously closing the gap he'd created. "Do you . . . do you have a business card?"

He cocked his head a hairbreadth.

"A friend of mine is . . . um . . . thinking about hiring some entertainment for a party she has coming up. And . . . uh . . . maybe if you're still in town, she could hire you."

Liar, liar, pants on fire . . .

Seconds accumulated as he stood there, his gaze moving between Winnie and the lake. Finally, he reached into his back pocket for his billfold and handed her a card.

"Th-thanks. I'll be sure she gets it."

With barely more than a shrug of acknowledgement, he shoved the billfold back into his pocket and stepped onto the path he was hell-bent on taking.

"It—it was nice, um, *interacting* with you," she called out in a desperate attempt to keep him there longer. But it was no use. He merely offered her the same salute he'd given Lovey and continued down the path, his back growing smaller and smaller before he finally disappeared into the grove of trees surrounding the east side of the lake. Still, when she spoke, she modulated her voice on the outside chance he could somehow still hear her. "He's hiding something, Lovey, I just know it."

A subtle thump against her calf yanked her focus down to the ground and the tabby staring up at her with large golden eyes. "What? You think I'm wrong?"

Lovey cast what could best be described as a pointed look toward the area in which George had been sitting and then stared up at Winnie once again, waiting.

"What? What are you trying to tell me that I'm not . . ."

Reality ushered in a laugh she hadn't realized she'd needed until that very moment. Savoring the sudden lightness in her chest, she snapped her fingers in the direction of the parking lot and the waiting Dessert Squad. "Okay, okay, Your Highness, you earned back your tuna. Now let's get out of here and go get it, shall we?"

Chapter 10

Looking back, baking had always been her go-to therapy. Measuring ingredients, experimenting with flavors, and eliciting moans of pleasure from all who ate her creations had gotten her through some of the more trying stages in life.

She'd baked her first chocolate soufflé the day she realized she was the only one in her new school who hadn't been invited to Cindy Farcus's birthday party.

She'd made her first crème brûlée the day she was told by a local baking competition she was too young to enter.

And she'd inadvertently created her first Dessert Squad menu item (Don't-Be-Blue Berry Pie) five months earlier while working through the horrors of finding her neighbor's body within hours of closing her bakery for the very last time.

So it wasn't really a surprise that after a long day at work and an even longer evening spent staring at her phone in the unrealized hope Jay's name would suddenly appear on the screen, she was wrist-deep in flour, determined to make the kind of chocolate chip cookie capable of curing the world of all its problems.

Shifting her focus to the assorted chips she'd arranged across the counter, she tried to calculate the winning percentage between semisweet and milk chocolate, but every time she thought she had it, the sound of Lovey licking herself set her back to square one.

"Any chance you could lick a little quieter?" Winnie asked.

Lovey retracted her tongue, stared at Winnie for a few seconds, and then jumped off the windowsill bed to resume her bath next to Winnie's feet.

Winnie was mid–eye roll when the stench hit. "*Good grief*, Lovey, what is that—that *smell*?"

Again, Lovey retracted her tongue, taking the offending stench with it.

"I mean it—what is that . . ." The question died off as her gaze moved from Lovey, to the empty tuna can on the counter, to Lovey's licked-clean bowl, and, finally, back to Lovey. "That stench! It's you!"

Hisss . . .

Completing her eye roll, she added the combination of chips to the mixing bowl and powered on the electric mixer, her nose willing the smell of butter, eggs, and flour to gain the upper hand over Lovey's tuna breath. When the dough was at the desired consistency, she traded the mixer for her favorite scooper, rounded up two dozen perfectly sized balls onto each of two waiting pans, and popped them into the preheated oven.

Eleven minutes later, she pulled out the pans and stared down at the cookies she suddenly had no interest in eating alone. But considering the time (nearly eleven o'clock) and the snoring coming through the vent in her floor, her self-made therapy session was officially over.

"So much for curing the ills of mankind." Winnie gathered up the dirty bowls and spoons and headed over to the sink, only to stop, midstep, as her gaze wandered out the window and over to Bridget's house and its *lit* living room window.

Dropping the items into the sink, she bypassed the dish detergent and, instead, reached into the cabinet for the plate given to her by Bridget and Mr. Nelson as a just-because gift the previous month. Etched with a whimsical pattern of fairy dust around the edges, her favorite part of the squeal-inducing surprise had been the sentiment spelled out across the plate's center: *Magical Tastes Make Magical Moments.* The second she'd unwrapped it, it had become her favorite possession. The fact that she'd been given it by people she loved so deeply simply made it all the more special.

With the plate piled high, Winnie crossed to the door and stopped, glancing back at Lovey as she did. "Are you coming, Your Highness?"

Lovey responded by leading Winnie down the steps, through the front door, across the porch, down the steps, and around the side yard to Bridget's back door. Winnie knocked once, twice, and then stopped as she saw Bridget's face appear beside a parted curtain panel.

Winnie lifted the cookie plate into the air and smiled as Bridget opened the back door. "Oh, you are a dear, Winifred. You heard my telepathic message, didn't you?"

"T-telepathic message?"

"The third toe on my left foot started aching about ten

minutes ago. I tried to ignore it until it became so bad it blurred my vision." Bridget wiggled a finger greeting at Lovey and then stepped back to allow Winnie and Lovey access to her kitchen.

Winnie waited for Lovey to enter and then stepped into her friend's kitchen and closed the door. "And now?"

"I'll soldier through the pain, dear. It's what I do." Bridget released a dramatic sigh and then limped (favoring her right foot, mind you) her way through the kitchen and into the living room, looking back over her shoulder every few steps to highlight her pain with a wince. "It is reassuring to know that you're so in tune with my health you'd check on me despite the late hour."

Winnie started to point out she'd merely seen the woman's light on and wanted companionship, but opted, in the end, to keep that nugget of information to herself. Instead, she turned her attention to the cat now circling Bridget's feet. "How come no one ever warned me about the lingering effects of tuna fish on a cat's breath?"

Slowly, Bridget lowered herself onto the chair at her computer desk and patted the brown and white tabby onto her lap. "Is your new momma finally trying to make friends with you, Lovey?"

"It's never been a question of trying, Bridget. I've tried. Countless times. Bribery doesn't work in that regard. Trust me on this." Winnie sank onto the rocking chair closest to her friend and gazed down at the cookie-topped plate.

"Then why the tuna?" Bridget asked.

"Because she earned it."

Nuzzling her nose to Lovey's, Bridget made a few soft clucking sounds and then turned her focus on Winnie. "I thought she was already using her litter box . . ."

"She was, she is, and she better never stop." She held the plate of cookies into the gap between their chairs and basked in the responding crackle of excitement that lit her friend's otherwise tired eyes. "No, I gave her tuna as a reward. For buying me that extra time with the poet this morning, and then with the mime earlier this evening."

Bridget pulled her hand back, mid–cookie reach. "You spoke with the mime, dear?"

"As much as anyone can speak with someone who communicates with his eyebrows and his hands, yes. I saw him out at the lake and Lovey decided he looked like someone she wanted to get to know."

"And?"

"Thanks to her, I found out he's not married, doesn't have kids, and he hails from New Jersey."

"How did you find out he was from New Jersey if he doesn't talk?"

"It's amazing what one can draw with little more than a stick and a dried patch of dirt."

"Anything else?"

"Nope. All conversation, for lack of a better word, ceased the moment I asked if he'd known Sally Dearfield prior to his arrival at the retreat. The second I asked that question, he started tapping on his watch and pretending he had somewhere really important to go."

Bridget plucked her cookie off the plate, took a quick bite, and swiveled back around to face her computer. "Hmmm . . . I haven't gotten to him yet, but maybe he went to Charlton School of the Arts, too."

"Charlton School of the Arts?" she echoed.

"Yes. It's a secondary school for students with a gift in the arts—performing, visual, or written." Bridget's fingers tapped the keyboard with ease and then retired to her lap (and Lovey) as a website devoted to the school flashed up on her screen. "So far, I can say with certainty, that the poet and the comedian both attended the school during the same time frame, although they only had one overlapping year. I was just getting to the magician when you knocked."

Winnie shifted the plate onto the end table to her left and scooted the rocking chair closer to Bridget and the computer. "So, at the very least, we know that two of them knew each other before the retreat started. Now, if we can only figure out if they knew Sally, somehow."

"Done."

Winnie ricocheted her gaze off the school's home page and back onto Bridget. "Done?"

"Paul Blark, the *Herald*'s obituary writer, is on vacation in the Caribbean with his pregnant girlfriend, and so Sally's obituary fell on me." Bridget leaned her head against the back of her desk chair and let her eyes drift closed. "Among the items I found about her life was mention of a lengthy career as a secretary at the Charlton School of the Arts."

Winnie sucked in a breath. "Are you serious?"

Without opening her eyes, Bridget nodded. "Seems she worked there for thirty years before retiring this past spring."

"I take it she was working there during the same time period Colin Norton and Ned Masterson were attending the school?"

"She was."

Winnie reached across her friend and moved the cursor across the website's masthead and its various tabs— Location, Programs, Admission Requirements, Faculty, Staff, Famous Alumni . . .

She clicked on the last tab, a dozen or more faces smiling

back at her from professional headshots. A few of the faces she recognized from book jackets and music sites, but a few she simply didn't know. She took in the names listed along with the photos and recognized one right away.

Abby Thompson, the puppeteer, smiled out at her from the screen, her time at the school recorded beneath her photo. Spying Bridget's notebook next to the screen, she compared the dates listed under Abby's picture with the ones written in Bridget's surprisingly youthful writing.

Abby's attendance dates didn't match with the poet's or the mime's, but they did overlap with the time Sally had worked at the school.

"Well, what do you know?" Winnie murmured. "An hour ago, we had nothing. Now, thanks to your genius, we can connect three of them to Sally for sure . . ." Winnie scrolled down past the last picture to a smattering of names highlighted for their mention in the news. The lengthy list took a few moments to skim, but sure enough, Colin Norton and Ned Masterson made the list as did the final two names associated with the current clientele at the Silver Lake Artists' Retreat.

"Bingo! We've got 'em all!"

A click on Abby's headshot, as well as on each of the four names highlighted in the section below the pictures, led to subsequent links—show reviews, question-and-answer articles, and a handful of special appearances. Nothing jumped out at her as being a red flag, but there would be time for that later. At least now they knew for certain that all five of the people found standing around Sally Dearfield's body did in fact know her beyond the confines of the Silver Lake Artists' Retreat.

"I have to say, Bridget, you are a genius!" When the

accolades went unacknowledged, she swung her attention back to the chair to find her friend sleeping peacefully, the pace of the woman's breath a near-perfect match to the quiet hum of Lovey's.

Rescuing the half-eaten cookie from the woman's hand, Winnie set it on the desk, closed out of the art school's website, powered off the computer, and made her way over to the double-wide trunk that doubled as a coffee table. Inside, she located Bridget's favorite summertime blanket and gently unfolded it across her friend's legs.

"Are you staying here for the night, Lovey, or are you coming home with me?" she whispered.

Lovey lifted her head off her paws, blinked up at Winnie, and then slowly lowered her chin back to its starting place.

"Okay, suit yourself." She draped the blanket across the chair's armrests to allow Lovey a way out, and then brushed a gentle kiss across Bridget's forehead. "Good night, my sweet friend. I'll show myself out."

Chapter 11

Winnie tossed her keys and rescue bag onto the kitchen table and gestured in the direction of the empty windowsill bed. "Lovey still isn't back yet?"

"Nope. But Bridget called and said she'd have her back after lunch." Renee pitched the lifestyle section of the newspaper onto the ottoman and stood. "You've got another delivery for two o'clock. The patient is reportedly quite stressed about a pending visit from her in-laws."

"Stressed, huh?" Winnie crossed to the sink and pumped two drops of soap into her hands, glancing back at Renee as she did. "Who called in the emergency?"

"The woman's husband."

"Any favorite tastes? Allergies?"

"No allergies." Renee wandered into the kitchen and over to the order pad situated next to the phone. "As for favorite tastes, the husband mentioned vanilla, strawberry, banana—"

"Goin' Bananas Foster—done." Winnie turned off the

faucet, dried her hands with a paper towel, and then turned to find Renee trying awfully hard to stifle a laugh. "What? No good?"

"You scare me. Truly."

"Why?"

"It's like you have an endless dessert bar in your head, twenty-four/seven." Renee plucked three bananas from a bowl on the counter, held them up, and then returned two at Winnie's direction. "I picture your mind as having all these desserts showcased on shiny plates. You know, with spotlights shining down on each one as it slowly spins around and around."

"Funny, but that's how I picture your brain in relation to shoes. To each her own, I say."

She shrugged off Renee's answering laugh and began firing off ingredients as they took a turn in her mental spotlight. "One banana, half a tablespoon of lemon juice, one tablespoon of unsalted butter, an eighth of a cup of dark brown sugar, an eighth of a teaspoon of ground cinnamon, a tablespoon of banana liqueur, an eighth of a cup of white rum, and half a pint of vanilla ice cream."

Renee moved from cabinet to cabinet assembling the required measuring spoons, cups, and ingredients. "Do we *have* banana liqueur?"

She made a face at her friend. "It's a potential baking ingredient, isn't it?"

"Oh. Right. I forgot who I was talking to for a moment."

It was Winnie's turn to laugh. "Anyway, since this will pretty much be made right in front of our patient, we really need to just make sure I have everything I need on-site, including the portable burner."

"Roger that." Renee transferred all nonperishables to the

rescue bag and then pointed at the refrigerator. "Hey, how about I make us both a sandwich since we don't have to worry about baking right now?"

Like Pavlov's dog, Winnie's tummy gurgled at the mere mention of food. "Yeah, sure. That sounds great. I'll take a ham on rye, but there's roast beef, too, if you'd rather have that. In the meantime, I'll grab the pretzels."

"And the cookies."

"Cookies?"

"The ones I found in the cookie jar while you were on the last rescue." Renee removed the ham from the refrigerator and placed it on the counter next to the cutting board. "I wish I could just say they *look* really good, but considering I've already eaten two, I'll just go ahead and tell you they're awesome and I want more."

Winnie located the pretzels on the top shelf of the pantry and carried them over to the table. "That's good to hear. I brought a plate of them over to Bridget's last night and she fell asleep before she even finished one."

Renee removed four slices of bread from the bag and topped two of them with ham. "What were you doing over there?"

"It was either that or bake another dessert."

Looking up from her nearly complete task, Renee's eyes narrowed on Winnie. "Uh-oh. What's wrong?"

"Am I that transparent?" She plucked two water bottles from the refrigerator and joined Renee at the table. "Seriously?"

"When it comes to late-night bake-athons, yes." Renee took a spot on the far side of the table, lifted her sandwich from her plate, and shook it at Winnie. "I thought those bags under your eyes were a bit darker than normal this morning."

Laura Bradford

"*Than normal?*" Winnie echoed, helping herself to a pretzel. "Gee, thanks."

Renee took a bite of her sandwich and then set it back on her plate. "So? What gives? Is it Jay?"

She took another pretzel and nibbled off the salt. "Partly."

"He still hasn't called?"

"No."

"Men. They're as fickle as the day is long," Renee mused. "If they weren't so adorable, I'd say forget them all."

Winnie considered her friend's suggestion and realized it had merit. Still, they were talking about Jay—a man she was pretty much crazy about. "California is three hours behind us. Maybe it's more a case of him not wanting to call too late."

"Okay, but what is he *doing*? I thought this trip was for Scream Queen to spend time with her mother. Shouldn't Jay have oodles of free time while that's happening?"

This time the merit in her friend's words was harder to explain away. Instead, she merely shrugged and took a bite of her own sandwich. "Oh, hey, did I tell you I'm getting a bit of a reputation at Silver Lake High School?"

Renee stopped chewing. "As . . ."

"The second coming of Lady Tremaine?"

"Wait, I know this!" Renee hijacked a pretzel from the bag and broke it in two before popping it into her mouth. "Lady Tremaine was Cinderella's evil stepmother, wasn't she?"

Winnie nodded.

"And you're getting that reputation because . . ." The words trailed from Renee's mouth only to pick back up as her eyes widened with understanding. "Wait. Scream Queen goes to Silver Lake High School, doesn't she?"

"She does, indeed."

"So you're being painted as an evil witch at school. How do you know this?"

"Do you remember the rescue I did yesterday afternoon?" Winnie asked as she finished her sandwich and took a sip of her water. "The Black-and-Blue Cookies?"

Renee stopped nibbling and waited.

"Seems the patient knows Caroline. And when she realized who I was in relation to her, she pretty much filled in the rest." Winnie pushed the cookie plate over to Renee, waited while she took one, and then helped herself to one as well. "There's one positive, though. Our patient doesn't agree."

"Who would?" Renee's lip curled in disgust before she sought solace in her cookie. "Anyone with two eyes knows you've been nothing but amazing with the Scream Queen. She just doesn't want to share her dad. Period."

Winnie looked down at her own cookie, her appetite suddenly gone. "You've gotta stop calling her that."

"Calling her what?"

"Scream Queen."

"Why?" Renee challenged. "I'm quite sure she calls you worse."

Sadly, there was no argument to be made. Still, she had to keep her chin up. "I need to remember what Mr. Nelson is always telling me about Lovey. Who knows, maybe he's right. Maybe if I give it time, she'll come around."

"Is Lovey still hissing at you?"

Winnie's shoulders slumped. "Yes."

"How long have you had her now?"

"Five months."

"Maybe Mr. Nelson needs a new catchphrase." Reaching across the table, Renee plucked Winnie's cookie from her hands and ate it. "These are way, way, *way* too good to go to waste."

Sliding her empty plate to the side, Winnie set her elbows on the table and rested her chin inside her right palm. "Can we talk about something else for a while? Like maybe what's going on with you and Bob? Is the custody schedule working out okay?"

The glimmer of mischief that always seemed to hover around Renee disappeared. In its place was a hint of sadness that showed in her eyes, her mouth, her demeanor. "Insofar as there've been no issues, yes. But the nights when Ty is with him are seemingly endless."

"Dating from time to time would probably help that," Winnie suggested.

"Chocolate does just fine, thankyouverymuch." Renee ran her fingers through her white-blond hair and then shook it back into place. "Besides, if I couldn't hold my husband's interest, why would I think I could hold someone else's?"

"Because Bob is an idiot."

"Among many, I'm sure." Renee considered a third cookie but gathered their plates and empty water bottles instead. "Seriously, I'm not interested. My focus now is on raising Ty to be a good man. My future daughter-in-law will thank me one day."

Winnie wanted to argue, to point out all the reasons her friend shouldn't give up on romance, but maybe it was too soon. The ink had been dry on Renee's divorce papers for only a month or so longer than the Dessert Squad had been up and running. The thought of dipping one's toe into the dating pool after fifteen years of loving someone else had to be tough all on its own. Trying to do it after the aforementioned someone cheated on you had to make it even harder.

Reaching across the table, she squeezed Renee's arm. "One of these days, when you're ready, you'll see all the heads you turn on a daily basis." Then, without giving her friend a chance to pooh-pooh her comment, she moved on. "I saw your mime last night."

"My mime?"

"Yeah, the one who taught Ty how to skip rocks over the weekend."

There was no denying the dash of hope that momentarily pushed the pain from Renee's emerald green eyes. There was also no denying the way she shook it off and tried to play nonchalant. "Oh?"

"After I had the joy of hearing just how widespread Caroline's hatred is for me, I decided to stop out at the lake and unwind. But no matter how many times I told Lovey she needed to stay put, she didn't listen." Winnie shot her hands in the air. "Big surprise, I know. Anyway, she spotted the one lone person on our side of the lake and had to make friends."

"It was him?"

Winnie eyed the clock, then swung her leg over the bench and stood. "It was. We chatted a little—if you want to call me talking and him arching his eyebrow now and again chatting, that is. I tried to get a handle on his background insofar as any connection he could possibly have to the victim, but he shut down on me."

"Shut down on you?"

"He suddenly had to go at that exact moment." She carried the plates to the sink and the trash to the wastebasket and then washed her hands again. "But I got his card before he left. It's on my desk."

"Do you think there really is a connection? I mean, beyond just being at the retreat when Sally died?"

Winnie dried her hands on a paper towel and then turned her attention to the cold items that needed to be packed into the cooler for the next rescue. "Thanks to Bridget and her nose for news, I *know* there's a connection."

Renee met Winnie at the center island and took the ice cream from Winnie's hands. "You get the portable burner, I'll finish packing this stuff up."

"Thanks, Renee." She made her way over to the pantry and the section she'd carved out for special equipment. Once she located the portable burner, she returned to the center island for her rescue bag and the cooler. "So now I know he attended the same special arts school where Sally worked for more than three decades. The other four did, too. But all that does is show prior knowledge of the victim. I'm going to need a whole lot more than that before I can finger her killer."

Glancing up at the clock, Renee patted the bag and then helped Winnie hoist it up and onto her shoulder. "You better go. I'll call you if we get another order."

Chapter 12

The second they stepped inside the entryway of Luigi's, Winnie lifted her chin and savored the aromatic medley of warm bread, garlic, and marinara sauce. While she still preferred the now-defunct Mario's for her weekly pizza night with Mr. Nelson, the newer, hipper Italian eatery was beginning to grow on them.

"Mmmm . . . I say we get an order of garlic knots before our pizza." Winnie took in one more deep breath and then met her housemate's smile with one of her own. "What do you say, Mr. Nelson? Are you in?"

"Don't gotta ask me twice." Gesturing her forward with his non-cane-holding hand, he led the way past the vacant hostess stand and over to his preferred booth in front of the large picture window overlooking Main Street.

When they were settled on their respective sides—Winnie with a view of the stationary dessert tray, and Mr. Nelson with a clear shot of the women coming in and out of the yoga studio next door—he tucked his cane underneath his feet. "I about fell over when Bridget told me she wouldn't be joining us. Can't remember a time her jaw hasn't been flappin' a mile a minute across this very table."

It was true. In the nearly two years since they'd established their weekly pizza night, none of them had missed an outing. They pointed to their shared love of pizza as the reason, but they all knew the tradition meant so much more. For Mr. Nelson, the outing was a chance to see and be seen. For Winnie, it was a chance to be waited on while enjoying time with two of her best friends. For Bridget, it was likely a tie between not wanting to miss something and knowing that, despite the ribbing she suffered at the hands of Mr. Nelson, she was treasured by both him and Winnie.

A cloud of something Winnie couldn't quite identify shifted across Mr. Nelson's face, taking with it his normal jovial mood. "You ain't keeping something from me, are you, Winnie Girl?"

She paused the carafe of water above his empty glass. "Like what?"

"Like maybe one of those winces she's always making, or one of them pains she's always yakking about, is something real?" His pale blue eyes moved between the water she'd added to his glass and the tabletop Parmesan cheese before slowly making their way back to hers. "She ain't getting ready to check out on us, is she?"

"If only Bridget were here now," Winnie said, grinning. "If she was, she'd be able to see with her own two eyes that you care about her."

"About *that* hypochondriac?" A series of chest-puffing, hand-flicking, head-shaking movements gave way to a lowering of his stubbled chin and, finally, a whisper. "Serenity

Lane wouldn't be the same without her, Winnie Girl. I might forget all the reasons I've been a bachelor all these years if she wasn't around to remind me with nearly every word out of her big mouth."

Winnie's laughter was cut short by the genuine concern etched across every feature of her friend's face. "She's fine, Mr. Nelson. Really. She's just covering a library board meeting for one of her coworkers. I told her I'd bring her home a slice of pizza and a piece of that tiramisu she keeps hoping will be good but never is."

"That's because her skull is so dang thick." He took another sip of his water and then leaned his upper body across the top of the table. "You're not gonna tell her I was asking about her, are you?"

"Would it be so awful for Bridget to know you don't hate her?"

"Yes!"

She considered putting up an argument but knew it was futile. Besides, if Mr. Nelson and Bridget quit arguing, half (okay, maybe 99 percent) of her daily entertainment would cease to exist. In the end she gave him the nod he was seeking. "Your secret is safe with me."

"I knew I could count on you, Winnie Girl." He patted the top of her hand and then retracted his to summon Katrina, his favorite twenty-something waitress, over to the table.

"Hiya, Mr. Nelson . . . Winnie." Katrina cheeked her wad of gum on the right side of her mouth and wiggled her fingers at Mr. Nelson as if he were a six-month-old child. He, of course, responded in kind (with a side order of drool to boot) before she looked back at Winnie. "Where's Ms. O'Keefe this evening?"

"Working."

"When *I'm* that old, I plan on living out the rest of my days on a beach somewhere in the middle of Tennessee," Katrina said, working her gum toward her left cheek. "Anyways, you want your usual? Large pie with just cheese on one side and sausage and pepperoni on the other?"

Mr. Nelson met Winnie's eye and guided it back to the leggy brunette with his enamored grin (and not-so-sly once-over). "She's purty *and* smart, ain't she, Winnie Girl?"

She resisted the urge to groan and, instead, added an order of garlic knots before Katrina bounced off in the direction of the kitchen.

When he was sure she was out of sight (and he made triple sure), he leaned forward again, dropping his voice to his version of a whisper (translation: full voice). "When she comes back, should I tell her there're no beaches in Tennessee?"

"Nah. It's her dream, not yours." Winnie wrapped her fingers around her water glass and released a long sigh, the last of the day's busyness exiting her neck and shoulders once and for all. "I can't even begin to tell you how good it feels to just sit here . . . with you . . . and not have to worry about anything except whether we should save a garlic knot for Bridget."

"She don't need to know we got knots."

"Are you sure?"

"You say that like you doubt me," he groused.

"No, I say that like one who *knows* your secret-keeping ability. Or lack thereof."

He waved her words away with a weathered hand and then lifted his water glass into the air between them. "If you can keep a secret about what I asked earlier, then I can keep a secret about your garlic knots. Heck, I keep secrets all the time."

She felt her eyebrow arch and confirmed it in the reflection of the silver napkin holder at her elbow. "About what?"

Swiping his hand across his mouth, Mr. Nelson looked left toward the sidewalk, right toward Katrina and the tray of soda glasses she was readying for transport to another table, and finally back to Winnie as he attempted (and failed) another whisper. "I know you were keeping time with someone other than your professor last night."

"I—I—"

"Now, don't you worry none, Winnie Girl, I didn't say nothing to anyone."

A glance around the dining area confirmed the sensation of a half-dozen or more sets of eyes being trained on their table. She swallowed. Hard.

"Except maybe Cornelia . . . and Harold . . . and—" He stopped, tapped his chin in thought, and then nodded. "My barber, Lenny. But that's it."

"You are a locked vault, Mr. Nelson. A. Locked. Vault."

The age spots on his cheeks elongated with his smile. "See? I can keep secrets."

This time when she sighed, it had absolutely nothing to do with releasing the day's tension. "For the record, I wasn't keeping time with anyone. I simply stopped out at the lake to clear my head after my last delivery of the day and ended up talking to that guy Renee was telling us about over the weekend—you know, the one who taught Ty how to skip rocks."

"The hand flapper?" Mr. Nelson asked.

She gave into the giggle spawned by the visual accompaniment to the man's verbal assessment. "*Mime*, actually, but yes. Him."

His eyes widened before narrowing in on Winnie. "Does Renee know you're keeping time with him?"

Groaning, she dropped her head onto the table.

"Does she?" he asked again.

Lifting only her eyes, she peeked up at her dinner companion. "I wasn't keeping time with the mime, Mr. Nelson. Not in the way it sounds like you're implying . . . and likely implied to Cornelia, Harold, and your barber when you weren't saying nothing to anyone, of course."

He straightened up in his seat. "You're a poet and you didn't even know it, Winnie Girl." A wink followed. "See what I did there? I said you're a *poet* . . . and you didn't even *know it*."

"Clever, Mr. Nelson." She pulled her head up off the table, bracing her cheeks with her hands. "The mime was sitting by the lake when Lovey and I pulled up. Lovey, being Lovey, had to make his acquaintance. I tried to get her to leave him alone and, well, since she hates me she didn't listen. So I passed the time by chatting with him. I chatted, he answered with his hands. When I asked him if he knew Sally Dearfield prior to arriving at Silver Lake Artists' Retreat, he pretended he had to leave and he did."

Take that to your barber . . .

They both leaned back from their perspective spots at the table when Katrina reappeared with their garlic knots, a side of sauce, and a pair of plates. Bypassing the whole plate routine, Winnie plucked a knot from the basket and popped it in her mouth, releasing a moan of pleasure in the process. "Oh. Wow. Good."

Mr. Nelson smiled up at Katrina. "I think we're good for now, sweetheart."

Winnie added a nod on the end of the man's sentence and then reached for a second knot. "You'd think I didn't eat all day with as hungry as I am at this exact . . ." A familiar face near the now-manned hostess stand distracted her from her thought and had her scrambling for a name to match. Annie—no, Gabby, no . . . "Abby!" she whispered across her third knot. "Abby Thompson! The puppeteer!"

"Puppet what?" Mr. Nelson volleyed back, sans anything resembling a whisper.

Uh-oh.

Before she could wave him off, though, Abby turned in their direction, giving them a bird's-eye view of the exact moment Winnie's identity registered in the woman's brain. Suddenly, any hint of a smile that had accompanied her into the restaurant was gone, in its place a tangible discomfort.

Hmmm . . .

Casting what she hoped was a nonverbal warning to her housemate, Winnie followed it up with a whispered, "Behave," and waved the woman over to their table. Any possibility the puppeteer would decline the gesture or pretend it hadn't been seen was eliminated when the hostess led her to the table behind theirs.

"Abby, right?" Winnie abandoned her latest knot to her still-stacked plate and swiveled her body toward the aisle.

"That's right." Abby's gaze swept across the table to take in Mr. Nelson before settling somewhere just above Winnie's head. "You're the baker."

"I am." Desperate to put the woman at ease, she pointed across the table. "Mr. Nelson, this is Abby Thompson. She's a puppeteer who's traveled the country with a suitcase of puppets."

Laura Bradford

Mr. Nelson stuck out his hand, waited for Abby to recip-
rocate, and then lifted her fingers to his lips for a kiss. "It's
a pleasure to meet you, Miss Thompson."

"I, um . . . thank you. You, too, Mr. Nelson."

"You can call me Parker." With obvious reluctance, he
released Abby's hand and jerked his chin at Winnie. "Been
telling this one the same thing since the day she moved in
upstairs, but she doesn't listen. Keeps calling me Mr. Nelson
like I'm some sort of old fart."

Winnie's laugh mingled with Abby's for a moment and
she let it. When it played itself out, she rescued her abandoned knot and took a bite. "Good thing Bridget isn't here
tonight, Mr. Nelson, because she wouldn't have let that comment go unchecked."

Then, turning her focus back on Abby, she added,
"Bridget is our next-door neighbor. She's eighty and she
refuses to cut Mr. Nelson slack about *anything*."

"If I sneeze too loudly, she yells at me. If I don't warn
her about the whoopee cushion I stuck under her seat before
she sits down, she yells at me. If I blink wrong, she yells at
me." Mr. Nelson rolled his index finger above the table.
"Nag, nag, nag."

Slowly but surely, the discomfort that had been so obvious on Abby's face when she spotted Winnie began to dis-
sipate, thanks to Mr. Nelson's histrionics.

"Fortunately for me," he continued, "I can tune her out
with a flip of a dial." He tapped the hearing aid in his left
ear and grinned. "Now all I need is a pair of window shades
for my eyes . . . that way I don't have to see her mouth moving, neither."

Abby laughed again, prompting Winnie to have to resist

112

the very real urge to lean across the table and plant a kiss on her housemate's cheek. Instead, she offered Abby the last garlic knot in the basket and silently celebrated when it was declined.

"Mr. Nelson, here, is retired navy. Twenty-five years, actually," Winnie said as he, too, declined the last knot. When Abby didn't react, Winnie helped herself to the leftover and continued, widening her conversational net to include the man now nodding his head with pride. "Abby visited your former naval station over the holidays. To entertain the sailors with her puppets and her marionettes. She's quite gifted at what she does."

Abby's left eyebrow hitched, but before she could speak, Mr. Nelson jumped back into the conversation, his interest piqued. "You were at the Charleston naval base?"

"I—I was." Abby pinned Winnie with a curious eye. "How did you know that?"

"I read it."

The beginnings of a smile inched the corners of her mouth upward until the pride Abby felt was on full display. "So someone other than my mother actually caught that mention of me in *Performers' Weekly*, huh?"

"*Performers' Weekly?* Really? Wow, that must have been pretty pinch-worthy . . ."

Abby drew back, her smile still in place. "I take it you read about it somewhere else?"

"On the Charlton School of the Arts' website. When I clicked on your picture."

"Y-you're familiar with Charlton?" Abby asked, her smile fading.

"I wasn't until last night. Bridget, the woman we were

just telling you about, came across it while writing Sally Dearfield's obituary."

Like a lamp that was suddenly powered off, Abby's face drained of all color, prompting Winnie to slide out of the booth and onto her feet as the woman turned and made haste toward the door. "Abby? Are you okay?"

Chapter 13

Night had fallen across Serenity Lane, taking with it the buzz of hedge clippers, the whir of Harold Jenkins's motorized scooter, the jingle of Con-Man's leash as Cornelia walked her beloved sheltie from one end of the road to the other, and the near-constant exchange of greetings delivered over porch rails. Judging by the darkened first-floor windows Winnie could see from her rocking chair, she guessed the vast majority of her neighbors had retired to their bedrooms for the night.

She'd thought about it off and on all day—the notion of escaping to bed with a paperback in one hand and a bowl of popcorn in the other. But after the interesting turn of events at dinner, she knew there was no way she could settle her brain down enough to read, let alone sleep.

"I'm telling you, Bridget, the key to what happened to Sally is that school." She scooped a handful of popcorn from the bowl Mr. Nelson gave her and then passed it across to the woman seated in the next rocking chair. "I can feel it in my bones."

A burst of exhaled air off to her immediate right was followed by the sound of Mr. Nelson's hand smacking his forehead. "Ah, Winnie Girl, did you have to go and get her started on all of that?"

"What are you talking about, Mr.—"

"I wish that's *all* my bones were doing right now, dear. If it was, I could sleep without interruption and move without pain. But, alas"—Bridget sighed dramatically—"it's not to be."

Mr. Nelson shook his head at Winnie. "Now, look what you went and did to a perfectly good night . . ."

Taking advantage of Bridget's ongoing ailment list, Winnie peeked at Mr. Nelson, readied her silent apology, and then swallowed it as his hands flew upward to the collar of his button-down shirt and began desperately patting the area around the top button.

"Mr. Nelson? Are you—"

"Popcorn? I didn't know there'd be popcorn!"

Dread propelled her out of her rocking chair and over to the steps as her friend and employee stepped onto the porch, an unusual aura clinging to the woman's sneaker-clad body.

Sneakers?

"Renee, what's wrong?"

"What makes you think something is wrong?" Renee crossed in front of Bridget's rocking chair and dropped onto Winnie's.

"You mean aside from the fact that it's nine thirty on a Wednesday and you're wearing . . ." She paused, swallowed, and continued, her voice shaky. *"Sneakers?"*

Mr. Nelson leaned forward, pulling his gaze off Renee's

bosom just long enough to inspect her feet. Bridget, too, took in the spectacle while Renee waved away Winnie's concern.

"I'm being practical."

"Practical?" Winnie echoed. "You?"

Renee helped herself to a handful of popcorn from the bowl Bridget offered and popped one, two, three pieces into her mouth, chewing each one much like a squirrel nibbled on acorns. "I live a mile away, Winnie. That's two miles round trip. I'd be brought up on shoe-abuse charges if I tried to make that trip in any of my stilettos."

"Wait." Winnie craned her neck around the porch upright and did a mental inventory of the driveway (just the Dessert Squad) and the street (nothing). "You walked?"

Renee popped two more pieces of popcorn into her mouth and nodded. "I figured it would be good exercise."

"Walking around the block after dinner is good exercise, Renee. You just walked a mile . . . in the dark."

"I didn't eat dinner."

"You didn't eat . . . ?" The words trailed away as Renee's shrug, coupled with the downward cast of her eyes, filled in the blanks. "I have some leftover pizza in the house if you'd like some."

Even with the limited light, there was no mistaking the way Renee's eyes lit up or the way the rocking chair pitched forward as she stood. "Carry on. I'll be back in a few."

When she was gone, Mr. Nelson motioned Winnie over to his chair. "While she's gone, would you go inside my place, Winnie Girl, and bring me the tan-colored box that's on the bottom shelf of my television cabinet?"

"Sure thing, Mr. Nelson."

She followed the jet stream left in Renee's pizza-seeking

wake but turned left into Mr. Nelson's place rather than heading up the stairs to her own. It took less than a minute to find the requested item and carry it back to the porch, where it was snatched from her hands by a clearly desperate man.

Flipping the lid open, he pointed down at the plethora of clip-on bow ties inside. "Which one, Winnie Girl?"

"Mr. Nelson, you don't need a bow tie," she protested, mid-laugh. "It's almost bedtime. Consider it your version of Renee's sneakers."

He extracted a purple and white polka-dot tie and held it against his striped shirt. "How about this?"

"No, I think—"

"Winnie, this smells and looks positively divine." Renee's sneakers smacked against the stairs and sent Mr. Nelson's bow tie–holding hand up to his collar.

Snap went the tie.

Thump went the box.

The screen door smacked against the exterior wall and Renee emerged, pizza in one hand, a diet soda in the other. Lovey, obviously awoken from her windowsill slumber, was at her feet. "So what's shaking on Serenity Lane this evening?"

Mr. Nelson tossed his shoulders back and made a show of looking down at his collar.

Before Winnie could even complete her eye roll, Bridget lolled her head against the back of her rocking chair and murmured something under her breath. For the most part, the eighty-year-old's rant was unintelligible, but an occasional word (like *pathetic* and *brainless*) was pretty clear.

If Renee noticed, she didn't let on. Instead, she made her way back to Winnie's chair, stopping to acknowledge Mr. Nelson's bow tie as she did.

Mr. Nelson, in turn, puffed out his chest with pride.

Oh brother . . .

"Anything *exciting*?" Renee added once she, and her pizza, were settled.

Winnie lowered herself to the top step and rested her back against the closest upright. "Mr. Nelson and I ran into Abby Thompson at Luigi's this evening."

Renee looked at Winnie over top of her pizza slice. "Why does that name sound familiar?"

"She's the puppeteer staying out at the retreat center."

"Did she have her puppet with her?" Renee asked.

"No."

Renee took a bite and then paused, her cheek full. "I thought it was kind of weird the way she was moving that puppet's mouth when she was reacting to Sally's death. Like the puppet was talking for her."

"I know. I thought that, too." Winnie closed her eyes and allowed herself a moment to simply take in the night air. "But maybe it was force of habit. Kind of like it is for me when we eat dessert out at a restaurant and I start critiquing it, ingredient by ingredient. What I do know for certain is that she was none too pleased when I brought up her connection to the victim."

The gentle creak of Bridget's rocker came to a stop. "The same connection they *all* had to the victim."

"I wonder if they knew one another prior to this week," Winnie mused. "I mean, I know they didn't all attend the school at the same time—some were long graduated before the others attended—but I wonder if they knew each other from schoolwide reunions or something."

Bridget scanned the floor of the porch until she located Lovey and then patted the cat up and onto her lap. "I was wondering the same thing earlier this evening, so I did a little checking on the school. Seems they have a strong alumni network that not only supports the school financially, but also benefits the students in terms of networking and, sometimes, getting that first big break after graduation."

"So maybe they know each other that way?" Winnie suggested.

"Maybe. Hard to know without asking them directly."

Winnie looked up at the stars and tried to imagine Jay looking out at the same ones in California. Then again, it could still be considered dinnertime on the West Coast . . .

Shaking the interloping image of Jay and his ex-wife laughing together across a white linen tablecloth from her thoughts, she willed herself to remain focused, to be in the conversation happening on the porch rather than the one in her head. "Based on how that worked with the mime and the puppeteer, I'm not holding out hope we'd get anything useful."

"But you asked them when leaving was an option, didn't you?"

She gave Renee her full attention. "Meaning?"

"Didn't you say you asked the good-looking one if he knew Sally prior to this week while he was sitting on the edge of the lake bed?" At Winnie's nod, Renee continued, stopping every few words to chew her latest bite of pizza. "He didn't *have* to stay . . . so he didn't. Sounds like that was the case this evening with Abby, too."

Mr. Nelson pointed the end of his cane at Winnie. "She's right, Winnie Girl. When you asked her about that school, she hadn't ordered yet. In fact, she hadn't even sat down yet. So it was easy for her to just go."

It made sense. But really, what was the alternative? Tie them down before she asked them certain questions?

"I get what you're saying, but a person can walk away from a conversation anytime they want, can't they?"

Bridget stopped rocking once again, earning Winnie a death glare from Lovey in the process. "Not if those questions come in a public forum."

"What kind of a public forum?"

"Well, like Beans, for starters."

She stared at her neighbor. "Beans? What on earth could Beans possibly have to do with any of this? Besides the fact that I'm now craving a mug of their coffee?"

"It's summertime, Winnie." Bridget resumed the steady pace of her chair much to Lovey's delight.

"And?"

"Tomorrow is open mic night at Beans."

"Okay . . .

"The owners have asked Mr. Masterson to serve as emcee for the event."

She sat up straight as Bridget's words registered. "As in Ned Masterson, the comedian?"

"One and the same."

She took a moment to process the news, but it was Renee's voice that brought it home. "Maybe you could ask whatever question you want during the Q and A they always do in the middle of the show."

"Ain't gonna be easy to turn tail and run when you've got a coffee shop of people hanging on your every word." Mr. Nelson cleared his throat, straightened his bow tie, and gestured toward the popcorn bowl Bridget had set on the floor beside her purse. When Renee passed it to him, he acknowledged her gesture with a wink.

"This is perfect!" Winnie declared, rising to her feet. "I mean, I know that only helps with one of them, but one is better than none at this point."

Renee worked her pizza down to the crust and then pointed it in Winnie's general direction. "Come Saturday afternoon, you'll have two."

"Two?"

"That's right."

"How do you figure that?"

Renee gnawed on the crust for a moment and then dropped it onto her paper plate. "Well, I'm kind of hoping I can talk you into helping me with an impromptu party I've decided to throw for Ty."

"Ty's birthday isn't until October," she reminded her friend.

"I know. But he's been through a lot this year with the divorce and the split time between Bob and me. I thought a just-because day with his friends might be a nice thing to do."

Winnie wandered closer to Renee and met the woman's eyes with the reassuring smile she knew was needed. "I think it's a fabulous idea. I'll help in whatever way you need me to—just name it."

"Desserts?"

"That goes without saying."

"An extra pair of eyes?"

"Done."

"Pick up and return the entertainer I hired?"

"You hired an entertainer?" Winnie repeated.

Pitching forward on her rocking chair, Bridget reached into the back pocket of her jeans, pulled out a small rectangular card, and handed it to Winnie. "You told me you put this on your desk and I couldn't resist checking it out."

Winnie took the card and held it up to the porch light, a smile spreading across her face as she read the words aloud. "'George Watkins. Mime. Birthday parties, corporate events, retirement parties, special events . . .'"

Chapter 14

She was less than a foot from the Dessert Squad, with Lovey in tow, when she heard the telltale thump of his cane as he stepped onto the porch from their shared vestibule. Turning, Winnie balanced her latest rescue on her right forearm and waved.

"Good morning, Mr. Nelson. I didn't hear you snoring last night. Did you sleep okay?"

Poking his head beyond the porch rail, he shrugged his narrow shoulders. "Where you off to this morning?"

"A dessert rescue." She lifted the plated cake level with her face and then set it on the top of the ambulance. "It's a kuchen."

"A what?"

"A kuchen—like a coffee cake of sorts."

He nodded. "And whatcha calling it? For your rescue?"

"A Kootchy-Kootchy-Koo Kuchen." She glanced at her wristwatch and willed herself to relax. After all, she always padded her departure time in case of an unexpected delay. "My customer apparently needs a bit of cheering up. So I'm delivering an edible tickle."

"A pickle? Who orders a pickle?" Mr. Nelson shouted.

Winnie tapped her ear and waited for Mr. Nelson to get the point. He, in turn, fiddled with his hearing aids. When she saw his hand drop back to his side, she repeated the misheard word. "I'm delivering an edible *tickle*."

In lieu of his usual nod, he caned his way down the stairs and over to Winnie. "I was thinking about your little dilemma last night, Winnie Girl."

Keenly aware of her decreasing delivery window, she retrieved the dessert from the roof of the ambulance and carried it around to the back of the rig. "What dilemma is that, Mr. Nelson?" She unlatched the back door, set the dessert inside its waiting container, and secured her rescue bag in a holder to its left.

"Trying to find out things from people who don't want to talk to you."

"Meaning?"

Mr. Nelson trailed her back around to the driver's-side door. "The mime, the puppeteer—them folks."

With a snap of her hand, she opened her door to admit Lovey, and then slid into position behind the steering wheel. "That's going to change, remember? I'm going to hit up Open Mic Night at Bean's tonight to see what I can find out from the comedian, and then I've got Ty's party on Saturday with the mime."

"But that's only two of 'em. You've got three more, don't you?"

She pulled her keys out of the inside pocket Bridget had sewn into her uniform top and inserted the correct key into the ignition. "True, but opportunities haven't presented themselves for those three . . . yet."

"I can help."

A vibration from the same pocket had her reaching for her phone and checking the text display.

You're going to be late!

She leaned forward enough to catch a view of her second-floor window and, sure enough, Renee was looking down at them. "Mr. Nelson, you don't need to worry about this stuff. I'll figure it out."

"I want to help. I'm not any good at computers like Bridget is, so I can't do none of that inline research stuff she's always babbling on and on about."

"Online," she corrected.

His brows furrowed. "Huh?"

"You just referenced Bridget's research. Only you said 'inline' instead of 'online,' and it's *online*."

"Online, inline, offline—it's still like listening to a foreign language to me. I know nothing about that stuff." Something about the lack of sparkle in his eye caught Winnie off guard, but before she could inquire about it, he continued, his voice void of its usual happy lilt. "And I don't have a kid to throw a party for like Ms. Ballentine does. But that don't mean I can't help. Why, I can—"

Winnie looked from Renee, to Lovey, and back to Renee, before coming up with just the right words. "Mr. Nelson, trust me, your comic relief last night helped tremendously. There's enough heaviness in the world these days. Being able to inject the kind of lightness that makes people laugh the way you do? That's a gift. One I treasure."

"I just know you've got a lot on your plate, Winnie Girl, what with your business . . . and your young fella . . . and . . ."

She knew he was still talking. She could see his mouth moving out of the corner of her eye. But the moment he referenced Jay, her thoughts were off and running.

On yet another night that came and went without a call . . .

On the blanks her brain had insisted on filling in while she tossed and turned through the night . . .

On—

Her phone vibrated in her hand.

You have five minutes to get across town!

Tossing the device onto the seat alongside Lovey, she turned the key and listened to the answering hum of the engine. "Mr. Nelson, I really have to go."

"But I—"

Another vibration.

Go!

"Why don't you go inside, Mr. Nelson, and turn on the news. Maybe you'll get an early sighting of your favorite weather girl." Reaching across the gap between her body and the open door, Winnie wrapped her hands around the handle and pulled it closed. Then, slipping the gearshift into reverse with her right hand, she blew a kiss to her housemate as she maneuvered the ambulance off the driveway and onto Serenity Lane.

A kiss he didn't catch, or return.

She was halfway to the ambulance when the jingle of her phone from deep inside her purse mocked her full hands.

"Great, just great," she murmured. Shifting the plastic dry cleaning bag and the uniform tops it contained from her left hand to her right forearm, she fumbled inside her purse until she had a visual of the phone's screen.

Renee . . .

She contemplated letting it go to voice mail, but her curiosity won out. "Hey, Renee, what's up? I swung through the grocery store to replenish the ingredient cabinet and now I'm just leaving the dry cleaners. We'll be back at the house in about ten minutes—twenty if we stop for a milkshake at Jake's."

"If you do, get me banana." Renee paused and then rushed to amend her order. "Wait! No! Make it a peanut butter chocolate chunk shake."

At the ambulance, Winnie nodded at Lovey through the partially open driver's-side window and then carried the dry cleaning around to the back. "Text that to me when we get off so I don't get up to the counter and order banana." Wedging the phone between her cheek and her shoulder, she opened the gate and thrust her uniforms inside.

"Roger that."

She made her way back around the ambulance, unlocked her door, and slid in behind the steering wheel before Lovey got any bright ideas. "So if you're calling to check on the delivery—it went well."

"Your driveway gabfest didn't make you too late, did it?"

"Thankfully, no. Thanks, no doubt, to the traffic light gods who kept things green the whole way there. I pulled into the woman's driveway two minutes ahead of schedule."

"I'll take credit for that," Renee said. "The way you two were yakking, I suspect you'd still be here if I hadn't pestered you with those text messages."

Winnie inserted the key into the ignition and listened as the engine hummed to life. "Yeah, thank you for that. Though, I think I might have hurt Mr. Nelson's feelings by running out on him the way I did."

"Puh-lease. Like you could ever do anything to get that man upset with you."

"Said the pot to the kettle." Yet even as the retort left her mouth, she knew Renee was right. Mr. Nelson enjoyed flirting with Renee, but he treated Winnie like gold. "Maybe I should pick up a shake for him, too. Strawberry."

"He's not here."

"Hang on a sec, I'm putting you on speaker so I can drive." She hit the Speaker button, set the phone down next to Lovey, and piloted the car toward Main Street. "Okay . . . so where were we?"

"The shake for Mr. Nelson. I wouldn't bother. He's not here," Renee repeated around a yawn. "Master Sergeant Hottie showed up about twenty minutes after you left."

At the mouth of the parking lot, Winnie turned left and headed toward Jake's. "Did Greg say what he wanted?"

"No."

"Hmmm . . ." She felt the smile spreading across her face and confirmed it in the rearview mirror. "The Dessert Squad wasn't in the driveway, so if he came inside it wasn't to see me . . ."

"I may drift off to sleep to fantasies like that, but in the cold light of day I'm not blind. *You* might be, but *I'm* not."

She slowed as Jake's Milkshake Shack came into view and silently marveled at the way Lovey (an ice-cream enthusiast thanks to Mr. Nelson) placed her front paws on the driver's-side door and peered out at their destination as if she knew . . .

"Winnie? You still there?"

"Um . . . yeah. Sorry. I was distracted by Lovey. She's like a savant when it comes to Jake's."

"Smart cat. Anyway, when are you going to realize Master Sergeant Hottie only has eyes for you?"

"You're nuts, Renee. Greg knows I'm with Jay and he gets it. You know this. We've been over it a bazillion times." She flipped on her blinker, turned into the drive-thru lane of Jake's, and took her place in line. "Maybe it's like *I* said—maybe he was there to see *you*."

The car at the front of the line placed an order and moved forward, prompting Winnie and the rest of the order line to move up one car length.

Getting closer . . .

"Considering he didn't come upstairs, I highly doubt it."

She stopped salivating and concentrated on her friend. "Then why was he there?" she asked.

"To pick up Mr. Nelson."

There was no denying the dread that ignited in Winnie's chest and spread outward to every nook and cranny of her body. "Wh-what happened? Is he okay? Did . . . did he fall?" A movie reel of worst-case scenarios fast-forwarded through her mind's eye, making it difficult to breathe. "It was that damn top step, wasn't it? The one from the sidewalk onto the porch?"

"Whoa. Slow down, Winnie—"

"Please tell me he was lucid, please?"

"Good grief, Winnie, relax! Master Sergeant Hottie wasn't here in an official capacity. He wasn't wearing his paramedic garb, he wasn't driving the ambulance, he wasn't here like that at all."

Relief sagged Winnie against the seat back. "Thank God."

"He parked at the curb, walked toward the house in all his hotness, and disappeared out of my sight line," Renee explained amid another pair of yawns. "By the time I located anything even remotely resembling lipstick in your bathroom cabinet, I heard him back out on the front walkway again. With Mr. Nelson."

Winnie inched the Dessert Squad up until she was next in line for the order window. "Where were they going?"

"Since I'm not the one on Sergeant Hottie's personal speed dial, I can't answer that. I wish I was, so I could . . . but I'm not, so I can't." Renee's voice lowered for a moment, indicating a shift in position of some sort. "You there yet?"

"There?"

A sigh filled her ear. "At Jake's, dummy."

"Oh. Yeah. I'm next in line to order."

A notable silence filled the cabin, followed by a quick vibration atop Lovey's seat. Leaning over, Winnie fixed her gaze on the seconds-old text message.

PB Choc Chunk. Large.

Chapter 15

They were a little over a mile from home when Winnie's phone vibrated next to a milkshake-staring Lovey. Keeping her eyes on the road, she reached over and hit the Speaker button.

"I'm almost there."

"Oh, how I wish *that* were true."

Her foot let up on the gas pedal all on its own. *"Jay?"*

"You sound surprised."

She could feel Lovey's eyes as they left the cardboard milkshake carrier in favor of studying Winnie's face. "I—I guess I am."

Something that sounded an awful lot like a sigh filled her ear before a more tired version of his voice returned. "And I'm sorry about that. I really am. I've wanted to call you a dozen times these last few days but—"

"Then why haven't you?"

It was a fair question, wasn't it? Still, she sucked in her breath as she waited for his answer.

"It sounds like I'm on speaker."

"Because you are." She turned right at the four-way stop and continued. "I'm driving."

"Are you on the way to a rescue?" he asked.

"On the way home, actually."

"Can you pull over somewhere for a few minutes? So we can talk?"

She considered telling him she could almost see the street sign for Serenity Lane, but refrained. After all, there would be no chance of Renee overhearing if she did as Jay asked. Then again, if the ominous tone in his voice was some sort of foreshadowing of things to come, she might want Renee within earshot.

Decisions . . .

Decisions . . .

When Serenity Lane did, indeed, come into view, she asked the tie-breaker question she couldn't swallow down anymore. "Are we okay?"

"Of course, we're okay! Why would you think otherwise . . . ?" His words gave way to silence and then, "Ah, Winnie, I'm so sorry. I thought I was doing the right thing by not weighing you down with my problems, and instead I made you doubt my feelings for you. I'm so sorry."

Relief propelled her over to the curb, joy had her shifting into park. "I didn't want to believe it. Hated it, in fact. But when you were so distracted by the arrival of Didi the last time we spoke . . . and then you didn't call back . . . I was afraid you were falling—" She stopped, grabbed her milk-shake out of the carrier, and took a fortifying (and, whoa—

so, so good) sip. "Anyway, it doesn't matter. You're here now—or as here as you can be when you're on the other side of the country."

"How are you?"

"Better now." And it was true. The past few days had felt off—like a part of her happiness was missing in action.

"Have you had to create any new rescue desserts?"

She took another long pull of her shake, savoring the cold as it slid down her throat. "Two. Goin' Bananas Foster—the patient's husband thought she needed a little de-stressing, and Black-and-Blue Cookies for a young girl on Silver Lake High School's soccer team."

"Oh? Who?"

It took her a moment to recall the name, but, eventually, she did.

"Hey, I know her!" The tension she'd heard in his voice at the beginning of the call began to ebb. "She's a friend of Caroline's."

Not knowing what else to say, she returned to her shake.

"Did she make the connection when she saw you? You know, that we're dating?"

Oh, she made the connection, all right . . .

She made what she hoped was a noise of assent around her straw and willed him to accept it and move on.

He didn't. Instead, he rephrased. "Did she know who you were?"

A glance at the passenger seat showed Lovey's golden eyes trained on Winnie's cup. Covering the phone, she addressed her furry copilot. "You'll get some, Your Highness. When we get home."

Hisss . . .

"Or maybe you won't," she hissed back.

"Winnie?"

Pulling her hand off the phone, she made herself answer the question he was refusing to let go. "She knew me, Jay."

A pause and then, "That doesn't sound like a good thing."

"She was thrilled with her cookies—don't get me wrong. But when the rescue was wrapping up, she let me know I wasn't what she expected."

"Meaning?"

The telltale gurgle of an impending empty cup greeted her latest suck on the straw and she sank back against the seat, defeated. "Can we just move on to something else?"

"Winnie . . ."

"We already know Caroline isn't my biggest fan so it really shouldn't be a surprise that—"

Even from the other side of the country, she could tell Jay's exhale was made up of equal parts frustration and fatigue, and she hated it. "I'm sorry, Jay. I really am."

"Don't. I'm the one who should be sorry."

"For?" she prodded.

"Not raising a child with more confidence and respect than this."

"She'll come around." The words were no sooner past her lips when the smile started. "Look at me—channeling Mr. Nelson . . ."

"Better not let Bridget hear you." He sighed again. "Winnie, I'm afraid the stuff with Caroline is about to get worse. Much worse."

She felt her smile wilt. "Why?"

"This trip. It hasn't gone the way I'd expected it to go."

She swallowed, sans milkshake. "Meaning . . ."

"Didi's charm was on full display the moment she showed up at our hotel room that first day. She walked into our room gushing and she hasn't stopped since. She's showered Caroline with new clothes, a new hairstyle, painted fingernails, fancy meals in a private room here at the hotel, a private showing of Didi's next film—in Didi's home theater, no less—and on and on. And Caroline? She's taken to it like a duck to water."

"I—I thought you were enjoying your visit with Didi, too." She hated the uncertainty she heard in her voice but it was too late to pull it back. Instead, she tried to soften it with an explanation. "I mean, the few times we *did* speak you always sounded so happy when she showed up."

"Do not mix happy for polite, Winnie." He groaned so loudly she knew Caroline couldn't be in the background. His words simply served as verbal proof. "I don't know what I was hoping for when I agreed to this trip. I don't know if I was hoping for Caroline to embrace reality where Didi is concerned, or if I just wanted to make her smile the way she used to before . . ."

She waited for him to continue. When he didn't, she took the ball and ran. "Before we met."

"Before I had something to do when she was at dance . . . or hanging out with friends . . . or whatever," he corrected. "Because that's what this has been the last four months, Winnie. You and I—building a relationship—around Caroline's schedule. She's sixteen, and I only take you out when she's otherwise occupied."

"And that's worked fine, Jay."

"But I don't want *fine*, Winnie," he argued, his voice rising. "You're amazing. You're fun. You're creative. And you're *kind*! There's not a reason on the face of this earth that my daughter should be so hostile toward you."

She returned the empty cup to the carrier and her hand to the gearshift. "There's one." When he said nothing, she filled in the blank. "You are her everything, Jay. You have been her whole life—most especially since Didi walked out on her when she was five. I'm not sure I'd be all too crazy about sharing you if I was her, either."

"I get that. And it's why I've agreed to your idea about confining our dates to those times Caroline is busy, anyway. But all that's done is result in her doing less with her friends." His voice fell away only to pick back up with an almost strangled quality. "You could have been so good for her—a real positive female role model."

Could have been . . .

Past tense.

A murmur of voices, followed by a burst of laughter, filled the cabin, signaling the end to Jay's privacy. "Dad! Dad! Wait till you see what Mom found of yours!"

"Winnie?" he said, his voice quiet.

"You have to go. I know." She blinked against the sudden moisture in her eyes and prayed it wasn't evident in her voice. "I'd offer to pick you up at the airport tomorrow, but I'm guessing that wouldn't go over too well."

"Probably not, but I'll—"

"Daaaddd!"

His earlier sigh was back, only this time, the frustration that had costarred alongside fatigue, simply bowed out. "We'll get through this, Winnie."

And then he was gone, the silence left in his wake deafening.

She dropped her rescue bag onto the counter, tossed her empty cup in the trash, and thrust the cardboard carrier into Renee's outstretched hand. "Here. Enjoy."

"Don't you want yours?"

"Nope. I already drank mine."

Renee squealed. "You brought me *two*? Winnie Johnson, you are the best boss ever."

"No, I'm not. The kid-sized one is for Lovey." She retrieved the smaller of the two cups from the carrier and worked her finger around the underside of the lid. "*After* I drink it down to the soupy part at the—"

Renee's stiletto clacked against the floor in a stamp. "Winnie! My shake is *melted*!"

Winnie stared into Lovey's cup and tried to think past the sudden roar in her ears. "I—I . . ."

"You didn't come straight home, did you?"

Movement beside her leg brought her eyes down to the floor. Lovey blinked up at her. Giving in, she carried the cup over to the center island, located a clean cat bowl in a nearby cabinet, and filled it with a few lickfuls of melted ice cream.

Lovey, in turn, was purring before it even hit her food mat.

For a moment, Winnie simply watched as the brown and white tabby lapped up the melted ice cream with reckless abandon. Any calm the sight managed to restore in her head, though, was wiped away by a second, louder stamp.

"Winnie! How could you stop with a perfectly good milkshake in the car?"

Slowly, she lifted her eyes until they mingled with Renee's. "Jay called when we were on our way home."

Curiosity replaced irritation on Renee's face. "Oh?"

Winnie nodded.

"And?"

"It was good to hear his voice." It was a simple response, but no less true.

She followed Renee's gaze back down to the melted milkshake and readied the apology she owed. But before she could get it out, Renee shrugged a what-the-heck, deposited a straw into the thick liquid, and began to drink, her eyes rolling back in her head as she did. "Mmm. . . . So. So. Good."

"I'm glad." Winnie pointed toward the order pad in its usual place on the kitchen table. "Any more rescues?"

"Uh-uh."

Crossing to the little table just inside the front door, she rummaged through the stack of waiting mail.

Electric bill . . .

Phone bill . . .

Ad for a new bakery (joy!) opening up in the neighboring town of Vester . . .

Cable bill . . .

A letter for Mr. Nelson—

She pulled the letter from the pile and held it up. "Mailman goofed again. Is Mr. Nelson back from wherever he went with Greg yet?"

This time, Renee's lips parted around her straw just long enough to give a real *no*.

Setting the letter beside her own stack of mail, Winnie made a face. "Weird."

When Renee slurped down the remainder of her shake, she wandered into the living room and dropped onto the ottoman. "Mr. Nelson is a cool dude. You know this. Maybe they're just hanging out—having a guy's day or something."

Winnie looked again at her housemate's name scrawled across the front of the envelope and then turned and made her way over to the couch. "Hanging out with old people isn't really Greg's thing, remember?"

139

Renee gave her a long, pointed once-over. "Am I detecting a note of jealousy?"

"No, it's just weird." Pulling her calves up and onto the couch next to her, Winnie hugged a throw pillow to her chest. "Mr. Nelson knows I'll take him anywhere he wants to go. If I'm not around, he calls one of his friends from the VFW hall. And if all else fails, he can usually coax Bridget into being his driver, provided he agrees to be a taste tester for whatever dinner she's trying out."

"A fate worse than death, from what he's told me," Renee interjected.

"True. But still, why call Greg, of all people? I mean, aside from an occasional brainstorming session here, they don't really know each other all that well."

Renee inspected her nails, declared them in need of a fresh manicure by way of a deep sigh, and then pointed at Winnie across the coffee table. "I take it the phone call with Jay didn't go well?"

Something about her friend's voice stirred up the same unsettled feeling she'd had as her call with Jay was ending. Only this time, instead of blinking away tears, she found herself clenching and unclenching the pillow. "It seems this trip only served to make things worse where Caroline is concerned."

"Meaning?"

"Meaning, before she was hanging on to the *ghost* of what she wanted her mother to be."

Renee's eyes narrowed to near slits. "And now?"

Winnie found a loose thread on the edge of the pillow and wound it around her finger until the tip turned white.

Smart . . .

Slowly, she unraveled herself from the pillow and ad-

140

dressed her friend's question. "And now, the living, breathing incarnation has stepped up to the plate and is swinging for the fences with private movie showings, fancy meals, a hairstylist, et cetera."

"I like what you did there. 'Stepped up to the plate. Swinging for the fences.' Ty would be even more gaga over you than he already is."

She stared at Renee. "Ty is gaga over . . . *me*?"

"Duhhh." Renee rolled her eyes and then patted the edge of the ottoman in an attempt to lure Lovey into the room. When Lovey finished licking whatever residual ice cream she could find along the edges of her mouth and its neighboring fur, she acquiesced, throwing a glare in Winnie's direction as she did.

"You little stinker! Who do you think just gave you that ice cream?"

Hisss. . . .

"Do you see the level of ungratefulness I deal with from this cat?" she said, her voice rising. "It's mind-blowing!"

"I think it's kind of cute," Renee said. "Endearing, actually."

"Cute?" she echoed. "Endearing? Are you kidding me?"

"No."

"Explain."

Lovey pushed her head against Renee's hand. Renee, in turn, rewarded the cat for her efforts with a scratch between the ears. "Well, it's like the sparring between Mr. Nelson and Ms. O'Keefe. And the way Harold Jenkins tries to be so sly on that electric scooter of his when he's following behind Cornelia Wright and her dog. It's their thing, you know? If it stopped—if Mr. Nelson stopped yanking Ms. O'Keefe's chain . . . and if Harold stopped stalking

Cornelia—things would feel wrong. Like the world slipped off its axis or something."

"So you're saying it would feel *off* if the cat I feed and shelter suddenly stopped hissing at me?"

"Yeah."

Winnie pondered that for a moment and then dismissed it with a flick of her hand. "Don't try to excuse away that tyrant's behavior."

Renee reached down, plucked Lovey from the carpet, and settled the cat into her lap. "Let's move along, shall we?"

Winnie was pretty sure she nodded. But she wasn't positive. It was hard to nod and shoot death glares (at Lovey, of course) at the same time.

"Sooo, I take it the Hollywood Hag is spoiling her kid for a few days," Renee said. "Are you really surprised by this?"

"No. Yes. Maybe . . ."

"It's easy to be Roller Coaster Riding Mommy when you haven't seen your kid for eleven years. And it's even easier when you only have to play that part for three or four days. It's one of the aspects of divorce with kids that everyone seems to think they're immune to until they get a crash course from a former spouse that is suddenly nothing like the person they married."

"Bob does this?" she asked.

"All the time. Before the divorce, he was pretty strict with Ty. But since the divorce, if Ty acts up in school and I enforce a punishment, Bob buys him a pony."

Winnie sucked in a breath. "Bob bought Ty *a pony*?"

"No. I'm speaking metaphorically. But whether it's a real-life pony or a trip to the ice-cream parlor complete with a pat on the head . . . it's the same thing—undermining."

"But that'll only hurt the kid in the long run," Winnie protested.

"True. But that requires long-range thinking and caring. There's always one party who is incapable of doing that." Renee filtered Lovey's left ear through her fingers and then moved on to the right. "It's sad. But I'm determined that I'm going to keep Ty's best interests at heart at all times—even when that puts me at a disadvantage against Bob's games."

"Good for you." Winnie considered everything Renee said and then brought it back to the original subject at hand. "But I don't think that applies here. I think Didi is just trying to make up for lost time."

"Which she can't do inside four days."

"I wouldn't be so sure of that." She swatted the pillow off her lap and stood, her destination changing at the whim of her feet—the window, the fireplace, the window, the fireplace . . . "Jay said Caroline has been nonstop smiles since they got to California."

Renee moved on to Lovey's back, gliding her hand from the top of the animal's head all the way to the end of her back. "The treatment Scream Queen is getting from Mommy Dearest right now is like a numbing gel, Winnie. That's all. And like all numbing gels it *will* wear off. When it does, all the same issues will still be there. Maybe even worse."

"Meaning?"

For a split second, Winnie wasn't sure Renee heard her. But before she could repeat the question, her friend looked up, the resignation in her green eyes palpable. "Her resentment of you is about to get a whole lot worse."

Chapter 16

"You're starting to weird me out a little."

Releasing her hold on the living room curtain, Winnie turned to find Renee shaking an emery board in her general direction. "I am? Why?"

"You've been standing at that window for close to ten minutes now, just staring out at the road like some sort of psycho." Renee tucked the top of her fingers inward, filed her pinky, and then pointed the board at Winnie again. "I know you two are tight, but are you always this over-the-top with him?"

Winnie took one last glimpse through the sheer fabric and wandered into the kitchen, the approaching five o'clock hour lessening the chance of another rescue call. "Can we not talk about Jay and Caroline for a little while? I think I'm all talked out about that for the moment."

"I wasn't talking about Jay."

Winnie turned. "Then who?"

"Mr. Nelson. You've been watching for him like he's some sort of teenager who's blown his curfew."

She started to deny the assessment but, instead, dropped onto the kitchen bench and dug her hand in the bowl of chips Renee had left out after her lunch. "They should be back by now, Renee."

"If you don't know where they went, how can you know when they should be back?" Renee tossed the emery board onto the coffee table, whispered something in Lovey's ear, and then, when the cat jumped down from her lap, stood.

"What did you just say to her?" Winnie asked between nibbles of her chip.

Renee joined her at the table and the bowl of chips. "That I wanted a chip."

"And she just gets down?"

"That's right."

"How come she doesn't do that when I need to make the bed?"

"Because you're you, and I'm me." Renee stacked two chips on top of each other and then ate them whole, grinning at Winnie as she did. "That's as good an explanation as I can give."

She rolled her eyes and then steered back to the original conversation. "Even if Greg took him to the VFW hall or to shoot the breeze with his friends at the bingo hall—which is unlikely considering *tomorrow* is bingo day, not today— they should have been back by now."

"Maybe they went hiking or something."

"*Hiking*?" she repeated. "Did you really just say *hiking*?"

Renee stopped chewing to match Winnie's raised nostril. "Um, they're men, are they not?"

"Mr. Nelson is seventy-five and uses a cane."

Renee's nostril returned to its original starting position. "Okay, so maybe they didn't go hiking . . ."

Winnie reached for another chip, only to grab her phone off the table instead. "You know what? I'm going to call Mr. Nelson myself. See if maybe he needs a ride home from wherever it is he's gone."

"He doesn't have a cell phone, Winnie."

"Ugh. Right. I forgot that little fact for a moment."

"Besides, if Greg picked him up, wouldn't he drop him off, too?" Renee asked.

"Probably, but I'd rather be sure."

"And they call *Mr. Nelson* nosy . . ."

Ignoring her friend, Winnie scrolled through her contacts and stopped on Greg's number. "I'll just check with Greg."

"Nosy, nosy . . ."

She held the phone to her ear and silently counted the rings.

One . . .

Two . . .

Three . . .

Four—"Hey, Winnie! I was just getting ready to give you a call."

Something that felt an awful lot like dread squeezed her chest. "Did something happen?"

Silence gave way to confusion. "Happen? No. Why?"

"Because Mr. Nelson isn't back yet. And I—I was just getting worried."

The second round of silence lasted a bit longer. "I take it Renee saw me pick him up?"

"She did." When he said nothing in response, she swallowed. "Look, I know he's a grown man and all, but . . ."

Propping her elbow atop the table, she dropped her forehead into her hand and sighed. "I'm usually the one who takes him where he needs to go."

"Hey, I was surprised he called, too. But I wasn't working so it wasn't that big of a deal to swing out to your place, pick him up, and drop him off at the retreat center."

She snapped up her head. "Did you say retreat center?"

"I was curious myself, but it makes sense, you know? I mean it's not like Silver Lake is overrun with professional magicians."

"*Magicians?*" Winnie echoed as she sought to make sense of what she was hearing. She came up short. "I don't understand."

Greg took what sounded like a sip of something before answering. "Apparently, Mr. Nelson has always had a fascination with magic—bunnies emerging from hats, quarters appearing behind ears, ladies being sawed in half, and that kind of stuff."

Reality dawned like a slap to the face. "Wait. Are you saying he went out to that retreat center to see if"—she swung her leg over the bench seat and scurried into the bedroom for her list of suspects, her gaze zipping down the names—"Todd Ritter would do some magic tricks for him?"

"Not *do. Teach.*"

"And what? He just called this guy and said, *Please teach me some tricks?*"

"No, we just stopped by the center, asked for Todd's cabin number, and then stopped out there to see if he was game. And he was."

Her head was beginning to spin. "Okay, so where is he now?"

"Who? Mr. Nelson?"

She lowered herself to the edge of her bed and tried to get ahold of her thoughts. "Yes. Mr. Nelson."

"I picked him up about thirty minutes ago and took him into town."

"To?"

"To grab a bite to eat with one of his VFW buddies before the comedy show at Beans this evening."

The comedy show at Beans . . .

"Which brings me to why *I* was going to call *you*."

She looked up as Renee peeked around the corner, a worried expression on her friend's face. Holding up her index finger, Winnie returned her attention to the man still speaking in her ear.

"Mr. Nelson mentioned you're planning to go?"

"I am," said Winnie.

"Okay, so I was wondering if maybe we could go together."

"You're wanting to go together?" Renee's answering intake of air echoed around the room, momentarily stealing Winnie's attention. She forced it back onto Greg as she continued. "To the comedy show?"

"Yeah. When I was overseas, the USO sometimes brought comedians over for us. Half the fun was enjoying it alongside everyone else."

There was no ignoring Renee's emphatic nodding unless Winnie closed her eyes. But even with her eyes closed, her answer was still the same. "Yeah, sure, that works. It'll be fun."

Then, once a meeting time and place had been established, she lowered the phone to her bed and peered up at Renee. "I was going, he was going—it's no big deal. Really."

"Can I do your hair and your makeup?" Renee asked over the staccato clap of her hands. "Please? Please?"

Diving backward onto her mattress, Winnie stared up at the ceiling and groaned.

"What? Consider it *my* version of a rescue . . ."

Winnie groaned louder. "The only rescue I need is from you and this ongoing campaign of yours to get Greg and me together."

"Is that so wrong?" Renee bypassed the bed and headed for Winnie's closet.

Winnie closed her eyes at the telltale scrape of hangers moving left and right across the bar. "When I'm dating someone else and you know this? Yes."

"I like Jay—don't get me wrong." Hanger sounds ceased, momentarily indicating something was getting a once-over. "In fact, I think the two of you are pretty much a perfect match."

"So then, what's the problem?" Slowly, she opened her eyes, her gaze moving across the ceiling and down to her friend. "Why are you constantly pushing Greg at me?"

The hanger sounds commenced again—a shove to the left, a shove to the right. "One of these days, we're going to do a massive overhaul of this closet."

"We are?"

"We sure are."

"And that means what, exactly?" Winnie asked.

"Everything gets replaced."

Winnie had to laugh at that. "Um, I'd need a little cash to be able to do that, Renee. And until we're up to six rescues a day, I don't see that happening anytime soon."

"It'll happen. We're adding more rescues every week."

"True." Struggling up onto her elbow she watched as

Renee paused on a whimsical peach-colored dress Winnie'd actually forgotten she had. "Ooh. That wouldn't be too much would it?"

Renee pulled the dress all the way out of the closet and held it up against herself. "For an evening out with Master Sergeant Hottie? No."

"This isn't *a date*, Renee."

"I know that, and you know that. But maybe, if word were to get back to Jay that made *him* think it was, that wouldn't be such a bad thing."

She sat all the way up and held up her hands. "Whoa. Stop right there. You're pushing Greg at me so I can make Jay jealous?"

"Not jealous, per se, but maybe something that will wake him up and make him get off the pot, so to speak." Renee draped the dress across the bottom of Winnie's bed and then returned to the closet to inspect Winnie's very limited inventory of shoes.

Winnie dropped her hands to her side. "Meaning?"

"You're either dating or you're not." Renee held up an off-white kitten heel, turned it to the right and left, and then flung it back into the closet. "If you *are*—then the two of you need to stop this only-dating-when-Scream-Queen-is-otherwise-occupied stuff because it's accomplishing nothing. And if you're *not*—then there's a perfectly amazing and oh-so-hot specimen waiting in the wings for you as we speak."

Propelled by yet another groan, Winnie dropped back down onto the mattress. "First of all, Renee, I'm not interested in Greg whether there's a Jay or not. He's a great guy, and a good friend, but he's not my type. Second of all, with that in mind, don't you think it would be kind of cruel to let

Greg think there's a chance when there's not? And last but not least, I've had my fill of the Caroline situation for the day."

"You're letting that kid win."

"Renee . . . please."

It was Renee's turn to groan, only hers carried components of a sigh as well. "I just don't want to see you get hurt, Winnie." Her hand emerged from the closet with a pair of espadrilles. After a closer inspection, she set them on the floor next to the bed. "That kid doesn't want to share. She's made that rather obvious, don't you think?"

There wasn't anything Winnie could say to that, so she mulled it over in her thoughts instead.

"And now that Hollywood Hag has catered to Scream Queen's every whim this week, things are only going to get worse."

Winnie sat up again. "If Jay and I are committed to this, we'll find a way to make it work. For all of us."

"You sure about that?" Renee stood and faced Winnie. "Because while I think Jay is a nice guy, my loyalty and my concern is for *you*. Always."

"Thanks, Renee, I really appreciate it. But I'm a big girl and I'll be okay no matter what."

Renee tapped a finger to her chin and then used it to point at Winnie. "And Mr. Nelson is a big boy. Yet that doesn't stop you from worrying about him, does it?"

Touché.

Winnie slid up and onto her feet, grabbed the dress, and headed toward the bathroom to change. At the door, she turned and smiled at her friend. "You're the best, you know that?"

"Of course I do." Renee paused her primping and posing long enough to point at Winnie once again. "That said, there's no amount of buttering up or distracting that's going to get you out of the inevitable."

"I have a feeling I'm going to regret this question, but what inevitable might that be?" she asked, laughing.

"I'm doing your hair. *And* your makeup."

Chapter 17

If the way Greg's Adam's apple slid up and down his throat was any indication, Winnie had made a bad call on the dress. Yes, it was cute. Yes, she'd gawked at her reflection a time or two (or ten) when Renee had finished her makeup and hair. And yes, she'd hit Record on her phone so she'd never forget her first catcall as she was walking through the parking lot behind Beans. But until that exact moment, she hadn't thought about the mixed signal she might be sending the handsome paramedic by wearing it.

Great . . .

"Keep it light, keep it friendly," she murmured to herself as Greg's hand shot up into the air and motioned her over to the four-top table he'd secured a few feet from the make-shift stage set up for that evening's comedy show. At the table, she found her smile and a seat catty-corner from Greg's. "Look at you, securing a table in front . . ."

"I, uh, got here early enough, I guess." He pushed in the

chair he'd obviously been sitting in before her arrival and moved to the one directly opposite hers. "You look amazing, Winnie. Wow."

She gave what she prayed was a carefree smile and willed her voice to match. "Renee all but smacked my favorite jeans and cami from my hands when it was time to get ready. She said there are so few events in Silver Lake that I need to take advantage of them when they come."

Propping her elbows on the table, she rested her chin in her hands and shrugged. "Frankly, I think she just missed her calling in life."

"What calling would that be?" Greg asked.

"To roam the halls of a prison, smacking inmates' hands with a nightstick."

Greg's eyebrow rose with amusement. "You think Renee should have been a prison warden?"

"That or a stiletto-wearing pit bull." She straightened up and looked around the coffee shop at the smattering of familiar faces she saw across the top of the display case at Delectable Delights on occasion—folks who used to stop by for a coffee cake on the way to work, or to pick up cupcakes for their kids' birthdays. "It might sound a little weird, and I'm not trying to get all deep on you, but sometimes, when I'm somewhere like this, I can't believe how much my life has changed in the past four months or so."

"You mean with the Dessert Squad?"

"That's a big part, sure. I mean, if you back up five months, I was spending most of my waking hours just down the road from here—in a place that's now a pool hall. I baked all morning, stocked my cases, and tried to figure out how I was going to be able to meet the increased rent on the shop. I was so sure my baking days were numbered." She brought her focus back on Greg and was relieved to see a cessation of movement inside his throat. "Now, thanks to the generosity of an old friend, I'm not only baking, I'm getting to take it to a whole new creative level and loving every minute of it."

He leaned back in his seat and nodded. "And the other part?"

"Adding you to my circle of friends, adopting Lovey for lack of a better word, and"—she paused—"meeting and getting involved with Jay."

She watched his gaze drop to the table but only for a moment. When his attention returned, the charged atmosphere was replaced with something more familiar and comfortable. "Think you can top that in the second half of the year?"

"I'll be content with status quo for a little while." Winnie waved her hand at the chairs beside them and then peeked around the room once again. "Any sign of Mr. Nelson yet?"

"Nope."

"He *was* okay when you picked him up from his so-called magic lesson, wasn't he?"

Greg cocked his head to the side, eliciting a domino of sighs from every female in their immediate vicinity. Greg, of course, didn't notice or didn't care. "He definitely had a lesson, Winnie. He showed me one of his new tricks the second he got in the car. He messed it up a little, but he tried."

Again, she surveyed the room and again, she found no sign of her housemate. "He may have learned something but that's not why he was there."

"It wasn't?"

"No." She waved away Greg's surprise while swinging

her gaze toward the door. "You see, it all makes sense now. He wasn't *asking* me if he could help get to the bottom of what happened to Sally Dearfield out at that retreat—he was *telling* me. And I brushed him off."

A quick glance back at Greg revealed a note of understanding on his face. "Ahhh, so that's why he was a little quieter than normal. Maybe even a little sad."

It was her turn to swallow slowly. But for a very different reason than the attire of the person seated across the table (although, truth be told, Greg looked amazing in a short-sleeved henley that showcased his toned upper arms and chest). Shaking her head at her insensitivity, she followed the motion with a smack of her forehead. "Ugh. Ugh. Ugh. I hurt his feelings."

"Winnie, he's a grown man."

"A grown man who was trying to talk to me," she mumbled.

"Mind if I sit with you, Winnie Girl?"

Startled, she snapped up her head to find the seventy-five-year-old in question, smiling down at her. "Mr. Nelson, I—I didn't see you, I'm sorry."

"It happens." He gestured his non-cane-holding hand at the chair next to Greg's and, at their collective nod, lowered himself onto it with the help of his cane. "I'm curious how this fella is gonna react when you start pumping him with questions about his past. People who are hiding things don't take too kindly to unexpected inquisitions."

Greg looked from Winnie to Mr. Nelson and back again. "'Unexpected inquisitions'?"

She cleared her throat, her focus never leaving her neighbor's face. "Yeah, I just have a few questions for the comedian during the Q and A the Beans' folks usually have at events like this one."

"What *kind* of questions?" Greg asked.

"You know, if he killed Sally Dearfield and all." Mr. Nelson rotated his head to catch a glimpse of the chalkboard menu hanging behind the register. "So what's good here besides coffee? 'Cause if I drink a cup now, I'll be pacing around all night."

Winnie stifled the urge to laugh and the even bigger urge to point out her friend's ability to sleep anywhere, anytime, and instead, rewound the conversation back to the pre-coffee stuff. "I have no intention of asking Mr. Masterson if he killed Sally. I'm simply going to see if I can hit on something regarding his relationship with the woman."

Pressing his lips together, Mr. Nelson nodded slowly. "By asking that question outright?"

"I'll disguise it. Like you did today."

Mr. Nelson's eyes shifted downward for less than a second before lifting to pin Winnie's. "Like I did today?"

"Greg told me about your sudden interest in taking a magic lesson."

Mr. Nelson slipped his hand into the front pocket of his trousers, pulled out a small red cup with a lid, and set it on the table. Then, with much pomp and circumstance, he re-tracted the lid long enough to show the cup's empty interior. "See? There's nothing there . . ."

"I see that."

He replaced the lid and slowly waved his trembling hand across it. "One. Two. And *threeee*!"

Following his eyes down to the cup as he removed the lid once again, she took in the still-empty interior while Greg leaned over and whispered something in the man's ear.

Clearly frustrated, Mr. Nelson tried the trick again. Still nothing.

"Mr. Nelson, it's okay, you'll get the hang of it at some point and *then* you can show me."

"I can do this, Winnie!"

She drew back at the unfamiliar agitation in his voice, but before she could recover enough to speak, Greg tapped Mr. Nelson on the shoulder and then made a twisting motion with his hand.

Again, Mr. Nelson replaced the lid. Then, mimicking Greg's not so subtle motions, he twisted the cup to the right. "One. Two. And *threeee!*"

Sure enough, a small white ball appeared in the once-empty cup.

"Ta-da!"

She clapped softly and then leaned across the table to squeeze her friend's age-spotted hands. "You did it, Mr. Nelson. Very nice!"

Slowly, he lifted his gaze to Winnie's. "You'd be surprised what I can do if I'm given a chance, Winnie Girl."

"Mr. Nelson, that's not fair," she protested. "I believe in you—always. You know that. I just don't want you worrying about this whole Sally Dearfield thing. It's really nothing for you to worry about."

"Is it something that's weighing on you?"

She shrugged a *yes*.

"It's keeping you up at night, ain't it?"

"I—I don't know . . . maybe a little."

He returned his magic trick to his pocket and positioned his hand atop his cane. "If I was having trouble sleeping because of something, you'd want to help me, wouldn't you?"

Touché.

"Mr. Nelson, I've got this covered."

"Bridget is helping you, isn't she?"

Reality dawned mid-nod and she threw herself against the back of her chair. "I'm sorry, Mr. Nelson, I wasn't trying to hurt you."

"I know that, Winnie Girl." Placing his weight atop the cane, he rose to his feet, tapped Greg on the shoulder, and then nudged his chin in the direction of the counter. "C'mon, young fella, let's get some snacks for the table before the show gets started."

She watched Greg stand and follow the man up to the counter, buying her time to breathe and collect her thoughts. She hadn't meant to slight Mr. Nelson, she really hadn't. She just hated taking him away from the things that made him happy—his one-man chess games, his ogling of Renee, his unofficial job as her lead (don't tell Renee) taste tester, and his bingo games. Yet even as she tried to rationalize her actions in that way, she realized she'd been selfish. In addition to wanting what was best for Mr. Nelson, she also liked his happy and unstressed self because of its contagious effect on her own life . . .

A flash of movement to the right of her outside elbow brought her self-reflection to an end just as Bridget's finger darted past her nose to point at the empty seat next to Winnie's. "Would you put my purse on that seat, dear, before someone decides to make their two-person table a three-person table with *my* chair?"

"Of course." She claimed the voluminous bag from her next-door neighbor and tucked it on top of the chair. "Have you eaten anything yet?"

Bridget rested her hand on her abdomen and made a face. "My stomach has been swirling all day. I tried soup. I tried

Laura Bradford

warm milk. I tried a few of those cookies you brought me the other night. But nothing has worked." A quick look to her left and her right was followed by a lowering of her voice to a whisper. "I looked up my symptoms online, dear, and I'm afraid I have a stomach tumor."

"Oh, Bridget, I'm sure it's not a tumor."

"Just because you deliver your desserts out of an ambulance, dear, doesn't mean you have a medical degree." Bridget took a moment to peruse the glass-fronted cabinet containing an assortment of cakes and cookies and then gestured toward their seatmates, who were now next in line to order. "I'll be right back, dear, that cinnamon coffee cake looks divine."

"But what about your stomach . . . ?" Winnie's question fell away as its intended recipient made a beeline for the counter and the cinnamon coffee cake that had made her forget all about her latest purported dalliance with death.

Winnie savored her ensuing chuckle and took a moment to really take stock of all that was good in her life. Sure, the whole Caroline situation was putting a cloud over her budding relationship with Jay, but other than that, she couldn't really ask for her life to be any better than it was at that moment.

The Emergency Dessert Squad was gaining more momentum with each passing week thanks to their growing list of satisfied customers. Renee, of course, was just as invaluable behind the scenes of the Dessert Squad as she'd been behind the counter at Delectable Delights. Mr. Nelson and Bridget (despite her often amusing but always insistent argument to the contrary) were in good enough health. And Winnie was able to keep up on her bills even if there was nothing left over after the last one was paid.

"So how's things going with Lovey?" Greg asked as he

reappeared beside the table with four lidded cups balanced in his arms. "Any improvement?"

So much for focusing on the positive aspects . . .

She freed him of two of the cups and set them down in the spots he indicated while he set the remaining cups in front of his spot and Mr. Nelson's. "Same old, same old."

He turned, grabbed two plates off the counter, and positioned them in the center of the table. "I got a plate of brownies and a plate of cookies. Mr. Nelson and Ms. O'Keefe are still at the register arguing over whether the third shared plate should have cinnamon coffee cake or lemon squares."

Following his words to the counter, she considered rescuing the barista from the ensuing verbal war, but opted to remain right where she was, with Greg. "Every once in a while, I catch Lovey looking at me with something other than pure hatred, but it never lasts long."

"Would you stop with that?" His rich laugh accompanied him into his seat. "I really don't think Lovey hates you, Winnie. She's just . . . I don't know . . . playing a little hard to get, is all."

"Then why doesn't she play hard to get with everyone else?"

"Like . . ."

"Like Mr. Nelson, Bridget, Renee, you, the postman, the garbage collector . . . Shall I go on?" Then, scrunching her face, she answered her own question. "No. I shouldn't. The list of people Lovey adores is endless. The list of people she detests is rather small—if you can call one name *a list*."

He looked at her over the lid of his cup. "Do you want me to talk to her?"

It was her turn to laugh and laugh she did. "Do I want you to *talk* to her?"

Laura Bradford

"Go ahead, laugh. But I've always had a way with animals. Heck, I actually was the only one in my entire platoon who was never spit on by a camel when we were in the desert. In fact, the camels actually liked me."

She took a sip of her own drink—a hot chocolate—and eyed him with open curiosity. "Okay . . ."

"It's like you with anyone over seventy years of age," he said, lowering his cup back to the table. "Animals just respond to me. Especially the female ones, oddly enough."

It was too late to rescind her sip as evidenced by the spray of hot chocolate that flew out of her mouth. But at least Bridget was on her way back to the table and therefore able to help quell the choke-cough combination that followed.

When the back slapping stopped, Winnie wiped up all visual effects of Greg's confession and shrugged. "Go ahead, talk to her if you want. It certainly can't hurt at this point."

"Talk to whom?" Bridget added the agreed upon (with *agreed upon* being a rather loose description) cinnamon cake to the center of the table and claimed the seat next to Winnie.

"Lovey."

Bridget narrowed her eyes on Greg. "You're going to talk to Lovey?" At his nod, she expanded her line of questions. "Why? About what?"

"He thinks maybe he can sweet-talk her into liking me." Winnie swapped her cup for a cookie and took a bite, her taste buds snapping to attention while the baking side of her brain began noting all the pluses and the negatives.

"Save your breath, young man. Some things simply can't be changed." Bridget sent an annoyed look in the direction of the man caning his way back to the table with a plate of

162

lemon squares in his free hand. "Like Parker, for instance. He was, is, and always will be a pigheaded fool."

They were still laughing when the manager of the coffee shop took the makeshift stage and welcomed the small but lively crowd to the latest installment of what had been coined "Thursday Night at Beans." The earnest twenty-something listed a few of the week's coffee specials and then rocked back on his heels. "Okay, now that that's out of the way, let's get on with the evening. All of us here at Beans are beyond excited to introduce, to the stage, a comedian you will no doubt be seeing on *The Late Show* in the not-too-distant future. For now, though, he's agreed to be here at Beans with all of us and I know he'll have you rolling on the floor before you've finished your first coffee. Let's give it up, everyone, for Ned Masterson. Ned, come on out here."

The applause built to a crescendo and then stopped as the man Winnie judged to be about forty lifted his hands into the air for quiet. "Thanks for the intro there, guy, but I've gotta correct you on the part about agreeing to be here. You see, the only reason I'm here is because I can't leave."

Pockets of laughter rose up around the room before Ned silenced the crowd with his hands once again. "No, no, seriously, folks. The past few days here have been everything I envisioned hell to be right down to the endless text messages from my ex-wife."

Mr. Nelson leaned across the table toward Winnie. "What's he saying about a knife?"

Shaking her head, she tapped her finger to her ear and waited as he adjusted the volume on his hearing aids. When he was done, Winnie rushed to repeat the joke before its answering laughter had subsided completely.

"But, hey, there was one thing I didn't expect to find here in hell," Ned said, egging on the crowd once again.

A male seated toward the back took the bait. "And what was that?"

"That the desserts would be so, so, *sooo* good."

Chapter 18

"Okay, so that didn't go exactly as I'd planned." Winnie consulted her rearview mirror and then pulled into the flow of traffic behind Bridget's no-frills four-door economy car.

Mr. Nelson stopped fidgeting with the top of his cane and wedged it between his seat and the passenger side door. "Life rarely does, Winnie Girl. That's what keeps things interesting."

"That's one word for what happened back there."

His soft chuckle filled the cabin only to disappear as Bridget slowed to a crawl for no apparent reason. "One of these days, that crazy woman is gonna kill someone with her driving."

"There's a raccoon, see?" Winnie pulled her hand off the steering wheel and pointed at the wild animal scampering across the road in front of Bridget's car. "If you ask me, Mr. Nelson, I think Bridget's eyesight and reflexes are still pretty good."

"Let's not go overboard, Winnie Girl." Leaning forward,

he ran his hand along the Dessert Squad's dashboard. "So old Gertie's ambulance is still going strong, eh?"

"No issues so far." At the four-way stop, Winnie allowed Bridget to clear the empty intersection before she, too, turned right. "So what did you think of Ned's comment about being lured to Silver Lake under false pretenses?"

"It wasn't a news flash, if that's what you're asking."

Mr. Nelson was right. From her Lovey-elongated encounter with Colin Norton the day after Sally's murder, she already knew about the bogus auditions for *Do You Have What It Takes?* All the question and answer session really did was verify that Ned had fallen for the same ruse. So really, she'd learned nothing from the comedian that she hadn't already known.

"I wish the Beans guy hadn't wrapped up the session before I had a chance to ask when, in relation to Sally's death, he learned the auditions weren't going to happen. Because if he found that out *before* her death, I can't figure out why he stayed. Why any of them stayed."

"Sure you can, Winnie Girl."

She glanced at her companion as they approached the next stop sign. "Sure I can, *what*?"

"Figure out why they stayed."

"What are you talking about, Mr. Nelson?"

"Think about it, Winnie Girl. When Bridget is hungry, what does she do?"

She didn't understand the shift in topic, but she played along, anyway. "She eats?"

"I mean when she's sitting on the porch with us and there's no food around."

"Oh. Okay. She drops little hints."

"*Little* hints?" he challenged.

She laughed. "You know what I mean."

"And when she doesn't feel as if we're paying attention to her?"

"She talks about her health issues." She turned left at the next stop sign and then right onto Serenity Lane. "But I don't get what any of this has to do with wanting to figure out why Ned, Colin, and the rest of the artists stayed."

"Think about his stand-up routine—the one topic he kept coming back to again and again."

Bridget's car continued to the driveway beyond theirs, while Winnie turned left. "I know he was really funny, but I don't remember any sort of theme running through his jokes."

"Remember the joke about his ex-wife and the hit man?" At her nod, he continued. "And the one about the bank manager and the influx of cash in his account?"

She nodded again.

"Don't forget the dirty one about the video camera and the coed . . ."

"That one was a little much." She pulled the key from the ignition and gestured toward the house. "Shall we continue this inside? I'm pretty sure I have a rhubarb pie with your name written all over it."

"Blackmail."

She pulled her feet back into the Dessert Squad and turned back to her friend. "Excuse me?"

"His routine followed themes—his ex-wife, his kids, his own childhood, dating, and the jokes he told stayed within those themes. Except for one notable exception."

"And that is?"

"The blackmail jokes. He tossed those in like Bridget tosses in food references when she's hungry."

"He didn't do that, did . . ." The rest of her sentence fell away as the truth behind Mr. Nelson's observation took root. "Wait a minute. You're right. I—I guess I sort of forgot about those jokes because they weren't as smooth as the others."

Mr. Nelson opened his door, planted the end of his cane on the driveway, and leveraged himself up and out of the car.

"Wait!" When he lowered his head back into eye contact range, she continued. "Do you really think that's the key to all of this? That Sally was blackmailing him?"

"I think she was blackmailing all of them."

It made sense. It really did. But . . .

She swiveled her feet back onto the pavement and met Mr. Nelson on the walkway up to their shared front porch. "If you're right, what on earth could she have had on five very different people that would have kept them here even *after* they knew the whole reality TV show thing was a lie?"

"I suspect the answer to that question isn't in their differences."

She froze her left foot on the bottom porch step and stared up at her friend. "You think it has something to do with the school where she worked?"

"I do, and so do you. Think about it, Winnie, you started talking about a connection between them from the very start."

"I did. But aside from having gone to a school where Sally worked, I haven't found any real connection between the artists themselves beyond a shared alma mater."

"Sally is the one who's dead, ain't she?"

For a long time she sat in the darkened kitchen, the only hint of light coming from the streetlamp on the other side of the road. All momentary disappointment over Mr. Nelson's preference for sleep over pie had long since faded against the constant replay of their conversation in her head. Try as she did to poke holes in his theory, she couldn't. Blackmail was the only thing that made sense. Why else would five able-bodied adults remain in a strange place under false pretenses?

They wouldn't.

Something brushed against her ankle and she looked down to find two golden eyes trained on hers. She braced for the hiss that was sure to follow, but it never came. Instead, Lovey jumped up onto the bench beside her and slowly lowered her midsection until she resembled a frozen turkey sitting atop a roasting pan.

Not sure what to make of the maneuver, Winnie remained perfectly still, even while her thoughts manifested themselves through her lips. "Let's suppose Sally had something on these five people—something big, something that could . . . I don't know . . . maybe ruin their careers. Why would she bring them here to drop that little bomb?"

She thought about that for a moment and then pushed the question aside. "If it had to do with something pertaining to the school, surely there would be more than five people, wouldn't there? Unless there's something different about these five? Maybe they have more net worth than other alumni?"

Lovey remained seated, eyes wide.

"Any idea on how we can begin to figure this stuff out?" she asked.

For the first time since Lovey appeared beside her leg, the cat moved her undivided attention off Winnie and fixed it, instead, on the computer monitor in the living room. Winnie, in turn, looked from the cat, to the computer, and back again.

"Okay, Lovey, you're actually starting to give me the creeps just a little bit." Then, without really thinking about what she was doing, she leaned forward and gently rubbed the area between the cat's ears (sans hiss).

Whoa.

Not wanting to tempt fate, she slowly pulled her hand back and gestured toward the computer. "I'm gonna take your advice, Lovey, and see what I can find on this whole mess. You're welcome to join me on the computer chair if you'd like."

Lovey stayed put.

Shrugging, Winnie stood, crossed to the computer desk, and pressed Power. While she waited for the machine to boot up, she liberated a pen from the top drawer and took a moment to jot a few potential search ideas.

Read the bios of successful alumni who weren't at the retreat—what's different about them?

Plug in Ned Masterson with Sally Dearfield's name—see if anything comes up. Do the same for the other four.

She tapped the pen to her chin while she reread her notes thus far. Then, after some careful thought, she added one more.

Research the attendance years of each of the five artists in relation to happenings at the school during the same time frame.

A second pass of her notes stirred up no additions and she turned her attention to the computer and her first stop in the research process—the website for the Charlton School of the Arts. This time, when the home page came up, she took a moment to really study what was obviously the school's signature building in much the same way the Cully Business Building was for Silver Lake College. Shifting her focus to the right, she noted the mature trees that surrounded the building like sentinels. It was a commanding scene if not maybe a little intimidating, as well.

She moved the cursor up to the top of the page and clicked on the Alumni tab. Sure enough, the same page that had been displayed on Bridget's computer appeared on Winnie's. A quick downward scroll reacquainted her with the faces she'd seen on her first visit to the page as well as a few more of the faces she'd seen standing around Sally's dead body three days earlier.

When she reached the bottom of the page, she scrolled back up to the top and clicked on the first alumni picture— a playwright from Missoula, Montana. Forty-year-old Sandra Moffitt boasted an impressive lineup of plays, some of which had been performed on stage in London (for the Queen) and in Rome.

Halfway down the page-long write-up, Winnie's heart skipped a beat. When asked who, at Charlton School of the Arts, had influenced her career most, Sandra Moffit pointed to none other than Sally Dearfield.

"I was always a shy kid. It's probably why I became a writer—it gave me a way to express myself in a manner I was comfortable with. But to succeed in this business, you have to deal with people to some extent. Ms. Dearfield helped me find my presence, my confidence. Once I did, there was no turning back."

"Interesting . . ."

When Winnie reached the bottom of Sandra's bio, she went back to the alumni page and clicked on the next picture. Forest Whitman, a thirty-five-year-old graffiti artist, had seen his work in the background of several major motion pictures over the past ten years. In fact, according to his bio, he'd won a few major awards for his work.

"Award-winning graffiti," she said aloud. "Who knew?"

A quiet meow from the kitchen had her laughing as she continued to read. When she reached the part about who, at Charlton, influenced him most, again Sally Dearfield's name all but jumped off the screen.

"I was a little rough around the edges when I came to Charlton. Sure, I'd gotten a scholarship to attend, but that still didn't mean I fit with the kids who could afford to attend without help. So there I was, with a big old chip on my shoulder that first week, and Ms. Dearfield pulled me aside and took the time to get to know me. Next thing I knew, that chip was gone and I was making friends. Real friends. Even now, I can look back at the work I was doing before Charlton and the work I've done since and see my growth as a person. Ms. Dearfield helped me do that."

Confused, Winnie scrolled up to the banner across the top of the page and clicked on the tab marked Staff. Although she knew Sally had retired from the school the previous fall, she couldn't help but hope that maybe the school had fallen behind on updating their site.

They hadn't.

In the spot assigned to the school's main secretary, a bright-eyed twenty-something smiled out at her from the confines of a standard faculty member photograph. Sagging against the back of the desk chair, she continued to scroll her way down the page, her attention flitting in and out (mostly in) until—

Bingo!

There, near the bottom, in a section devoted to retired faculty members, Sally Dearfield, in a powder blue blouse with a fancy collar, smiled out at Winnie in much the same way the woman's replacement had. Only instead of looking like a schoolkid herself, Sally looked like everyone's favorite aunt. The one who supports and loves her nieces and nephews as if they were her own children.

Sally's bio, while not as extensive as those of the alumni, talked of the numerous headmasters she served under during her decades-long career at the school. Quotes from past headmasters spoke of her dedication and work ethic, while quotes from faculty members and former students talked about her devotion to the student body. Virtually every student quoted spoke of the difference Sally had made in their life and the wings she'd given to their career.

At the end of the victim's bio, Winnie scrolled back up to the site's masthead and hovered her cursor over the Alumni tab. This time, though, instead of clicking on the third picture, she scrolled down to Abby Thompson's. Yes, she'd read the puppeteer's bio the other night at Bridget's, but it couldn't hurt to read it again, right?

Abby's bio read much like the playwright's and the graffiti artist's. It mentioned the year of her graduating class, her favorite teacher during her time at Charlton, the why behind her original interest in puppetry, and her successes to date in the field. When asked the question about who influenced her most during her days at Charlton, Abby simply said herself.

"Hmmmm . . ." Reaching across to her opposite shoulder, Winnie kneaded at the crick she felt forming. "So much for a perfect count. Still two for three isn't bad, right Lovey?"

She swiveled her chair to the right and stood, the crick in her shoulder now duplicating itself in her legs and back. "Wow. Yet another reason I was destined to bake for a living.

Ten minutes"—she leaned forward and took in the digital clock on the stove—"Whoa—really? *Thirty* minutes? No wonder I'm done."

Glancing back over her shoulder, she considered shutting the computer down for the night but left it on in case sleep proved elusive for yet another night in a row. Still, she pushed in her chair, neatened the mouse atop the mousepad, and shut off the floor lamp beside the desk. "Okay, Lovey, I'm heading to bed. Enjoy your hammock . . . or the chair . . . or wherever it is you sleep during the night."

Winnie made her way through the kitchen and into her bedroom even as her thoughts remained on Charlton School of the Arts. From everything she'd read so far, Sally Dearfield was adored by everyone during her time at the school—headmasters, teachers, cafeteria workers, the custodial staff, students, and even groundskeepers. So why would the five former students currently staying at Silver Lake Artists' Retreat despise her so much?

Sally lured them here under false pretenses . . .

"But why?" Bypassing the switch for the overhead light, Winnie flicked on her bedside lamp and lowered herself to the edge of her bed as Mr. Nelson's theory took center stage in her mind and on her tongue. "She wanted to blackmail them, that's why . . ."

The soft patter of Lovey's feet on the linoleum shifted her focus to the doorway in time to see the cat peek around the corner. "Oh no, you don't. Don't even think about trying to hiss me off this bed, Your Highness. This is *my* bed and I'm not giving it up tonight. No way, nohow."

Lovey took a tentative step inside the room and then stopped to lick her nether regions.

"Thanks for that image as I'm contemplating sleep,"

Winnie groused. Yet even as she flounced back against her pillows in disgust, she knew it didn't matter what Lovey or anyone else did at that moment. No, the notion of sleep was but a dream once again. Only this time, instead of wondering why Jay wasn't calling, she kept rewinding back to the car ride with Mr. Nelson, again and again.

There were no ifs, ands, or buts about it. The blackmail theory made sense. In fact, it was the only thing that made sense. Well, that and the fact that Sally must have been really angry about something to swap her beloved status for that of a blackmailer . . .

"At least Abby was smart enough not to hold Sally up as her reason for everything, eh, Love—"

Winnie sat up tall.

Nooo . . .

Like her former six-year-old self at news of a fresh bag of flour in the kitchen pantry, Winnie was off the bed and through the bedroom door faster than Lovey could lower her hind leg back to the ground.

Chapter 19

She was just punching in Renee's number when the voluptuous blonde strolled through the door with an open compact in one hand and a tube of lip gloss in the other.

"I know, I know. I'm late. Again. But I've got a better excuse this time."

Lowering the phone back to the table, Winnie ran a quick visual inventory of her friend and coworker.

Pixie haircut (as pixie-ish and flawless as usual) . . .

Emerald-colored eyes (no sign of the puffiness that coincided with a night spent thinking about Bob) . . .

Cute summer dress (formfitting and cleavage enhancing)—

"Mr. Nelson slipped out the front door and waylaid you out on the street again, didn't he?" Winnie swung her leg over the wooden bench and stood, her purpose and destination uncertain. "You really need to remind him that when he sees you at eight o'clock, it's because you're here for work."

"And crush his little bow tie–wearing heart?" Renee slacked her arm just enough to allow her purse to slip down to the floor before returning her attention to her reflection in the two-by-two-inch mirror. "That's *your* M.O. Winnie, not mine."

Winnie stopped en route to the window and eyed her friend again. "If you're referring to what happened on the driveway yesterday morning, I had a delivery to make, as you well know since you were the one texting me that little fact every two seconds."

Renee smacked her lips together, inspected the result, and then dropped her lip gloss and the compact onto the key table by the door. "See, now I thought you'd let that little poke roll right off your shoulders this morning."

"So you weren't being serious?"

"I. Wasn't. Being. Serious." Renee wandered over to the refrigerator, peeked inside, and emerged with an apple and a leftover piece of cinnamon cake from Beans. "Shouldn't you be bouncing off the walls with unrestrained excitement or something instead of being so—so *grumpy*?"

Winnie continued to the window only to turn around and make her way right back to the table. "I'm not being grumpy. I just didn't exactly sleep last night."

"Do you think that was advisable when"—Renee pulled the apple from her mouth and stared at Winnie—"Wait a minute! You were with Greg last night, weren't you?!?!"

"At the *comedy show*, yeah."

Renee chased a droplet of apple spray down her chin with her finger and returned it to her mouth. "Did he like the dress?"

"I don't know. I guess. Why?"

"D'uhhh."

"Would you please stop?"

Renee set the cinnamon coffee cake down on the island and then headed back toward the cabinets. "Humor me this one last question first—did you come straight home afterward?"

"Of course I came straight home, Renee. Where else would I go?"

Rolling her eyes, Renee returned to her apple and her daily inspection of any and all potential breakfast offerings. "Gee, I don't know. Silly me, I guess."

She ran her hand along the as-of-that-moment empty order pad and tried hard to keep the building yawn at bay lest it take on a domino effect. "I spent most of the night on that"—she pointed at the computer and yawned.

"Did Lovey steal your bed again?" Using her mouth as an apple holder, Renee reached into the cabinet, extracted a glass, and helped herself to orange juice. Then, with the glass in hand, she returned to the island and its view of the Lovey-topped window hammock.

Winnie followed Renee's gaze to the brown and white tabby blissfully unaware of the conversation unfolding around her sleeping form. "Actually, no. Believe it or not, she seemed to *want* to be near me last night."

Renee polished off the apple and tossed the core in the wastebasket. "Is she sick? Do we need to take her to the vet?"

"Gee, Renee, thanks, thanks a lot."

"Grumpy, grumpy . . ."

With a shove of her hand, she moved the order pad closer to the phone and lowered herself back down to the bench. "I'm not grumpy, Renee. Distracted? Yes. Grumpy? No. At least I'm not trying to be."

Renee gathered up her cake and her juice glass and joined

Winnie at the table. "Look, Winnie, I know you want today to be like something out of one of those old movies. Jay running through a meadow . . . arms outstretched . . . overcome with joy at the very sight of you . . . I get it, I really do. And I want that for you, too. But if it ends up *not* being that way, maybe you should see that as a sign and back off a little. This stuff with Caroline is his to figure out. And if he's unwilling or unable to unearth a little basic respect in that kid, then maybe you're better off knowing that now. Before you invest any more of your heart than you already have."

Winnie held her hands in the air. "Whoa. Whoa, slow down a minute. We weren't talking about Jay."

"Isn't that why you didn't sleep? Because you're excited?"

"Excited?" She heard the confusion in her own voice and waited for Renee to explain it away.

"Jay *is* coming home today, isn't he?"

Winnie's hands hit the table just before her forehead. "Oh no. I . . ."

Renee's ensuing gasp was cut short by her own words. "Are you telling me you forgot?"

"No, I knew when he was coming home, I just . . . um . . . temporarily misplaced the specific details."

"Which means you *forgot*."

Slowly, with the help of her palm, Winnie elevated her head off the table. "I temporarily misplaced the specific details," she repeated. "Kind of like you do with your start time each morning."

"Oooh, good one!" Renee took a bite of coffee cake, made a funny face, and then returned it to its to-go container. "Seems to me Beans is in need of an entire dessert menu rescue."

"It's not *completely* awful." Winnie pointed at the juice

glass and, at Renee's nod, took a quick sip. "It just needs a bit more cinnamon, some sort of streusel, a drizzle of icing, and a bit more milk."

Renee shoved the container to the side and reclaimed her orange juice glass. "I was late because I was putting goody bags together for Ty's just-because party tomorrow. I still need to find another little thing or two to put inside, but they're coming out cute, if I do say so myself."

"Oh, that's right." Winnie snapped her fingers. "I get to pump the mime tomorrow!"

"And you're going to make some cute desserts, right?"

Uh-oh . . .

"Yeah, yeah, sure. We can decide on those later. After lunch."

"You forgot the party, too, didn't you?" Renee accused.

"No. I temporarily misplaced the specific details."

Renee leaned forward and pointed her finger within centimeters of Winnie's nose. "Okay, Winnie, spill it."

"It?"

"Whatever is going on with you right now. You're being weirder than normal."

"'Weirder than normal'?" Winnie sat back in an effort to put a little distance between her nose and Renee's finger. "I think I should be offended."

"No, you should *talk*. Why were you on the computer all night?" Renee guzzled down the juice before sheepishly pulling the cake container back into reasonable reach-zone. "You weren't cyberstalking Didi, were you? Because if you remove the Botox and the fake boobs, she's really not all that wonderful."

"Cyberstalking Didi? No!" Winnie pinched off a piece of Renee's cake and popped it on her tongue. *Yup. Too dry.*

"I'm well aware of what Jay's ex looks like. I wouldn't even try to compete with that. I am what I am."

"Which is pretty darn amazing, thankyouverymuch."

Winnie smiled across the table at her friend, grateful for the woman's unwavering loyalty. "You're biased, and we both know this, but I love you anyway."

"I love you, too." Renee pointed a chunk of cake at Winnie. "Now, spill! If you weren't cyberstalking the ex, what were you doing on the computer all night long?"

"Figuring out a motive." Winnie stretched her arms above her head and gave in to another yawn. "Think I found it, too."

"I've been telling you this all along, Winnie," Renee said between nibbles. "Scream Queen wants you out of Daddy's life—that's the motive."

Swinging her leg over the bench, Winnie stood, only this time, instead of heading for the window, she motioned for Renee to follow her into the living room. "No, a motive for Sally Dearfield."

"You figured out why she was murdered?"

"Not specific enough to know *who* just yet, but I'm pretty sure blackmail led to her demise." With little more than a glance at the computer, Winnie sat down on the couch and propped her feet on the ottoman.

Renee abandoned her empty juice glass and headed straight for the overstuffed armchair that doubled as one of Lovey's favorite sleeping spots. "You think someone was blackmailing her?"

"No. I think *she* was blackmailing *them. All* of them."

Throwing her leg over the armrest of the chair, Renee pinned Winnie with an inquisitive stare. "Because . . ."

"Because of all the former alumni with special mention

on the Charlton website, these five were the only ones who didn't point to her as a reason for their success. And I do mean the *only* ones."

"You're kidding, right?"

"No. The alumni page highlights graduates who have gone on to work in their chosen art. Each one of those graduates has a pretty extensive bio on that page. There are probably thirty of them. And everyone but the five people who were in that room when Sally was murdered lavished praise on Sally in their bio—she encouraged them, she believed in them, she gave them confidence, et cetera, et cetera. But Ned, Abby, Colin, Todd, and George? Not so much as a word about Sally. And they've been successful. Quite successful, actually."

"Okay, so they slighted her. Big deal. Can't she be happy about the other twenty-five people who *did* mention her? I mean twenty-five public *attagirls* sounds pretty good to me."

Winnie rested her head against the back of the couch and studied the tired-looking ceiling. As much as she hated to admit it, she needed to paint. Soon.

"Winnie?"

"Oh, sorry. The twenty-five-people thing . . ." She dipped her chin down until Renee was in her sight line once again. "I thought the same thing when I first figured out what was going on. But those five are likely the reason Sally didn't win the Unsung Hero award this past spring."

"So?"

"Apparently, it's a pretty big deal. Like a *national* big deal." Grabbing the throw pillow to her left, she hiked it onto her lap and hugged it to her chest. "Sally was actually one of two finalists who were flown to California for a big ceremony in March, I think. She lost to a custodian from an all-boys school in Oregon or someplace like that."

"That doesn't mean she lost because those five didn't mention her in their bios," Renee protested across her impromptu fingernail inspection.

"Maybe, maybe not. The school newspaper affiliated with the winner's place of employment specifically called out the man's unanimous mention by their alumni." Aware of a brewing headache, Winnie kneaded at the area above her eyes and forced herself to take long, deep breaths. "And the reporter was right. Every single graduate featured on their noted alumni page mentioned this custodian. Every single one."

Renee picked at the third finger on her left hand and then dropped it back down to her lap. "So you think she lured them all here because she was ticked off?"

"I do. And I think she used that whole ruse about the reality talent show as the way to get them here."

"Okay, so let me get this straight. You think one of them killed her because they realized she'd lied?" Renee asked. "Doesn't that seem . . . I don't know . . . *excessive*?"

Winnie pulled her fingertips from her temples and shook her head. "The reality show was how she *got* them here. Whatever she was using to blackmail them with is how she got them to stay. Or, at least, that's what makes the most sense so far."

"I must admit, I'm intrigued." Renee clicked her tongue against the back of her teeth and, sure enough, Lovey's head popped up. "I have a lap for you to sit on, Lovey."

"Let her sleep, Renee. We could get a rescue call any minute and then she'll just be all cranky when you have to get up."

Renee stopped clicking and, instead, crinkled her left nostril at Winnie. "Okay, Miss Stick in the Mud, tell me

183

your theory. What did she have on them—besides, of course, not pledging their undying love to her in a public forum?"

"I don't know. I still have to figure that part out." She traced the piping around the edge of the pillow and then tossed it back onto the vacant cushion. "At least now I have a direction to go in, though."

"You do realize she'd have to have something pretty good on them to make them stay, right? I mean, why else wouldn't they just get up and leave when the reason they came here in the first place turned out to be completely bogus?"

"My thoughts exactly."

Renee dropped her legs back down to the ground and rubbed her hands together in blatant anticipation. "So when do we start?"

"Start? Start what?"

"Digging."

Winnie grinned in spite of the headache that showed no sign of letting up. "How about tomorrow? At Ty's party?"

"You want to start with my mime?" Renee asked.

"I'm game if you are."

The sudden yet insistent vibration of Winnie's phone atop the kitchen table propelled Renee off the chair. A few feet from her destination, she turned and winked at Winnie. "You bring the desserts and I'll supply the shovels."

Chapter 20

With one eye on the clock and the other on the rolled dough she'd just set in the bottom of the tart tin, Winnie did her best to keep up with the volleying conversation between Renee and Mr. Nelson. But somewhere between the eyelash batting (Renee), bow tie straightening (Mr. Nelson), and eye rolling (Bridget), she was pretty sure she'd missed a few tidbits.

Part of her wanted to request a rewind, but the other part of her—the part that had agreed to one more rescue before the end of the day—knew there would be time to get the skinny on Cornelia Wright and Harold Jenkins at a later time.

For now, she just needed to finish the egg custard tartlets before four o'clock so she could be back in the kitchen preparing for Ty's just-because party by five. If she was, she was confident the treat menu she and Renee had drafted during lunch would come together flawlessly.

"Hey, I'm sorry, Winnie. I'm over here gabbing away and you're baking." Renee took in her lower-than-normal neckline and hiked her summer top up just enough to shield her impressive cleavage from Mr. Nelson's carefully manipulated vantage point. "Is there anything I can do?"

"You could brush this egg I just beat onto the pastry and then put the tin in the fridge for a few minutes while I make the filling." When Renee stood, Winnie moved on to the bowl with more waiting eggs and egg yolks. Flipping the hand mixer to its lowest setting, she added a bit of sugar while talking out the next few steps. "I need to warm the cream, pour it over this mixture, beat again, and then add a little vanilla."

Bridget tilted her chin toward the notepad she'd been writing in off and on all afternoon and peeked at Winnie across the top edge of her glasses. "My mother used to make egg custard. It was my father's favorite treat."

"Did you enjoy it?" Winnie asked as she moved on to warming the cream.

"My favorites always seemed to reflect theirs," Bridget replied, tapping her pen atop the notepad as she did. "Do you put grated nutmeg on top of yours?"

"I do."

Even from Winnie's position at the island, there was no mistaking the slight fogging of her next-door neighbor's glasses as the woman's chin dipped still farther.

"Bridget?"

A handful of seconds ticked away before Bridget cleared her throat, removed her glasses from the bridge of her nose, and polished them with the hem of her floral housecoat. When the glasses passed inspection, they were returned to her face. "Yes, dear?"

"Assuming the tartlets all come out of the oven the way they should, you can have the extra one."

Mr. Nelson leaned back in an attempt to catch another peek at Renee's chest. When his efforts proved futile, he furrowed his brows at Winnie. "I thought *I* was your taste tester, Winnie Girl."

"You are, Mr. Nelson. But this is a recipe you approved last summer."

"It is?"

"It sure is." When the filling was ready, she took the tin back out of the refrigerator, sieved it onto the waiting pastry crust, and sprinkled grated nutmeg across the top. When it was ready, she slipped it onto the center rack of the pre-heated oven. "You had me make a whole new batch for you the next day."

"Then if I like 'em that much, why are you giving the extra to Bridget?"

She pulled the towel from her apron's waistband and wiped her hands free of all trace of residual flour. "You got to have some potato candy earlier, yes?"

"What's that got to do with it?" he groused.

"Someone has to keep an eye on your sugar intake, and besides, it's a connection to Bridget's past. Let her have it."

Ever the peacemaker, Renee headed off any subsequent grousing by taking control of the conversation (with the help of her upper half). "Did you tell them what the name is?"

"Name?" Winnie asked.

"Of this rescue dessert."

"Oh. Right." She gathered up the dirty bowls and flour board and passed them to Renee, who was standing by the sink with a sponge and dish soap in hand. "The caller wanted something for an employee at the hardware store who always smiles at him when he walks by the shop on the way to work each morning. He said that employee's smile always helps start his day off right."

Bridget capped up her pen and pointed it at Winnie. "Wait. I think I can guess this one. Something about being a good egg, yes?"

Winnie grinned. "Yup. You're a Good Egg Custard Tartlets, to be exact."

"You're so clever, dear." Bridget tucked her notepad inside her purse and then turned her attention to the lemonade she'd requested upon arrival yet had failed to drink in any measurable fashion. "Someone calls with a problem and—*poof!*—you make a dessert perfect for the occasion. It's quite magical, actually."

Mr. Nelson craned his neck until he was sure Renee was busy at the sink and then quietly removed his clip-on bow tie. Then, hooking his finger in Bridget's direction, he winked at Winnie.

Uh-oh.

"You know that magic lesson I had yesterday, Winnie Girl? The one with that fella out at the retreat center?"

She looked around wildly for a way to divert the joke grenade Mr. Nelson was obviously getting ready to toss at the eighty-year-old quietly sipping her lemonade, but there was nothing. Even Lovey wasn't in her usual spot at the window. Before she could go hunting, though, Mr. Nelson broke out his infamous pot-stirring grin.

Bracing herself for the moment of impact, Winnie sucked in her breath and waited.

Mr. Nelson, of course, didn't disappoint.

"I asked him if he could teach me how to make someone

disappear but, seeing as how Bridget is still sitting here, I think it's safe to say I need a follow-up lesson."

Bridget lowered her lemonade glass back to the table, pursed her lips, and turned her best death glare in Mr. Nelson's direction. "You need a lot more than a follow-up lesson in magic, Parker."

Sizzle . . .

A snort of laughter from the sink sent Winnie scrambling for a diversion before Bridget could turn her angst on Renee. Before she could settle on a topic change though, Mr. Nelson cleared his throat and quietly put the pin back in the grenade. "Todd said something interesting yesterday when I asked him about his knowledge of magic."

"Oh?" Winnie noted the remaining time on the tartlets and took a moment to prepare the cooling racks atop the island. "And what was that?"

"He said he likes altering perception. That he gets a charge out of it."

Renee shut off the faucet and reached for the dishcloth next to the sink. "Bob and I went to a magic show early in our marriage. He liked to pretend he knew how the tricks were done. But he didn't."

"I've never been."

"Never been what, dear?" Bridget asked.

Winnie shrugged. "To a magic show."

Mr. Nelson braced the floor with his cane and slowly rose to his feet, his eyes shining with excitement. "I can fix that, you know."

"Fix what, Mr. Nelson?" Winnie mentally counted down the final twenty seconds on the timer and crossed to the oven door. A peek inside confirmed the tartlets were done and she transferred them to the waiting racks. "The magic show thing?"

"I may not be as good as Todd, *yet*, but I learned a few things yesterday that you might enjoy seeing." Mr. Nelson turned, caned his way over to the front door, and then paused momentarily before heading downstairs to his own apartment. "I just need to get a few things together, but I'll be ready by seven—eight, at the latest."

"You mean eight *tonight*?"

Nodding, he switched his cane to the opposite hand and reached for the stairwell railing with the other. "We'll do it out on the porch."

Renee shoved the now-dry mixing bowls into the cabinet and spun around, her eyes wide, her whisper fierce. "You're baking for Ty's party tonight, remember?"

Winnie pulled her gaze from Renee's and fixed it, instead, on Mr. Nelson as he began his descent. "Wait. Mr. Nelson? Can we—"

"Prepare to be amazed, Winnie Girl." And then, "Now I just need to find my top hat."

"You do that, Mr. Nelson . . ."

At the telltale click of the man's front door from the vestibule below, Winnie lifted her hand in the air, crossing-guard style. "Don't say it. Please. How was I supposed to crush that?"

"Like a bug, dear." Bridget looped her purse strap around her shoulder and stood, her impending exit leading her to the door, as well. "It's really the only way to deal with that man, or *any* man, for that matter."

Winnie listened as the elderly woman made her way down the steps and onto the front porch before grabbing her rescue bag and flinging it onto the counter next to the tartlets. "I know. I know. But don't worry, I'll make Ty's treats, I promise."

Silence filled the space between Winnie and Renee as they readied the bag and the dessert for the last rescue of the week. Then, when it was ready to go, Renee crossed to the table and the order pad containing the recipient's address. "It's on the other side of town. Not far from the soccer fields."

"Soccer fields. Got it." Winnie commandeered the slip of paper from her friend, wiggled into her uniform jacket, and hiked the rescue bag onto her shoulder. "Lock up and head home. I know you've got stuff to do before the big day tomorrow. I can clean up the rest of this stuff when I get back."

"You mean between the baking you still have to do and the magic show you'll be attending later this evening?" Renee quipped.

"I'll get it all done. I always do."

"I know you will, and I know you do." Renee followed her to the door and planted a kiss on her cheek. "But still, I'll finish cleaning up before I head out."

Winnie started to argue but stopped as her phone vibrated atop the key table. A glance at the screen yielded Jay's name.

"Winnie, you've gotta go."

"I know. I'll put him on speaker and talk to him as I drive, if necessary." She pulled the woman in for a quick hug and then bounded down the stairs, her phone at her ear. "Jay? You still there?"

"I am."

"Good, I was afraid voice mail had kicked in." At the bottom of the stairs, she repositioned the bag on her shoulder and headed onto the porch, the screen door smacking against its frame in her wake.

"You sound like you're on the move."

"Last rescue of the day." She made her way down the steps and over to the ambulance, the pitter-patter of feet on the walkway at her back letting her know she wasn't alone. "You're a Good Egg Custard Tartlets."

His laugh resonated in her ears and warmed her from the inside out. "That's clever."

"Thanks."

"Guess what?"

She walked around the back of the rig and deposited the bag and the tartlets inside. "What?"

"We're back."

There was no denying the thrill of excitement that coursed through her body as she pushed the gate closed and headed back around the car to the driver's side. "*Back*, back?"

His laugh reached through the line and made her smile, too. "Back, back. As in, sitting in my living room right now, as a matter of fact, and dying to see you as soon as you're done with this rescue."

She stopped mid-jig as the reality that was her evening crashed ashore. "Wait. I have to bake. And go to a magic show."

"A magic show? Where?"

"My front porch."

His laugh was back but it stopped shy of resurrecting the same in her. "Mr. Nelson, I presume?"

"Good guess." She slipped onto the seat after Lovey and inserted the key in the ignition. "And Renee is having a big just-because party for Ty tomorrow morning and I promised to make all the treats—ice-cream cone cupcakes, brownies, cookies, et cetera, et cetera."

"Okay, so slap an apron on me and I'll help. But, fair warning, I don't care about the whole raw-eggs-in-the-cookie-dough thing."

Her smile was back as was the image of the kiss she'd been thinking about off and on since Jay left for California. "Duly noted. I'll order pizza and we'll make a date of it!"

"Fantastic. This'll be good for Caroline."

She paused her hand on the gearshift. "Caroline?"

"I'm all done trying to compartmentalize. Caroline needs to see the way we are together, Winnie. So she knows it's real."

"So y-you're bringing"—she stopped, swallowed, and made herself continue—"*Caroline*?"

"If that's okay . . ."

She swallowed again, the taste of disappointment (and *fear?*) unpleasant on her tongue. "Oh. Yeah. Sure, it's okay. It'll be . . . fun."

Liar, liar, pants on fire.

Chapter 21

She'd just pulled her hair into a fresh ponytail when she heard the footsteps—one set propelled by enthusiasm, and the other heavy with dread—on the staircase leading up to her apartment.

"You can do this, Winnie," she whispered to her reflection. "Just be yourself. Pretend she's sixty instead of sixteen and you've got this . . ."

The faintest hint of fur along her ankles brought her focus down to the floor and Lovey. "I could use your help tonight, Your Highness."

Lovey replied with one slow blink before trotting out of the bedroom and toward the male voice now echoing through her kitchen.

"Winnie? We're here!"

Squaring her shoulders, Winnie took one last look at herself, finger-brushed the end of her left eyebrow down, and then left the safety of her bedroom for the great unknown. Yet the second she rounded the corner and saw Jay standing there, all nervousness gave way to unadulterated joy.

For a moment she couldn't move, her gaze riveted on the man now smiling back at her as she worked to find her breath.

Jay Morgan was, in a word, handsome. Not double-take-hot in the way so many women found Greg, but handsome in that classic, quietly wow kind of way. At six feet tall, he owned his height with a quiet confidence that was more about his age and his life experiences than it was about anything else. The sprinkling of gray in his otherwise light brown hair lent a distinguished aura to the thirty-nine-year-old. His strong chin, infectious smile, and friendly blue-green eyes simply completed the picture.

"Aren't you a sight for sore eyes . . ." He met her midway between the entryway and her bedroom door and scooped her up and into a hug. "Oh, I've missed you."

She buried her face in his shoulder and reveled in his smell, his nearness, and his warmth. "I've missed you, too."

And it was true, she had.

She'd been so busy bracing herself against the possibility of being hurt, that she'd almost convinced herself she'd be okay if Jay called it quits after reuniting with his ex. But there, in his arms, she knew it was a lie. Jay was the missing piece in her life she hadn't realized was missing before they met. Now, when he wasn't around, the hole he filled was so all-encompassing she wasn't sure how she'd been so oblivious to its existence in the first place.

Slowly, he lowered her back down to the ground, prompting her eyes to open on the clearly unhappy sixteen-year-old still standing in the open doorway.

"Caroline!" She parted company with Jay's arms and held her hand out to the girl. "It's good to see you. Did you have a fun trip?"

"I wish we were still there." Caroline inched her way into the entryway and around Winnie's hand. "Everything is so much better there. And I do mean *everything*."

Unsure of what else to do, Winnie brought her hands together in a quick clap and then hooked her thumb in the direction of the kitchen. "I thought maybe, instead of calling and ordering a pizza for delivery, we could each make our own. I stopped at the store and picked up all sorts of toppings so you can pretty much make your dream pizza."

"I like mine plain," Caroline said as she slouched against the nearest wall and cast a look of pure disdain at the topping-filled bowls Winnie had arranged around the island prior to their arrival. "And from Luigi's."

"Caroline!" Jay said, his voice sharp.

Winnie rested her hand atop his shoulder. "No, no, it's okay. I'll just place an order with Luigi's. Once it's ready, it'll only take a few minutes to drive into town and pick it up."

"No. I think making my own pizza sounds like fun and that's what we're going to do." He crossed to the island and the waiting bowls and took a moment to inspect each one, his smile returning as he pointed at the last few. "You have *ham*? And *pineapple*? I *love* ham and pineapple pizza!"

"Yeah, I—"

"Mom got you on that when you were dating, didn't she?" Caroline pushed off the wall and quickly closed the gap between the wall and her father with an almost-skip.

Jay's head snapped up, his cheeks red. "She introduced me to it but—"

"I'll put that on my pizza, too." Caroline's gaze moved across the island before landing on Winnie with a smirk. "After all, I am my father and my mother's child."

Winnie took a deep breath, counted to ten in her head, and then joined them in the kitchen, her smile wooden, at best.

Don't let her get to you . . .

"I made the dough when I got home from the store and it's chilling in the refrigerator." She opened the door and glanced back over her shoulder at her guests. "Are you ready to have a little fun?"

Jay's answering smile stopped short of his eyes. "We're ready."

As she transferred the dough balls to the counter, she gave a running commentary on the various ways they could flatten their dough. Jay, of course, opted to toss it in the air, narrowly missing a curious Lovey as he fumbled it on its way back down.

"Oops."

"Slick, Dad," Caroline mumbled as she pushed the heel of her hand into her own dough ball.

Winnie rescued the dough from the floor and tossed it into the wastebasket. "No pizza for you, mister." Then, before he could truly react, she returned to the fridge for another dough ball. "Just kidding. Here you go."

Again, he tossed it into the air, and again, it missed his hands on the way down. Only this time, instead of hitting the floor, it landed on the island.

A peek at Caroline revealed the faintest hint of a smile on the girl's otherwise expressionless face.

"Don't throw it so high, and move your hands like this." Winnie demonstrated with her own dough ball. When it was the way she wanted it, she rested it atop the pie pan and set it aside. "Okay, now try it again."

While not perfect, Jay kept control of the dough with the tip of his nose the only notable casualty.

This time, Winnie's clap was heartfelt as was the smile she couldn't hide. "Look at you! Look out, Luigi—Jay Morgan is in the house."

A giggle from just over Winnie's shoulder netted the first real smile on Caroline's face since her arrival.

"Oh, you think that was funny?" Jay teased. "How about you give it a whirl, dear daughter of mine."

"Mine is already flat." Caroline pointed at the dough now stretched across her own pie pan. "See?"

Jay crossed his arms and leveled a playful stare at his daughter. "But you did it the easy way."

"No, I did it the smart way."

"You mean the girly way."

Winnie sucked in a breath. "I'd say those are fighting words, wouldn't you, Caroline?" Then, without waiting for the girl's reply, she marched back to the refrigerator, extracted another dough ball, and handed it to Caroline. "Show him how it's done, kiddo."

"My pleasure." Caroline took the dough and flattened it a little the way Winnie had demonstrated. Then, with a quick glance at Winnie for confirmation, she lifted it into the air, gave it a few circular tosses and lowered it down to a waiting pie pan with a face-splitting smile. "And that's how it's done, *Dad*."

"Yeah, Dad." Winnie teased.

"Great, now you're ganging up on me." He snaked his arm around Winnie's waist and pulled her close. "I'm not sure I like two against one."

"You didn't mind it when Mom and I ganged up against you in that pillow fight the other night," Caroline said.

Pillow fight?

Caroline's eyes crackled with something Winnie couldn't place. "And you let Mom stay that first night."

"Caroline!"

Winnie steadied herself against the counter as Caroline's words exploded in her head.

Didi stayed? With Jay and Caroline?

"And you didn't mind it when Mom and I took turns trying to choo-choo train those green beans into your mouth earlier that same night, either."

Choo-choo train green beans into—

No.

Let it go. She's trying to shake you.

Winnie sensed Jay moving, even heard him clearing his throat over the dull roar in her ears, but beyond that, she was at a loss.

"Caroline, that's enough, young lady!"

Inhaling sharply, Winnie forced herself to refocus, to take control of the evening. "Um, so next up is the sauce. Just spoon on however much you want and spread it out as far as you want it to go on the crust." She hated the uncertainty she heard in her voice, but considering the tears that were amassing in the corners of her eyes, it was better than the alternative. "Then you can put whatever toppings you want on top of that and I'll pop them into the oven."

She did her best to focus on the steps as she'd outlined them, tried to lose herself in the fun of spreading the sauce and sprinkling the cheese, but her thoughts kept traveling back to the picture Caroline had painted—a picture very different from the one Jay had painted during their last real phone conversation before he'd left California.

Was Caroline telling tales? Or was Jay massaging the truth? And where, if anywhere, did that leave Winnie?

When her pizza was done, she carried it over to the pre-heated oven, the weight of Jay's eyes making her footfalls heavy. She knew he was waiting for eye contact so he could gauge the damage his daughter had caused, but she wasn't ready. Her head was still reeling from the things Caroline had said and the way they'd made Winnie feel.

"Okay, anyone else's done?"

"Mine is," Jay said, his tone hesitant. "Caroline?"

"Yeah, it's done." Caroline pushed the pan across the island to Winnie. "I opted to stick with plain. Ham and pineapple is Mom and Dad's thing."

Winnie slid her fingers under the edge of both pans, carried them to the oven, and slipped them onto the rack below hers. When the door was shut and the timer set, she turned around to find Jay shooting daggered stares at Caroline. Caroline, in turn, stared back in defiance.

Alrighty, then . . .

Somehow, they managed to make it through dinner, although the lightness Winnie had felt upon seeing Jay for the first time, and again when they were tossing the dough, was long gone. She tried to keep a conversation going, as did Jay, but it seemed no matter what topic they came up with, Caroline was determined to bring it back to her mother.

Finally, as dinner morphed into dessert, and dessert morphed into Winnie's need to bake, Jay's patience ran dry.

"Caroline, please. That's enough about Didi Evans. You've recounted every moment of the trip and then some."

The sixteen-year-old's eyes turned fiery. "Dad! You just said mom's name out loud!"

"What? You think I'd keep something like that from Winnie? C'mon, Caroline, knock it off."

The teenager's death glare widened to include Winnie even though her answer was directed at Jay. "But you've told *me* not to tell anyone."

A lot of good that did . . .

Winnie closed her eyes against the memory of Caroline's soccer-playing classmate and tried, instead, to put herself anywhere but where she was at that moment. Like maybe a beach somewhere . . . or standing in the winner's circle at a national pie-baking contest . . . or holding hands with Jay across a table at Beans.

"That's right, I did." Jay planted his elbows on the edge of the table and leaned forward until his daughter's attention was squarely back on him. "At *your mother's* request."

A flash of something resembling pain skittered across the teenager's face before being cast off by a shrug. "That's okay. After Mom does that interview with *Hollywood Tonight* she was telling me about, everyone is going to know I'm Didi Evans's daughter. *Everyone.*"

Chapter 22

Even if Winnie had never been to Renee's house (which she had) and had no idea where it was (which she did), there'd be little to no doubt she'd found the right place. It was the only house in all of Silver Lake that was, apparently, under siege by a dozen ten-year-old boys wearing swim trunks and darting behind trees, their hands heavy with water balloons.

For a moment, she simply sat there, beside the curb, watching as a smaller-than-average redhead crouched quietly behind a Bradford pear tree as a fellow partygoer unknowingly drew closer to his drench zone. Part of her wanted to warn the unsuspecting boy, but another part of her (the one that was still cranky from the previous evening) was having too much fun watching the redhead slowly cock his arm in preparation for his attack.

"Here we go, Lovey, watch this . . ." Without taking her eyes off the scene, she directed the tabby's attention across her lap and through the driver's-side window. "One . . . two . . . three—*Wham*! *Bull's-eye*!"

Unsuspecting Boy's resulting shriek sent the redhead running for the backyard for what was surely a blow-by-blow recap of the encounter. Provided Unsuspecting Boy didn't plug him with a water balloon before he made it across the side yard . . .

She breathed in the lightness of the moment, removed her foot from the brake, and steered the Dessert Squad all the way onto Renee's driveway. With a flick of her wrist, she shifted into park and turned off the engine, eyeing Lovey closely as she did.

"You ready to get your first taste of over-the-top craziness, Your Highness? Because if you think things get a little crazy when I'm baking sometimes, that's nothing compared to a gathering of ten-year-old boys."

Lovey stood up on the passenger seat and wagged the tip of her tail. The movement, in and of itself, wasn't earth-shattering, but considering it was the same thing the cat did when they arrived at each and every rescue, it said enough.

"Okay, don't say I didn't warn you . . ." Winnie dropped the keys and her phone into the inside pocket of the uniform she'd offered to wear despite it being a Saturday and shoved the door open. Before her feet even hit the concrete, Lovey was on the ground and sniffing her way across the front lawn.

A door just inside the open garage creaked open and Renee's perfectly tanned face peeked out. "Get in here quick! Ty and the rest of the boys are feverishly filling balloons with the hope of ambushing anyone and everyone within launching range."

"They wouldn't hit me! I have the desserts, remember?"

Whispers and giggles from the left side of Renee's house

revealed eight sets of eyes atop eight shiver-inducing grins peeking out at her from behind a nearby hedge.

Uh-oh . . .

Swooping her hands toward the ground, Winnie grabbed Lovey (mid-sniff) and dashed through the garage and into the small, yet protected, confines of Renee's kitchen. When she was sure they were safe, she closed the door and leaned against it, panting.

Hisss . . .

She lifted Lovey into her field of vision and shook her head. "I save you from certain dousing and you hiss at me? Are you serious?"

Hisss . . .

"Silly me, I thought she'd finally turned a corner on the whole hating-me thing." Winnie lowered the cat to the linoleum floor and let go, shaking her head as she did. "Remind me again why Gertie left me this ungrateful creature?"

"Because Gertie loved and trusted you and obviously felt you were the best choice to take care of Lovey." Renee stepped back, surveyed Winnie from head to toe, and then crossed to the kitchen counter she was obviously transforming into a lunch buffet complete with mini hot dogs, cheese sliders, and pizza balls. "Though, looking at you right now, I have to wonder if she wanted Lovey to take care of *you*."

Winnie smoothed her paramedic jacket down around her hips. "As if Lovey would ever take care of me. Puh-lease."

"You said she kept you company at the computer the other night, right?"

"Yeah . . ."

"And you said she's been following you around the apartment more the last day or so, right?"

"Yeah . . ."

"She's warming up to you, Winnie. Making sure you're okay."

Winnie had to laugh at the notion of Lovey as her protector, and laugh she did.

"I'm serious, Winnie. Animals sense when their owners are sad."

Slowly, and with as much stealth as she could muster, Winnie snuck her hand around the bowl of pizza balls and extracted one from the side. "What makes you think I'm sad?" she asked, hiding the finger food behind her back.

"I don't know. Maybe the circles under your eyes, the sparkle that's been AWOL from them for the past week, the fact that the smile that's normally plastered across your face hasn't been seen in days . . . You know, clues like that." Renee grabbed a small dipping cup from the first of two stacks, spooned a little pizza sauce into it, and held it out for Winnie to take. "That pizza ball you're holding behind your back will taste a whole lot better dipped in this."

Busted!

She took the sauce cup, dipped her pizza ball into it, and then popped it in her mouth. "Mmmm. And . . . as for . . . this notion I'm not happy"—she swallowed, helped herself to another pizza ball, and lowered it into the sauce cup—"I'm fine. I just didn't sleep too well last night."

"Oooh, you have your own personal refrain!"

"My own personal refrain?"

"You know, the repeating part of a song." Renee returned to the counter and placed a stack of napkins next to the paper plates and plastic utensils that denoted the start of the buffet line.

"I know what a refrain means, Renee. I'm just not sure what it has to do with me."

"The whole not-sleeping-well thing. It's been a daily oc-currence with you the past week." Renee loosened the lid on the apple juice container and set it back down next to the plastic cups. "And, to a lesser degree, off and on since you met Jay. Or, rather, since Jay's kid met you."

Winnie looked down at her overly sauced pizza ball, her appetite gone. "Can we not talk about that right now?"

"Talk about what, or should I say, whom? Jay or Scream Queen?"

"Either."

Cocking her head to the side, Renee pouted her lower lip. The effect, which would surely qualify as condescending on just about any other face, left Winnie wishing for a tissue and an enormous piece of chocolate. "I take it things didn't go so well last night?"

She knew she'd have to bring her friend up to speed soon, but not now. Not when she'd promised to help make Ty's just-because party a smashing success. She opened her mouth to say as much but closed it as her phone vibrated inside her pocket.

"Excuse me a sec." Winnie extracted her phone, noted Jay's name on the screen, and sent him straight to voice mail. Again. As the number beside the mailbox changed from three to four, she slipped it back into her pocket and delib-erately directed her attention toward something other than her gape-mouthed friend. "Anyway, I found something in-teresting during the time your mime was at Charlton School of the Arts."

Renee pulled a cheese slider off the top of the platter and nibbled her way around the sides, stopping every few sec-onds to shake it at Winnie. "I should protest this all-too-obvious topic change and demand you tell me what happened last night. But, in the interest of utilizing the limited time remaining before those boys come through my back door asking about food, I won't."

"Thank you." Winnie pointed at what remained of Renee's slider. "Is that good?"

Shoving the rest of the miniature hamburger into her mouth, Renee's eyes rolled back behind her eyelids. "Uh-huh. Ur is."

"Don't talk with your mouth full," Winnie teased. Then, at Renee's nod, she helped herself to a slider, too. "Anyhoo, check this out. Your mime didn't go to Charlton wanting to be a mime."

"Oh?"

"Yeah, his bio on the school's website said he came in wanting to be a magician."

"And what? He suddenly took a vow of silence?"

Winnie laughed. "I guess. Anyway, after rereading the bios of our five suspects, I decided to search the time frame each was connected with the school. Since I knew we'd be seeing George this morning, I figured I'd focus on him first. And, get this . . . During George's last semester at the school, a beloved teacher took her own life."

Winnie took in Renee's gasp and continued. "Now, I know this doesn't mean anything, but from everything I could find, this woman was a favorite among the students. Her death was so upsetting to the students, in fact, that the school borrowed grief counselors from as far away as two counties to help the kids in the wake of the news."

"Okay . . ."

"In a news article the very next day, each and every student interviewed talked about what a wonderful teacher this woman had been. Everyone except George. He actually complained about receiving a failing grade from her the previous semester."

Renee chased a few crumbs from her lips with a napkin and then balled it up and threw it in the trash can beneath the sink. "It's official. I seem to fall for guys who end up being insensitive jerks. My mother should be so proud."

"She should. Because the reason you fall for these guys is because your heart is bigger than pretty much anyone's I've ever known." She leaned forward, planted a kiss on Renee's cheek, and then gestured toward the gaggle of boys running toward the sliding glass door. "It looks like their tummies have finally caught up to the time on the clock."

"Grab a marker, will you? Maybe if we put names on the cups, they can hang on to them through dessert, too."

"Good idea. But first, I'll let them inside." Winnie crossed to the door but paused for a moment before actually opening it. "And you're absolutely sure you don't need me to swing out to the retreat center and pick up George? I mean, that's what we'd originally talked about."

"The secretary at the center called me this morning and said she'd drop him off," explained Renee. "So assuming that still happens, we're good."

"When is he supposed to be here?"

"Twelve thirty."

Nodding, Winnie wrapped her fingers around the handle of the door and slid it open. "Okay, boys, lunch is ready!"

With one big whoosh, the gaggle of boys swarmed past her and into the kitchen with one lone exception.

"Winnie!" Renee's only child wrapped his arms around Winnie and squeezed. "Mom said you made the desserts!"

"And Mom said you had me in the crosshairs of your water balloon fight, you little stinker." She tickled Ty's side and, when he jerked back with a laugh, she brushed a kiss atop his blond head. "You better watch out—revenge is sweet."

His eyes, so much like his mother's, sparkled at the challenge, and then he was gone, his feet running to catch up with his friends before the food disappeared. She watched him go and then turned and looked out at the backyard and the bits of colored rubber latex strewn around. For so many years she'd never allowed herself to think of being a mom. After all, she'd had little to no interest in dating for more than a decade. But once she met Jay, the thoughts had trickled in—baking sessions with a daughter, bringing home-made cookies to a son's soccer game . . .

It had been silly, of course. She and Jay had been dating for a little over three months—three months that had been carefully scheduled and planned around a sixteen-year-old who wanted absolutely nothing to do with Winnie.

So many nights she stared up at the ceiling trying to convince herself a clean break was best for everyone involved. But every time she was sure she was going to end it with Jay, her heart reminded her why she couldn't.

Something about Jay made her feel whole. When they were together, her laugh was truer, her smile fuller, her dreams endless. Surely that had to mean something, didn't it?

It means you're pathetic, that's what it means . . .

"Winnie? The cups?"

She shook herself back into the moment and slid the door closed. Renee was right. There was a job to do. Pulling the cap off the marker in her hand, Winnie retraced her steps back to the counter and the cups waiting to be marked with the names of Ty's friends. "Okay, let's get some names on these cups and then get down to eating, shall we?"

Chapter 23

"Hurry back, Mommy." Renee moved Lovey's front paw up and down in farewell as Winnie slowly backed the Dessert Squad down the driveway and toward the road. "I'll miss you."

"Not likely."

Movement in the passenger seat pulled her attention off Renee's front walkway and fixed it, instead, on the brown-haired, charcoal-eyed man gesturing first toward Lovey and then toward his own confused face.

"Why do I say that?" she asked.

At the mime's emphatic nod, she answered the nonverbal question she'd apparently interpreted successfully. "That cat? Lovey? The one who took to you the other day at the lake? Yeah, she doesn't exactly like me. And Renee knows this."

She shifted the car into drive and headed down the street, the neighborhood roads mandating a slow, easy pace and enabling her to play what was, essentially, a game of charades with her passenger.

He mimed whiskers (cat! cat!) and then pointed at Winnie, his forehead scrunched in confusion.

"Yes, Lovey is mine. Now." When the lines across George's forehead didn't budge, she filled in the blanks. "My friend Gertrude Redenbacher passed away earlier this year."

George's face fell in feigned sadness.

"She was old," Winnie explained as she slowed to a stop at a four-way intersection. When she was sure the coast was clear, she turned left. "Gertie lived a long life and she was excited to join her husband, who passed a few years earlier. Anyway, when Gertie died, she left me this ambulance—which her husband had been restoring prior to his death—and Lovey.

"This ambulance enabled me to continue my dream when I was forced to close my bakery due to a landlord who raised my rent so high I could no longer stay in business. And Lovey? Well, I bought her a windowsill hammock—which she adores—all her favorite foods—which she inhales—and have even given up sleeping in my bed more times than I can count so she can have it. Yet, here we are, nearly five months later, and her favorite pastime is still hissing at me."

Winnie stopped at the red light and, in conjunction with a sigh she hadn't meant to be so loud, pressed the back of her head against her seat. "I actually thought she was starting to warm up to me the last few days thanks to a nearly twenty-four-hour-long cease-fire in the hissing. But she was back at it again today."

George pointed at the traffic light a second before the car behind her blasted their horn.

"Everyone is always in such a rush, aren't they?"

He nodded.

She drove down Main Street, stopping every few feet to allow a pedestrian to cross. "See that place right there? The Corner Pocket? That was where my bakery was up until the beginning of March."

He pointed at the shingle with the pool hall's name and then scrunched his forehead at her again.

"It was called Delectable Delights," she said. "Renee worked there with me just as she does now. She makes the whole thing all the more fun."

His forehead relaxed with a smile.

"What you saw today at Ty's party? That's Renee pretty much twenty-four/seven. It's why watching her go through her divorce was so hard. She's supposed to be laughing and smiling, you know?"

When they reached the end of the downtown shopping district, Winnie turned right toward the lake. "And she'd probably kill me for telling you this stuff. But I trust you can keep this little conversation mum, yes?"

She laughed at her own question and then quickly followed it up with a shrug and an apology. "Sorry about that. I'm betting you get that a lot from people like me who think they're being funny. I didn't mean any harm. Really."

He waved her off and then moved his index finger in a backward motion.

"Rewind?" she asked.

A quick nod led to her next question. "What? The conversation?"

Again, he nodded.

"Rewind to what? Renee?"

A third nod had her smiling again. "She's a great friend. And an even better mom. Ty is one lucky kid, I tell you."

This time he shook his head and moved his finger in a slight forward motion.

"I rewound too far? Okay, let me think . . ." She stopped, revisited their conversation, and then picked it up in the only other area that made sense. "Her divorce with Bob?"

The nod was back.

"He traded her in for a slightly younger model." With the words came an overwhelming need to strangle her friend's ex. But since murder charges wouldn't be good for business—

Murder charges . . .

Ahhh yes, the reason she nearly fell off Renee's kitchen stool volunteering to transport George back to the retreat center in the first place . . .

Before she could steer the conversation in a direction meant to best utilize their time together, George was back to his miming.

It took a few tries, but eventually she got the gist of his question.

"Sure, Renee has had it rough. Even though the divorce isn't her fault, she still blames herself. I keep hoping the things I say will eventually drown out the doubt-filled voices in her head, but it doesn't always work that way."

George's nod was more reflective as he turned his attention on the scenery moving past his window at the forty-mile-per-hour speed limit permitted on the outlying road.

"Did you just stop talking the day you decided to become a mime?" Winnie took advantage of the empty road to really take in the man seated where Lovey usually sat. Somewhere in his mid to late thirties, George had an air of sadness about him that transcended the face paint designed to mask any real emotion. It was there in the downward slant of his shoulders, the eye contact that always seemed to lag south, and the lack of any perceptible glint in his eyes no matter how hard Ty and his friends had laughed during his show.

When he didn't move or react, she took her questions in a slightly different direction, hoping, if nothing else, to get a reaction. "Do you at least *miss* talking?"

"Every day."

His whisper, let alone its raspy quality, was so unexpected, so sudden, the tires on the right side of the ambulance actually left the edge of the road for a second or two before Winnie yanked the steering wheel to the left in compensation.

"Then . . . then, why don't you?" She looked from the road in front of them to the rearview mirror and back again. "Talk, I mean? Between shows?"

With his face still turned toward his window, he followed up his first two words with more. "Those voices that mess with Renee's head? Well, the ones in *my* head are relentless . . . *and right.*"

"Someone hurt you?" She checked the road ahead one more time and then took a moment to glance across the seat at her passenger.

"No."

Confused, she returned her gaze to the road. "I don't—"

"*I'm* the one who did the hurting," he said, his tone ripe with self-loathing. "With my words . . . my lies."

Now that he was talking, it was as if he couldn't stop. "I destroyed her marriage, her family, her life."

"George, I'm sure you're overstating whatever it is that happened."

"She's dead. Because of *me*. There is no overstating that."

Winnie felt her jaw clench in time with her hands. Did

she hang a U-turn and deliver him straight to the police station? Did she ask him to repeat himself while she slyly reached into her inside jacket pocket and hit Record on her phone?

Decisions, decisions . . .

"I knew I screwed up blowing off that last test, but I wanted to fool around like the other guys did. Looking back, I should have been grateful she didn't have me expelled for coming to class drunk that day, but all I could see was the hit to my transcript."

Transcript?

"I was so hung up on acing all my classes that the thought of that one blight on my report card sent me into a tailspin." He shifted in his seat but kept his face turned away. "I asked if I could do extra credit to pull my grade back up. But she said no."

Extra credit?

"I begged and pleaded but she wouldn't budge. And that's when I set my revenge in motion. I took pictures of her talking to the male faculty members—innocent conversations or walks to the parking lot that I spun differently in an anonymous letter to her husband. I started the gossip that spread like wildfire around a campus of kids who had nothing better to do between classes. Eventually, based on what I heard, the husband fell for the lies and filed for divorce. According to the note they found next to her body, she simply couldn't bear to live without him.

"My *lies* did that." He whispered. "*I* did that."

"Wait. You're not talking about Sally Dearfield, are you? You're talking about that teacher who died during your last year at Charlton, aren't you?"

His head jerked back as if he'd been slapped. And suddenly, the eyes that seemed so void of emotion throughout Ty's show crackled with first shock, then anger, and, finally, hurt. "You think *I* killed Sally?"

"I thought that's what *you* were saying," she said behind a pent-up exhale.

"I wasn't saying that!" He stopped, raked his hand through his hair, and then shifted forward on the seat.

"*Someone* killed her."

"I realize that." He brought his hand around to his mouth for a moment before letting it drift all the way down to his lap. "She made a lot of enemies in a very short period of time. One of them obviously struck back. But it wasn't me."

At the entrance to the retreat house, Winnie turned but didn't accelerate. "How did she make enemies?"

"She was angry because I kept her from getting some award she was after—we all did, from what she said." His voice, while still quiet, adopted more of a wooden quality as he continued. "Sally was out for revenge."

"Revenge?"

He nodded. "On us."

"What did you say?" she asked. "How did you react?"

"I told her I understood the knee-jerk reaction to exact revenge. But then I used the very thing she held over my head as an example of why she shouldn't."

A glance in the rearview mirror turned up no sign of a car behind them so she brought the ambulance to a stop in the middle of the driveway. "So Mr. Nelson was right about the whole blackmail thing, after all," she mused. "She really was holding stuff over your heads."

"She said she had proof that I'd written the letter to Mrs. Lowry's husband . . . that I'm the one who destroyed that marriage and, therefore, drove Mrs. Lowry to kill herself."

He took a deep breath and let it out, slowly. "She said she'd find a way to destroy my career with it."

"And you believed her?" Winnie asked.

"Of course I did. I know, better than anyone, what revenge can do."

"What did she want from you in exchange for keeping your secret?"

"Money. Lots of money." A tired laugh filled the space between them for as long as it took Winnie to blink. "Though, if she'd known how little I'd been making before I got here, she could have saved herself the postage stamp she used to entice me up here in the first place."

Winnie peeked in the rearview mirror once again. Still nothing. "Did she use the reality talent show audition on you, too?"

Momentary surprise gave way to a slow nod. "She used it on all of us. Same letter. Same ploy. And it worked."

"Do you know what she had on the others?"

Silence blanketed the space between them, prompting her to repeat the question.

"I only know of one for sure," he murmured.

"And?"

"At this time, I'm not at liberty to say."

"Even if it means righting an egregious wrong?" In the wake of yet another round of silence, Winnie considered everything she'd learned thus far and used it to formulate one more question. "Why didn't you tell the police that she'd been blackmailing you?"

"Fear, I guess. I don't know what she had on everyone else. My quest for revenge cost a woman her life. And Sally's quest for revenge cost her her own." He traced his finger across the hem of his cargo shorts and then stopped, his anguish raw. "What happens if something I say destroys another person's life?"

There was so much to absorb, so much to examine and figure out in relation to what happened to Sally. But even so, there was one thing she knew for sure—George Watkins didn't kill Sally. She knew that just as surely as she knew the reason he'd given up magic to become a mime . . .

"Maybe, instead of living a life in silence, you need to use your words to apologize—to the teacher's husband, to her family, and to yourself."

His eyes crackled to life again with an anger that didn't bow to hurt this time. "You say that as if apologizing for what I did could bring Mrs. Lowry back . . ."

"Remaining silent hasn't brought her back, either, has it?"

Chapter 24

Winnie leaned against the counter, her gaze following Ty as he raced out of the kitchen and through the open sliding door with Lovey close on his heels.

"That kid gives the best hugs, you know?"

"I do, and I'm glad. You looked like you needed one." Renee towel-dried the last of Winnie's dessert platters and stacked it atop the rest. "Is everything okay, Winnie? You seem distracted."

Winnie felt her smile falter but fought back by directing her friend's attention off her face and out into the backyard. Ty had commandeered a leafy branch and was dragging it through the grass in an attempt to get Lovey to play. Lovey, of course, responded on her own terms, alternating between aloof-spectator and attack-cat modes. "They're kind of cute together. Maybe you should keep her."

"Please. You talk a good game, but you've gotten attached to that cat."

"Attached?" Winnie redirected her attention to Renee and a kitchen that showed no signs of having hosted a dozen ten-year-old boys less than an hour earlier. "Don't you think you might be overstating things a bit?"

"Nope."

"How do you figure?"

"Easy. You came back to get her, didn't you?" Renee crossed to a wrapped plate on the counter next to the refrigerator, extracted two familiar-looking chocolate chip cookies, and handed one to Winnie. "Yes, I stashed aside a few of your cookies for myself while you were rounding the kids up for dessert. Sue me."

Winnie broke off a bite of the cookie and popped it in her mouth. "So what'd you think of George in action?"

"George?"

"Don't play dumb. You know who I'm talking about." Winnie pointed at the cabinet tasked with housing glasses and, at Renee's nod, helped herself to two while Renee secured the milk from the refrigerator.

When their glasses were filled, Renee led the way to the four-top table that looked out over the backyard via a bay window. "The kids loved him. In fact, after you left to drive him back to the retreat center, they took turns miming for me. Ty's friend Sam was actually pretty good at it."

"I mean, what's your read on him—as a person?" She broke off another piece of cookie and then chased it down with a gulp of milk. "Do you think he's trustworthy?"

Renee peeked out at her son. "I think he's good with the kids, and he certainly had a lot of patience with them. But it's hard to say much more than that when he doesn't speak."

"He spoke to me. On the way back to his place just now."

She shrugged off the shock Renee wore and made short work of her remaining cookie. "He was blackmailed. They all were."

Renee stood, grabbed the cookie plate from beside the fridge, and plunked it down on the table between them. "Tell me."

And so she did. About Sally's ploy to get these five Charlton alums to Silver Lake, the secret she was holding over George's head, and, finally, the woman's demand for money in return for her silence. Renee, in turn, took it all in while eating her way through the limited number of leftover cookies. When Winnie was done, Renee took another look at her son and then brought her elbows to the table and her chin to the pillow created by her hand.

"And you really don't think he's the one?"

"You mean the one who killed her?" At Renee's answering nod, Winnie, too, looked out the window. Only instead of watching Ty and Lovey, she found herself back in the Dessert Squad with George seated beside her in the passenger seat. "I don't. The anguish on his face was so real, so raw. And he told me what she had on him. I don't know why he'd tell me if he's the one who killed her."

"Does he know what Sally had on the other four?"

She forced herself back into her present surroundings and took another sip of milk. "He knows one of them for sure, but not the others."

"And that one?" Renee prodded.

"He wouldn't tell me." Winnie looked down at the remaining gulp or two of milk in her glass but stopped short of actually finishing it in favor of the thoughts she needed to verbalize. "But at least now the notion of blackmailing has been confirmed. Now we just need to track down the specifics as they pertain to each artist. Once we do, maybe we'll be able to figure out who retaliated with murder."

"So how do you propose doing—"

"Hang on a minute, I've got a call coming in." Winnie leaned forward against the edge of the table and retrieved her phone from the back pocket of her jeans. A glance at the screen had her shoving it back into its starting place and reaching for the last of her milk. "Go ahead, continue."

Renee pinned her with a stare.

"What?" She paused her glass en route to her mouth. "Continue . . ."

"You can't keep doing that, Winnie."

"I can't keep *drinking milk*?"

Adding a huffy breath to her eye roll, Renee crossed her arms and waited.

At a loss for what the issue was, Winnie splayed her hands at her sides. *"What?"*

"You can't keep playing games, Winnie. It's not fair. To you or to Jay."

"G-games?" she stammered around the sudden whoosh in her ears.

"If you want to end your relationship with Jay—end it. If you don't—then you two need to stop letting Scream Queen dictate the terms of your relationship. We've talked about this, remember?" Renee uncrossed her arms and helped herself to the last cookie. "What you're doing now—this ignoring-his-call thing? That's accomplishing nothing, zilch, zip, nada—"

Winnie released her hold on her glass and lifted her hands in surrender. "Okay. Okay. I got it. Point taken."

"You've got to talk to him, Winnie. If this matters to

him—if this matters to *both* of you, then you have to find a way to make it work."

Renee was right. Dodging Jay's phone calls was stupid. Childish, even. Winnie had never been one to run from problems. In fact, problems usually pushed her into action. So why change course now?

"You know I'm right, Winnie. It's written all over your face."

Slowly, she raised her gaze to Renee's. "Am I really that transparent?"

"To me? Yes. But that's because you're my BFF." Renee motioned toward the now-empty plate in front of them and then slumped back against her chair. "And as *your* BFF, you're supposed to stop me from eating everything in sight. No one will look at me twice if you don't."

"You can't walk down the street without getting double and triple takes."

"As if . . ."

Winnie pushed her chair back from the table and stood, hands on hips. "Renee Ballentine, you are a knockout. Any man with a brain in their head knows this."

"Not true. Bob didn't."

"I repeat, any man with a brain in their head knows this." She dropped her hands to her sides and came around the table to squat beside her friend. "Bob is a fool, Renee. His actions had nothing to do with you and everything to do with him."

"I want to believe that, Winnie. But it's hard. I mean, how could things go from so right to so wrong in the blink of a bimbo's eye?"

"If they'd been as right as you say, it wouldn't have." She followed Renee's gaze out the window and across the yard to the boy who was now lounging on the grass, staring up at the sky, with a contented smile on his face and Lovey's front paws stretched across his chest. "That little boy out there? You mean the world to him. And, when the time is right, you'll meet a man who feels that way about you, too. Because he *is* out there, Renee. And he wants to find you just as much as you want to find him."

Renee's eyes shone bright with tears she refused to shed. "Do you believe Jay is that man for you?"

"I do."

"Then get out of here and go make things right." Renee stood, pulled Winnie in for a hug, and then released her with a shove toward the sliding glass door. "You go get Lovey and tell Ty I need him in here to help get your platters and stuff out to the car."

Winnie stopped midway to the door and turned to look at her friend. "I love you, Renee. You know that, right?"

"Don't you dare make me cry, Winnie Johnson!" Like a bird preparing to take flight, Renee flapped her hands at her sides in an effort to remain upbeat and cheerful. "Don't you dare . . ."

Feeling her own eyes begin to mist, Winnie resumed her trek to the slider and stepped out onto the patio. "Okay, Lovey, it's time to go home."

Lovey looked from her, to Ty, and back again.

"Lovey, come on. We've got stuff to do."

Again, Lovey looked between the boy serving as her pillow and Winnie. When she didn't budge, Ty scooped her up and carried her over to the patio. "Lovey is a pretty cool cat, Winnie. She's really smart, too!"

Winnie reined in the urge to laugh out of fear it might come across as mocking. "Oh? What makes you say that?"

"When I said your name earlier, she looked right at you through the bay window." Ty dropped his emerald green eyes to the cat in his arms and smiled. "Didn't you, Lovey?"

"She—she did?" Winnie echoed.

"Uh-huh."

Interesting . . .

"Can you carry her to the car while your mom and I carry the plates and stuff?" She pulled the sliding door open and motioned Ty in first. "I'm sure Lovey would like a few more minutes with you."

"Yeah, sure, I can carry her!"

Winnie followed them into the house and through the kitchen, stopping briefly at the counter to claim the plates Renee was unable to hold. "The party came out great, Renee. And thank you for keeping track of Lovey while I took George back to his place."

"Thanks for *taking* George back to his place."

"My pleasure." Winnie followed Ty and Renee into the garage and out the other side to the Dessert Squad. Once the platters and plates were secured in back, she opened the driver's-side door and watched as Ty deposited Lovey inside.

"Catch you later, Lovey."

"Yes, you will." Winnie kissed Ty on the top of his head and then moved on to Renee's cheek. "And I'll see *you* on Monday morning."

"I'll be there." Renee wrapped her arms around her son and guided him onto the grass as Winnie slid into place behind the steering wheel. "I can stop and pick up some coffee on my way in if you'd like."

"You could, or I could ask Mr. Nelson to make us some," she teased.

"My mom says Mr. Nelson's coffee tastes like mud."

Pausing her hand atop the gearshift, Winnie laughed. "That's because it does."

"Oh! Oh! That's what I forgot to ask you about this morning." Renee guided her son back one more step and then smiled at Winnie across the top of the boy's blond head. "Did he really wear a top hat?"

Winnie drew back. "Did *who* wear a top hat?"

"Mr. Nelson."

Dropping her gaze to Ty's, Winnie tried to get a read on whether or not she was the only one clueless over the current topic of conversation. But before she could come to a conclusion, Renee brought her up to speed. "You know . . . For his magic show last night. I bet he was completely adorable."

"His magic show . . ." The words fell away as a reality that was too painful to voice aloud delivered a well-deserved sucker punch to her heart.

No matter how hard she stared at the first-floor windows of 15 Serenity Lane, there was no sign of Mr. Nelson.

No eyes peeking out at her from between the slats of his new blinds . . .

No waving from his favorite chair—the one positioned specifically for the purpose of watching the comings and goings of their neighbors . . .

No bang from the screen door as he caned his way onto the porch to welcome her home . . .

Winnie swallowed back the bile she felt rising in her throat and shifted her focus onto the passenger seat. "I hate myself right now, Lovey. I really do."

Lovey looked from Winnie to the front porch and back again.

"How could I have been so stupid?" She pulled the end of her ponytail in front of her shoulder and gave it a sharp tug. "He was so excited to show me the tricks he learned, and I forgot. How pathetic is that?"

Pretty stinkin' pathetic, that's for sure . . .

She took one last inventory of her housemate's front windows and then gathered her purse and keys and stepped onto the driveway. "C'mon, Lovey, we've got some serious apologizing to do."

Lovey paused in her journey across the front seat to pin Winnie with an irritated glare.

"Yeah, yeah, I know. *I've* got some serious apologizing to do." She watched Lovey jump onto the ground and then slammed the door shut. "Does it ever occur to you that we're in this stuff together now, Your Highness? That maybe I could use a little moral support from you once in a while?"

"I thought it was just old people who talked to themselves."

Winnie whirled around to find Harold Jenkins grinning at her from atop his motorized scooter. A quick scan of the road yielded Cornelia Wright and her sheltie, Con-Man, little more than a driveway and a half ahead.

"Good afternoon, Harold." She lifted her hand in what she hoped was a friendly wave. "Lovey and I were just having a chat, is all."

"It doesn't look like she's listening." He directed Winnie's attention back to the spot where Lovey had been less than a second earlier and, sure enough, she was gone.

She looked around frantically. "Where did she go?"

"She's waiting on the porch."

Winnie's search shifted to the aforementioned location and the golden-eyed cat peeking inside Mr. Nelson's living room window. Relief kicked in but not for long. "Thanks, Harold. I was afraid for a minute that I lost her."

She took two steps toward the porch and then turned back to the road. "Hey, Harold? Have you seen Mr. Nelson today?"

Harold tapped his finger to his chin in thought. "No, can't say that I have. In fact, when I was following Cornelia—I mean, going for a walk earlier—he wasn't sitting on the porch playing chess the way he usually does."

The bile was back. "He—he wasn't?"

"No. And I remember, because I had a joke all ready for him. A real good one, this time."

The guilt she'd been harboring since she left Renee's transitioned into something a lot more like dread as she looked, again, at the first-floor windows. Squinting, she tried to make out her housemate's form lurking behind strategically tilted blinds, but there was nothing.

"I'll take it from here, Harold, thanks." She repeated her initial wave and then hurried up the walkway and onto the porch, worry driving her steps to the (locked?) front door.

Once inside, she stopped at Mr. Nelson's door and knocked. Hard. "Mr. Nelson? Are you in there? I'm so sorry about last night. I really am. I—I guess I was so thrown by Caroline's behavior during dinner that I forgot about everything else. I'm sorry."

When he didn't answer, she pressed her ear to the door and knocked again. "Mr. Nelson?"

She counted to twenty and knocked again. "*Mr. Nelson*? Are you home?"

A glance at the ground confirmed she wasn't the only one worried. "Okay, Lovey, we're going in." Slipping her hand into her purse, she felt around for the extra set of keys Mr. Nelson had given her two years earlier. To date, they'd been used only to carry out the final moments of the surprise seventy-fifth birthday party she'd thrown him the previous fall.

She willed herself to focus on the joy in his face as he'd strolled into his apartment that day rather than the worry propelling her hand at that very moment. "C'mon, darn it . . . *Find. The. Key.*"

A vibration beneath her fingertips temporarily sidelined her search and she pulled out her phone.

"Hello?"

"Winnie, it's Greg."

"Greg, I can't really talk right now, I'm worried about Mr. Nelson and I'm trying to find the spare set of keys to his—"

"He's okay, Winnie."

She sagged against the doorframe. "Oh, thank God. I—I . . ." She stopped, swallowed, and started again as worry shifted back to guilt. "I think I may have hurt his feelings."

"You did."

Her cheeks flamed hot at the public confirmation. "He told you?"

"About the magic show you didn't come to? Yeah. He told me."

Holding her back to the wall, she slowly lowered herself down to the floor. "I didn't mean to blow it off, Greg. I—I just forgot. And I feel *awful*—worse than awful, actually."

"He'll get over it, Winnie," Greg said. "Are *you* okay?"

"You mean besides this intense guilt that's making me feel sick to my stomach? Yeah, I'm okay."

"So you really just forgot his show? Nothing was wrong?"

There's plenty wrong, she wanted to say. Not the least of which was a crumbling relationship with a man she treasured. But considering Greg's feelings for her, she kept mum. "I really just forgot."

"Okay, good. Not good that you forgot, but good that you're okay."

"I know what you mean." She covered the phone long enough to fill Lovey in, and then got back to Greg. "So where is he? I owe him an apology."

"I drove him over to the retreat center again during my relief."

"Why?"

"He wanted another magic lesson."

"Another magic lesson?" she echoed.

"That's right." Greg's voice faded out and then back in as he added, "I'm supposed to pick him up in about twenty minutes."

Bracing her feet against the ground, Winnie rocketed upward against the wall. "No. Sit tight. *I'll* drive out and get him."

Chapter 25

Winnie inched the Dessert Squad around the occasional rut in the thinly graveled road, ticking off each cabin through the windshield.

"Ned, the comedian . . . Colin, the poet . . . Abby, the puppeteer—or, wait, is that Todd, the magician?" She jerked the car to the right and came to a stop, her gaze traveling across the front seat, over Lovey's head, and out the passenger-side window to the line of identical rustic cabins that had necessitated one turnaround already. "I just cannot remember which cabin goes with which person . . ."

Sliding the gearshift forward, she scanned her way down the line in an attempt to pick out some sort of clue as to where she'd find Mr. Nelson. It wasn't the first one—that belonged to the comedian, her first-ever delivery to the retreat center. It wasn't the second one—that she knew, too, as a result of the post-murder sleuthing session that had landed her and Lovey in Colin Norton's cabin. It was just the other three she couldn't quite—

Wait. She and Renee had spotted George coming out of the last cabin and heading toward the main building via a rear walkway that first day . . .

"Okay, so Todd has to be in either number three or number four." Winnie shut off the engine and pointed at Lovey. "There's no rescue to be made. This is just about picking up Mr. Nelson and bringing him back home. So wait here, okay?"

She opened her door, stepped onto the road, and jumped back as Lovey, once again, defied orders by darting out and around the car. "Ugh! *Really? Now?*"

Shoving the door closed, she made her way around the hood of the car and onto the sidewalk that bordered the cabin side of the road. Lovey stopped, waited for her to catch up, and then headed in the direction of the third cabin.

Winnie hung back and split her attention between Lovey's guess and the cabin to her right, searching for any sign of Mr. Nelson. When she came up empty, she shrugged and followed the cat.

A low whistle drew her attention to the last cabin and the familiar face peering out at her from the partially open front door. She lifted her hand in a wave but pulled it back down to her side as he motioned her over.

Curious, she crossed the two makeshift yards between them with Lovey in tow. When she reached the mime's front stoop, he stepped back to allow her room to enter. "Hey, George, what's up?"

"I didn't expect to see you here today. Is everything okay?"

"Everything is fine," she said. "I'm just here to pick up my friend. He's taking a magic lesson from Todd Ritter."

"You mean the old guy with the hearing aids?"

Resisting the urge to fist her hands, she took a deep, cleansing breath. "Mr. Nelson is *seventy-five* and happens to need a little assistance with his hearing. He's also *tall* and *lanky*. But all that really matters is the fact that he has a heart of gold, don't you think?"

A featherlike swish against her leg stole her attention from the mime and redirected it to the patch of linoleum between their feet. "You want a cat?" she asked, pointing at the tabby. "Because you can have this one if you do."

George bent down, scratched Lovey between the ears, and then led Winnie down the short hall and into the cabin's galley kitchen. "I was hoping maybe we could talk."

"Talk?" She looked past him to the digital microwave clock and noted Mr. Nelson's impending pickup time. "I only have a minute or two, but sure, go ahead. What's up?"

He raked a hand through his hair, releasing a sigh as he did. "I thought about what you said this morning and I think you're right."

"About what?"

"That staying quiet isn't always the best option."

She felt her breath hitch. "Meaning?"

"I can't be a hundred percent sure on this because I only caught bits and pieces, but I think I know what Sally had on Todd." George dropped his hand to his face and the stubble that covered his lower jaw and chin. "If I'm right, and word got out, he'd be ruined."

Afraid to move, afraid to react too much, she merely grunted a response to let him know she was listening.

"Now, mind you, this guy is billed as a gifted magician. A lot is made of the fact he can make things appear and disappear in front of an audience of nonblinkers. Me? I don't think he's worthy of the press he gets, but there you go. Anyway, this reputation he has is why his shows sell out everywhere he goes. That, and the fact he's real big into the wow factor. Heck, he even brings a helicopter onstage and makes it"—he used his fingers to simulate air quotes—"*disappear.* But stuff like that costs money—money he didn't have when he was starting out."

"Okay . . ."

"So, from the bits and pieces I picked up during his blackmailing session with Ms. Dearfield, I'm pretty sure he made his start-up money selling drugs. A side job he may very well still have to this day."

She drew back. "And my friend is with this guy now?"

George splayed his hands and shrugged. "I wouldn't worry. He seemed fine when I saw him a little while ago."

"You're probably right." It was a lot to process, but still, she craved more. "And Todd has been able to keep this whole drug-selling thing under wraps this whole time?"

"Well, from everyone except Ms. Dearfield, apparently."

"Who could put him in jail with that information," Winnie mused as much for herself as for George. "Wow. No wonder he was willing to meet her demands."

She wandered into the adjacent parlor that, like the kitchenette, was virtually identical to the one in Colin Norton's cabin. Only instead of fan mail strewn across the simple desk, George's was empty save for a single paperback novel. When she reached the nondescript love seat, she lowered herself onto its narrow cushion and glanced back at George. "Can I ask you a question about that day?"

Hesitation tugged at his features before disappearing behind a determined swipe of his hand. "I never intended for her to kill herself, Winnie. I was just angry. I'd worked my tail off to prove to my old man I could graduate with straight A's and she—*I* messed it up."

"I was referring to the day *Sally* died."

"Oh." He remained in the kitchen but took a seat at the table and summoned Lovey to his side with a snap of his hands. "What do you want to know?"

"Did you see anyone around the teapot besides Sally? Someone who could have slipped the cyanide into that tea?"

"I was late to that little gathering so I couldn't say one way or the other." George ran his hand down Lovey's spine and then hiked his right ankle atop his left knee. "What I can tell you is that when I got there, everyone was drinking something. Yet, not more than a few minutes later, she was the only one who was dead."

Winnie sat with that tidbit as another piece of the puzzle dropped into place. "So the cyanide was added specifically to *her* cup . . ."

"Makes sense to me." George dropped his foot back down to the floor and stood. "I guess I better let you go so you can pick up your friend at Todd's place."

A glance at her watch had her on her feet and headed for the door. "Which cabin is his again?"

"Next door. Number four."

"Number four—got it." She snapped her fingers the way George had and waited for Lovey to follow. Lovey, of course, took her sweet time, stopping to sniff the carpet, the linoleum, the chairs, and the baseboards before heading out into the late-afternoon sunlight. Winnie watched her scamper down the walkway and then turned back to George. "Actually, one more question, if I may. When Renee and I got to the main building that day, we heard voices. Like normal talking. It wasn't until we stepped into the doorway that someone gasped."

"We weren't expecting to see *you*."

She drew back. "So that gasp really was for our benefit?"

He nodded.

"Then you already knew Sally was dead . . ."

"We did."

"Why didn't anyone scream when it happened?" She heard the confusion in her voice and knew it had to be mirrored on her face, as well. "Why didn't you or anyone else pull out their phone and dial 911?"

George leaned into the doorframe and shrugged. "I can't answer that for anyone other than myself."

"And *your* reason?"

"Shock, fear, relief, opportunity . . . Take your pick. They all applied."

She stared at him as she tried to make sense of his words. *"Opportunity?"*

"Sally's death put me back in the driver's seat."

The driver's seat. An odd choice of words but accurate, nonetheless. Without Sally in control of his secret, it was up to George when or if he owned up to his part in his teacher's suicide.

Chapter 26

She waited until Mr. Nelson was settled in his seat, with Lovey atop his lap and his cane at his feet, before she finally spoke, her voice shaky even to her own ears.

"Did . . . did you have fun?"

Turning his chin toward the passenger-side window, he nodded.

"Did you learn any new tricks?"

He shrugged a second, shorter nod.

Winnie maneuvered them around the handful of ruts leading to the main road, the guilt she'd managed to push aside during her sidebar conversation with George resurrecting the lump in her throat and the excessive warmth in her cheeks. "Mr. Nelson, I'm so sorry. I—I wish I had some sort of noble reason why I didn't come to your magic show last night, but I'd have to lie to do so and I'm not built that way. Never have been."

She took advantage of oncoming traffic and her inability

Laura Bradford

to turn right to reach across the seat and rest her hand on his knee in the hope he'd finally look her way. But he didn't.

"As you probably noticed while you were preparing your show, Jay and Caroline came over for dinner and to help me make the desserts for Ty's just-because party." When Mr. Nelson didn't move, she returned her hand to the steering wheel and her eyes to the break in traffic she needed to turn onto the outer road. "And we were all going to come to your show, too."

"So why didn't you?"

Wooden or not, the fact that she'd earned a response of any kind gave her the courage to continue. "And I was looking forward to it. Really."

Slowly, deliberately, he turned, his eyes wide with . . . *disbelief*?

She tried to swallow but it wasn't easy.

"If you ain't built to lie, Winnie Girl, you ain't built to lie."

"Mr. Nelson, I was excited to see your show!"

Hurt muscled its way past disbelief only to vanish momentarily behind pinched eyes. "I heard you and Renee talking after I left. Heard it through the same vents that keep you up with my snoring some nights. I know she was after you about taking on too much. And I know the only reason you agreed to come was 'cause you didn't want to squash my feelings."

"Mr. Nelson, I . . ." Winnie let go of the argument she couldn't win. Mr. Nelson wasn't dumb. "I didn't want to hurt your feelings by turning you down *last night*. It wasn't about not wanting to see your show at all. I like magic. And I suspect I'll like it even more when it's *you* who's doing all that hocus-pocus."

"Real magicians don't say *hocus-pocus*," he groused.

"Sorry. I didn't know." She lifted her face to the breeze caused by the forty-mile-per-hour speed limit and welcomed its tonic for her still-warm face. "Please, Mr. Nelson, you have to believe I wanted to see your show. I just should have asked you to wait until tonight or tomorrow night, instead. Biting off more than I can chew sometimes is a problem I need to work on. Always has been. But even as I say that, I know I could never say no to making desserts for Ty's party . . . or going to dinner with you and Bridget . . . or an invitation to a magic show. I want to do it all. And I fully intended to do it all last night, but considering the evening's players, I should have anticipated things going awry . . ."

She hated that her voice broke, hated even more that the same lump of guilt that had made it difficult to talk off and on over the past several miles, had chosen just that moment to let through a strangled sob.

Shifting his knees left, Mr. Nelson reached inside his pocket and pulled out a two-foot- . . . no, three-foot- . . . no, four-foot-long handkerchief in a rotating rainbow of colors. When he reached the end, he mumbled something about the wrong pocket, stuffed it all back inside, and handed her a standard handkerchief instead.

"I'm sorry, Mr. Nelson." Winnie wiped her eyes quickly and then handed the handkerchief back to her friend. "I really just want to apologize for hurting you last night. That's the last thing I'd ever want to do."

She felt him studying her as she turned left at the four-way stop and then right onto the next street. But he remained silent.

"Please say you forgive me, Mr. Nelson," she pleaded. "Please? I'm truly, truly sorry."

He waved her words away and then rested his hand atop Lovey. "Eh, don't mind me, Winnie Girl. I've just been indulging in a bit of a pity party lately."

"Pity party? Why?"

"I guess I'm finally waking up to my age, the way Bridget is always sayin'."

Slowly, she wound her way past a line of parked cars and then turned left at the next stop sign. "I don't understand."

"Now, I hate to admit this out loud—and I'm gonna trust you won't repeat this—but that old biddy is right." He stopped, wiggled his tongue around his mouth as if he tasted something bitter, and then scratched Lovey beneath her chin. "A person really does become unnecessary when they get old."

She jerked the car to the right and stopped. "Unnecessary? Are you kidding me?"

Lovey yawned, stretched, and stood, her golden eyes canvassing their surroundings. When Winnie didn't move, the cat looked at Mr. Nelson.

"What do I do with my days, Winnie Girl?" Mr. Nelson countered. "I plan my day around a television weather report!"

"You think the weather girl is cute. What's wrong with that?"

He pursed his lips, nodded, and then brought it all to an abrupt stop. "I play chess by myself."

"Because no one wants to lose against you!"

The answering puff of his spindly chest was short-lived. "You can't even walk up the stairs to your apartment without me trying to waylay you with some nonsense."

"That waylaying thing? That's a matter of perspective, Mr. Nelson."

His brows furrowed beneath the frame of the reading glasses he didn't need to be wearing. "You lost me, Winnie Girl."

"Do you really think I bump my foot on that first step *by accident*? Every single time?"

"Some women are just a little clumsier than others. There's no shame in that."

It felt good to laugh. "Oh, Mr. Nelson . . . no one could be that clumsy."

He lowered his chin to see her but lifted it again as she reached across the seat and plucked his glasses from his face. "Are you saying you hit that stair on purpose?"

"It makes sure you hear me, doesn't it?"

"I'd hear anything if I was standing at the door waiting."

The momentary confusion sparked by his words gave way to the kind of tears she wasn't in a rush to hide. "Then I guess you need time with me as much as I need time with you."

"Winnie Girl, you're young. What do you need with an old fool like me?"

"Guidance, understanding, experience, love . . . need I go on?" She rested the side of her head against the seat back and tried to bring her narration in line with the memories playing out in her thoughts. "When I moved here, two years ago, I had no one. It was just me and that bakery. But you welcomed me to this town . . . to Serenity Lane . . . to our home as if I was family. You calmed my nerves on my first day of work, celebrated with me when I didn't mess it up, willingly taste-tested every new recipe I tried, and brought me into your circle of friends without a moment's hesitation. You mean the world to me, Mr. Nelson. I'd be lost without you."

He tried to shake off her words, but there was no denying

the pride that grabbed hold of his demeanor and made him sit up tall. "You have fellas, Winnie Girl."

"If you mean Jay—time will tell. If you mean Greg—he's my friend, yes. But you're the puff of air that sends me on my way each morning and the warm hug that welcomes me back home each and every time I return. There's no replacing that, Mr. Nelson. Not for me, anyway."

"You really mean that, Winnie Girl?"

"I really mean that, Mr. Nelson." She leaned across the seat and whispered a kiss across his weathered cheek. "I love you, Mr. Nelson. You are absolutely, positively *necessary* to me."

He captured her hand inside his own and squeezed it gently until the shine in his eyes disappeared. "I love you, too, Winnie Girl. More than you can ever know."

"Then I'm one very lucky girl." With a quick check of her side mirror, Winnie pulled back onto the road and headed toward Serenity Lane. "So, do I still get a magic show in the near future?"

"If you want magic, I'll give you magic."

She turned right, left, and then right one more time, the sight of the Serenity Lane sign one block over akin to a cold glass of water after a day trekking through the desert. "What do you think of me making some popcorn when we get back and then hanging out on the front porch for a while? Maybe Bridget will be around and she can join us."

"I think that young fella would probably rather have you to himself for a little while."

"Young fella? What young—" She stopped as Mr. Nelson's finger guided her attention off him, through the break in the Rickmans' hedges, and onto the lone figure sitting on the top step of their front porch. *"Jay?"*

"I don't know what happened between you two last night, but I know he's crazy about you, Winnie Girl. It's written all over his face every time he so much as looks at you."

She took advantage of the Rickmans' hedges and pulled the Dessert Squad alongside the curb once again. "How do you know something happened last night?"

"I might not always be the sharpest tack in the box, but I did catch the fact that the daughter was part of the mix. And I heard the hurt in your voice." He stroked the top of Lovey's head but kept his attention on Winnie. "It ain't getting any better, is it?"

Oh, how she wished she could dispute his words with stories to the contrary, but she couldn't. Not even close. So, rather than paint a picture that didn't exist, she merely shook her head. "I thought maybe, after that party we had in the spring, we were poised to make some progress, but it just never happened. She said all the right things to throw Jay off the scent, but her actions haven't matched."

"She'll come around, Winnie Girl. You watch and see."

"You've been saying that since the beginning, Mr. Nelson. About her *and* Lovey. And neither one is showing any sign of"—she simulated air quotes with her fingers—"coming around."

Mr. Nelson stilled his hand midway down Lovey's back. "Why do you think this little lady insists on accompanying you on all your rescues?"

"I don't know—boredom, I guess? Though really all she does is sleep in that seat the way she is on you."

"Something she could do at home with Ms. Ballentine."

"Your point being?" she prodded.

He resumed his petting (much to Lovey's satisfaction). "She accompanies you because she loves you."

Her answering snort echoed around the car, earning her a dirty look from Lovey in the process. "*Love* is not a word I'd use to describe her feelings for me."

"I would. In fact, I'd go so far as to say Lovey is well aware of the fact you're her new owner. But she loved Gertie first and then, one day, Gertie was gone. Maybe she's just protecting her heart, too."

She waited for him to continue, to fill in the blanks left by his words, but he didn't. *"Too?"*

"I've never been a little girl, so I can't say for sure, but I *was* a little boy once. And I can't imagine what it would have been like to have my father or my mother choose a career or a way of life over me. I suspect something like that would have scarred me pretty bad."

Instinctively, her gaze left the elderly man's face and traveled back through the break in the hedges to the house they shared. She hated being a cause of tension in Jay's life. She really did. Yes, she was crazy about him, in love with him, even, but didn't that mean she should want what was best for him?

"I just want him to be happy, Mr. Nelson. The way he was when I met him at the college that first day." At the feel of Mr. Nelson's hand on hers, she pulled her attention back into the car and onto her housemate. "I guess just because he's *my* Mr. Right doesn't mean I'm his."

"Let's hope not." Mr. Nelson smacked his free hand atop his knee and snorted back a laugh. "You said you can't be his Mr. Right—get it?"

Her confusion must have been written all over her face, because he continued. "You're a woman. So you're right, you *can't* be his *Mr.* Right."

She forced herself to smile, to even laugh a little, but her heart wasn't in it. Fortunately, Mr. Nelson didn't seem to notice as he continued to amuse himself with his joke.

Returning her hands to the steering wheel, she checked the side mirror and made the turn onto Serenity Lane. "I think you're right, Mr. Nelson. I think a rain check on that popcorn might be wise. Jay and I need time to talk."

"Mind if I hang on to Lovey while you do?" Mr. Nelson asked. "I sure could use someone to practice my magic on before I do my show for you."

Jay's head popped up as they approached the house. But thanks to the tilt of the late-afternoon sun, she couldn't quite make out his expression.

"Winnie Girl? Did you hear me?"

Had she? She wasn't sure . . .

"Can you say it again?"

"Can I hang on to Lovey while you talk to Jay?"

She turned onto the driveway and rolled to a stop next to the stately pin oak tree. Out of the corner of her eye she could see Jay rise and make his way down the short set of stairs to the walkway below. "Um, yeah, sure. I'm sure she'd love to spend a little time at your place. I—I'll come by and get her when we're done."

"No rush. I enjoy the company." Then, placing his hand atop hers on the gearshift, he squeezed. "The best things in life don't always come the easiest. Remember that, Winnie Girl."

Chapter 27

There was no denying the disappointment that emanated from Jay as she bypassed the cushion beside him to perch atop the ottoman on the opposite side of the coffee table. But she needed strength to do what needed to be done and his nearness would only make that more difficult.

It's like a Band-Aid—just pull . . .

She felt her lower lip begin to tremble and steadied it between her teeth. "Jay, I think we—"

"They say that life-changing events come equipped with souvenirs—images, sensations, even *scents* that linger for years after the actual moment has come and gone." Jay leaned forward, his blue-green eyes studying her face with such intensity, she actually shivered. "And it's true. Even now, sixteen years later, I can still hear Caroline's first cry and feel her newborn skin against my hand."

"I know and that's—"

"Likewise, when I revisit the moment you appeared in

my office doorway with that first cookie, my heart skips a beat just like it did that day. And that smile? I can still feel the edge of my desk inside my hand."

She tried to ignore the sudden tightness in her throat but it was there. "The edge of your desk?"

"I grabbed it to keep from falling out of my chair."

"Jay, I—"

"Don't you see, Winnie? I can still feel that desk in my hand and that skipped beat of my heart because that very moment was one of *my* life-changing events. *You* are one of my life-changing events."

Blinking against the sudden burn in her eyes, she willed herself to stay on track. To yank now and cry later . . . "This isn't going to work, Jay. Not the way it needs to in order for you . . . *and me* . . . to be truly happy."

He reared back as if struck but rebounded to close the gap between them with two long strides. When he reached the ottoman, he lowered himself to its armchair and gathered her hands inside his own. "That's just it, Winnie. I *am* truly happy. *With you.*"

"There's no way that's true." She tried to wriggle free of his grasp, but he held tight. "Your daughter hates me. How can that make you happy?"

"It doesn't. Not even close. But her actions can't change how I feel about you. They just can't." Releasing his hold on one of her hands, he lifted his palm level with her eyes and then closed it against his chest. "Life-changing souvenirs, Winnie. From *you*."

She felt her resolve weakening and willed it to remain firm. "Just because something is life changing doesn't mean it's good. Bad things are life changing, too."

"There's nothing about us that's bad, Winnie. Nothing."

"Okay, but I imagine you can still recall the moment you met Didi, and *that* didn't work out." The words circled around to her ears and made her cringe. "Wow. Look, I shouldn't have said that. It was out of line."

"Why shouldn't you say it? It's fair." He raked his free hand through his hair and then brought it back down to cover hers. "Funny thing is, I've actually thought about that point. Many times. And you know what? I can't recall the moment I met her. I mean, I know where and when, but there's no *wham* moment. And even when I think of the moment Caroline was born, the souvenirs are all about her . . . not her mother.

"Don't you see?" He lifted her hands to his chin. "This is different. Powerful."

"Yet, on a trip you insisted was all about your daughter, you're having pillow fights with your ex-wife, letting her stay in your hotel room, and allowing her to feed you?" This time, when she tried to tug her hands free, he obliged. "C'mon, Jay . . . Something isn't right here. And I, for one, don't want to live my life in someone else's shadow."

"The pillow fight Caroline mentioned wasn't a pillow fight at all. When Caroline got in from some private shopping thing with Didi, she tossed a pillow at me. I tossed it back. That's it. And Didi, being Didi, booked us a suite—with a room for Caroline, a room for me, and a living room in between. Didi fell asleep on Caroline's bed one night. I was in my own room—on the other side of the suite."

She studied him closely, looking for any sign he was massaging the truth, but there was nothing. Still, Caroline had been so smug . . .

"And the green-bean thing my pot-stirring daughter referenced? Didi made mention of the way I used to try and get Caroline to eat the veggies she didn't like as a baby.

Caroline, of course, decided it would be fun to use that tactic on me with the green beans room service failed to cook properly."

"But she made it all sound like . . ." Unable to continue, she simply stopped.

"Like there was something there that isn't," he said. "And hasn't been for sixteen-plus years."

Rising to her feet, she wandered over to the fireplace and the assorted pictures that graced its mantel—Mr. Nelson celebrating a particularly grueling chess game he'd won against himself, Bridget cuddling Lovey, her and Jay sitting on the porch step looking at each other with such joy she had to look away. "*Caroline* is sixteen, Jay."

"You're right, she is."

"But you just said—"

"I know what I said. And if Didi was standing here right now, she'd tell you the same thing." Jay scooted forward on the chair but remained seated. "Within a few weeks of getting married, we knew we'd made a mistake. We were just way too different in everything from likes and dislikes, to life goals. But instead of being honest with each other and ourselves, we decided to solve the issue with a baby. All that did, of course, was hold off the inevitable a little longer."

"Does Caroline know this?"

"No. And Didi and I promised each other she never would." Pushing off the chair, Jay stood. "I believe there's a reason for everything. The reason Didi and I got married when we were the most ill-suited people on the face of the earth was so Caroline could be born. It's the only thing that makes sense.

"Likewise, the only reason I placed an order for a cookie I really didn't need back in March was so I could meet you."

Laura Bradford

She ran her hand along the edge of the mantel and then wiped off the dust on the side of her jeans. "So you—as head of Silver Lake College's business department—could check out the crazy new business in town."

His laughter grew closer until he was within arm's reach—a reach he used to pull her close. "I thought that was the reason. But the moment I laid eyes on you, I knew it was much, much more than that."

Taking advantage of the cover afforded by his chest, she permitted a single tear to fall from each eye before she stepped back. "I don't want you being pulled between your daughter and me."

"Winnie, it's only a matter of time before she sees how awesome you are."

"She doesn't *want* to like me, Jay. Don't you see that?"

"Tough."

For the first time since she spotted him through the Rickmans' hedges, she found herself getting angry. And while she tried to keep it in check, she knew she wouldn't be able to hide it completely. "So? What? You force me on her? Make her come over here for dinner and to bake? Because, let's be honest, that was so successful, wasn't it?"

"Then what do we do?" he asked as he lifted their picture off the mantel and turned it toward her. "Because *this* right *here*? It's too special, too one of a kind to end. For *any* reason."

Her eyes drifted down to the picture, to the way he looked at her and the way she looked at him . . .

Jay was right.

There had to be a way.

"Mr. Nelson says we need to give it time," she said, her voice barely more than a whisper.

The faintest hint of a smile played at the corners of his

250

mouth. "I always knew he was a smart man. Now I know he's the smartest."

"The smartest, eh?"

"Well, next to me, of course."

She smiled through the tears that no longer gave a hoot about coverage. *"You?"*

"I ordered that cookie, didn't I?" He returned the frame to the mantel and then pulled her close once again, his breath warm against her forehead. "We'll get through this, Winnie. I promise."

She held her final wave for as long as it took Jay's car to reach the end of Serenity Lane and then backed away from the window, the emotional roller coaster that had been their time together leaving her in a pretty good place.

Were things solved? Not necessarily. But knowing that she meant as much to Jay as Jay meant to her certainly helped. At least in the spirits department.

The vibration of her phone against the top of the kitchen table nixed all further thoughts of Jay and replaced them, instead, with an image of her next-door neighbor, thanks to the picture app she'd found during one of her more recent sleepless nights.

"Hi, Bridget."

"I know what Abby's secret is."

"Are you serious?" With the help of her toe, Winnie nudged the bench back from the table and sat down. "How?"

"I got the voice mail you left when you were on your way back to Renee's to pick up Lovey." Bridget let loose a few audible winces but stayed on point. "I was finishing up my column and couldn't break my concentration."

"I understand."

"Anyway . . . *ohhhh, ohhhh* . . ."

"Bridget? Are you okay?"

"I—I'm fine, dear. My back is simply protesting the grocery bag I carried in while you and Parker were out doing whatever it is you were doing together this afternoon."

Uh-oh . . .

"I thought about reaching out to you when the pain became too much, but . . . I didn't want to interrupt your time together . . . or the bite to eat you must have stopped to have . . ."

Grateful for the exterior walls and the side yard that separated them, Winnie dropped her head onto the table and tried not to sigh directly into the phone. "Mr. Nelson had another magic lesson at the retreat center this afternoon and I was his ride home."

All moans of pain ceased. "No meal was involved?"

"No meal was involved."

"You came straight home?"

She considered mentioning the pair of curbside chats along the way, but decided it was best to keep those to herself. "Yes."

"Oh."

"Is there something I can do to help you with your back?" she asked.

"Wouldn't you know, the pain has subsided, dear. But I'll let you know if that changes. Anyway, after I listened to your message confirming the whole blackmail thing, I decided to do a little digging of my own."

"On the computer?"

"Partly. That gave me the questions to ask when she was sitting across from me at my desk."

Winnie lifted her head. "You had her in your office? How?"

"Under the guise of an article about her puppetry, of course."

Of course . . .

"I noticed, during the prep work I did before her arrival, that much of the attention she's garnered was born on the exquisite detail of her puppets—puppets she claims to have designed herself—and the vibrant stories they tell. Yet when I had her here and started asking specifics about her process, it became clear to me she was full of hooey."

"I don't understand."

"During the fall semester of Abby's last year at Charlton, she studied abroad. In Salzburg. While she was there, she ventured off one weekend to a small, economically challenged outlying town. There, she met a man named Mohsen Bietak, a grocer who reminded her of her grandfather. The two struck up a friendship during the months Abby was in Salzburg and she came to learn of his penchant for woodworking. When she told him of her dream to be a puppeteer, he surprised her with a marionette he'd made. Better yet, he used that marionette to tell her the kind of stories that stick with a person . . . the same *exact* stories that have put her on the marionette map in this country."

"Surely she's given him credit all this time, yes?"

"Mohsen Bietak's name has never come up in even one of Abby's interviews . . . until now. And only because I figured it out myself."

Winnie shivered despite the July temperatures that warmed her apartment to almost saunalike status. "Tell me you didn't confront her, Bridget . . ."

"I can't, dear."

"Can't confront her or can't tell me you didn't?"

"I'm a newswoman. Of course I confronted her."

"*Alone?*" she snapped.

"It's a Saturday, dear. The paper only runs on a skeleton crew."

"So someone else was there . . ."

"In the bowels of the building, perhaps." Bridget yawned in Winnie's ear and then followed it up with a dramatic stretch. "But danger is part of the job."

Winnie tapped her fist on the table's edge in frustration and stood, her destination as much about peace of mind as anything else. When she reached the window that afforded a view of her neighbor's parlor, she willed the light shining through the partially drawn curtains and the voice in her ear to ease the sudden knot in her chest. "Did she get angry when you confronted her?"

"No, she cried like a little girl who'd been caught with her hand in the cookie jar."

She cried . . .

"I take it this will destroy her career?"

"Destroy? Probably not. She could have the greatest stories in the world at her disposal and still make them fall flat if her puppetry skills weren't good. But they are. And she needs to see that as enough."

"Doesn't sound like a motive to kill someone," she mused.

"I agree, dear. But *someone* had one."

Winnie took one last look at Bridget's house and then wandered back across the kitchen toward Lovey's empty food dish. "Does she have any idea what Sally was holding over the poet or the comedian?"

"No. But she's willing to help so she can go home."

She continued over to the floor vent and listened. No snoring.

"Winnie?"

"I'm still here." She listened one more time and then headed for the front door. "She could just tell the cops herself. Unleash *them* on the whole blackmail angle . . ."

"She doesn't want her secret getting out before she can tell her parents, face-to-face."

"Ahhh, and she can't tell them face-to-face until the killer is found and the rest of them are cleared to leave Silver Lake." With one hand on the phone and the other on the railing, Winnie descended the stairs and stopped outside Mr. Nelson's door. "Did she have any ideas on how she might be able to help us?"

"As a matter of fact, she does. And it involves a very specific window of opportunity."

Winnie knocked once, twice, and then dropped her hand to her side. "Care to share?"

"How does access to the master key sound?"

The smile that normally accompanied the telltale sound of Mr. Nelson and his cane froze midway across her face. "*Master key*? To *what*?"

"The cabins."

The thumping stopped just as her heart began to pound. "*Which* cabins?"

"All five of them, dear."

Chapter 28

They were barely out of the driveway the next day when Renee let out the kind of squeal that might have netted some unwanted attention if 90 percent of the people on Serenity Lane weren't either hard of hearing or napping. "I don't know about you, Winnie, but I'm feeling all Thelma and Louise right now, aren't you?"

A cough from the backseat drew Renee's eyes to the rearview mirror and a hint of red to her otherwise tanned cheeks. "Oh. Right. Sorry about that, Bridget. I'm feeling all Thelma, Louise, and . . . Nancy Drew."

"Aw, c'mon, can't *I* be Nancy? *Please*?" Winnie stole a glance at Bridget through the split between Renee's front seats and then waved the semiserious question away before her neighbor could even respond. "I still can't believe we're doing this. Breaking and entering is a crime."

"Only if we get caught, dear." Bridget pulled a notepad from her oversized purse and flipped it open to the first page.

"Which we won't. And besides, it's not really breaking and entering if you have a key. Which we do."

"A key only one of them knows we have." Winnie swung her gaze back onto the road before fixing it on the woman behind the wheel. "You sure you're okay with all of this? Leaving Ty with Mr. Nelson? Letting us drag you into something none of us should be doing in the first place? And using your car while we do it?"

Renee turned left at a four-way stop and then right at the next street. "Do you know what I had planned for the day before you called? Laundry. Smelly ten-year-old soccer boy laundry. So, really, getting to do something that will allow me to inhale without gagging is a welcome surprise."

"Glad we could help." Winnie pointed out the next direction and then, realizing Renee knew how to get to their final destination, dropped her hand back to her lap. "Based on what Bridget is telling me, we have a very specific amount of time to work with, so I think it makes the most sense for us each to take a cabin. If we come across something we think is important, we'll ring each other's cell phones."

The sound of turning pages drew Winnie's attention to the backseat occupant once again. "Does that sound good to you, Bridget?"

"I'm thinking, if we stick together, we can go through each cabin faster and without the worry of having to stop and call every time something looks remotely interesting."

"That makes sense. We'll do it that way, then."

Renee slowed to allow a pedestrian to cross the street and then returned her attention to the rearview mirror. "So whose cabin are we going to check out first? The hunky mime's?"

"Winnie has already vetted him, and I've already vetted the puppeteer, so the focus is on the other three."

The squeal was back. "Vetted? Oooh, this sounds so official, doesn't it?"

"No, *official* would have us driving a police car and wearing blue," Winnie pointed out, only half joking.

Renee, in turn, dropped her chin to her chest to allow a quick self-inspection and then returned her attention to the road in time to make the necessary turn onto the outer road. "I figured black was best for being discreet."

"And your choice of footwear?" Bridget challenged.

"I opted for my three-inch stilettos instead of the four-inch. They're easier to run in if that becomes necessary."

Bridget leaned forward as if she were going to tie her shoe but, instead, used the opportunity to roll her eyes and make a face outside the watchful eye of the driver. When she caught Winnie staring, she merely shrugged and returned to her original starting place.

"Anyway, let's go over what we know so far." Winnie stopped, held her index finger in the air, and cocked her head toward the floor. Sure enough, her phone was vibrating inside her purse. "One second, ladies . . ."

She glanced at the screen and felt the smile that raced across her mouth in response. "Hi, Jay."

"Hi, yourself. Did you sleep well last night?"

"Hardly." Then, realizing how that could be misconstrued in light of their ongoing situation, she rushed to clarify. "I'm just helping Bridget with a little problem."

She didn't need to turn around to know at least one of Bridget's eyebrows had shot upward.

"Anything I can help with?" he asked.

"No, I think we'll be fine." The turnoff to the retreat center was growing closer by the minute but still, she wasn't ready to say good-bye. "So, um, what are you doing today? Anything fun?"

"The big interview is supposedly going to run on this evening's installment of *Hollywood Tonight*. Caroline will be glued to the television, waiting for her mother's segment, I'm sure." And then, after a momentary hesitation, he continued. "You could come, too. I'd love that, actually."

"Jay, I—"

"No, hear me out. We could sit in the kitchen and talk while she's waiting for the interview. When it comes on, we could either watch it with her or stay in the kitchen and keep talking. Makes no difference to me."

"Thanks, but I think you should probably watch it with her. And besides, I kind of owe Mr. Nelson a magic show."

"A magic . . ." His voice disappeared for a moment only to return in between groans. "Oh no. We blew that off on Friday night, didn't we?"

"We sure did."

"Oh, Winnie, I'm so sorry. We got so sidetracked with Caroline's antics that I lost sight of everything else. Was he upset?"

"He was. But we talked and he's forgiven me. However, I promised him when I dropped off Lovey this morning, that I would be front and center for his magic show at eight o'clock this evening."

"Ready to be amazed and dazzled," Renee interjected.

Winnie laughed. "That's right, I promised I'd be front and center *and* ready to be amazed and dazzled at eight o'clock this evening."

"That didn't sound like Bridget just now."

"Because it wasn't. That was Renee. She, too, will be

attending tonight's evening of magic with her dapper young man, Ty."

"And Bridget?"

She peeked over the seat at Bridget and simply waited for her answer.

"I'll be there. But I won't clap."

Jay's laugh tickled Winnie's ear and reignited her smile once again. "I heard that."

"She'll clap. Somehow, someway, I'll make her clap."

"Good luck with that one." The sound of his breath in her ear warmed her all the way down to her toes. And when he spoke again, it was as if his words provided the hug she craved more than anything at that moment. "Anyway, I don't want to ruin all your girl time by keeping you on the phone too long, but if you find yourself with a little time on your hands at any point between now and the magic show, give me a call, okay?"

"I will." She shifted the phone to her opposite hand and peered out at the passing scenery. "I'm really glad you called, Jay."

"Good, because I've been thinking about you since I woke up."

"Oh? That's nice to hear." And it was. Even though she knew Jay had feelings for her, and had for several months, it never hurt to get verbal confirmation. "I'll talk to you later."

When she was sure the call had ended, she leaned over, shoved the phone back into her purse, and straightened in her seat, the smile she felt on her lips reaching deep inside her soul.

"So I take it you two talked things out?" Renee asked.

"Last night. We still have an uphill climb where Caroline

is concerned, but we're going to climb it together." She felt the car slow as the turnoff for the retreat center came into view, igniting a fresh new set of nerves and the shiver that accompanied them. "Bridget, are you absolutely *sure* they all went to Beans for breakfast?"

"Abby confirmed it via text message not more than ten minutes ago. She said the shuttle bus driver had just dropped them off and that he said he'd be back to get them at one thirty."

Winnie directed all eyes to the dashboard clock as Renee navigated the first rut in the retreat center's driveway. "Okay, so that means we have two hours, tops. If we can find what we need to find in *half* that time, even better."

Winnie was rooting through a stack of magazines in Ned's sitting room when Bridget let out a yelp from the cabin's modest bedroom.

"Bridget?"

"I found something!"

Dropping last year's issue of *Modern Art* back into the misshapen basket at her feet, she met up with Renee in the hallway and, together, they headed down the short hall and into the lone bedroom.

"He caused an accident." Bridget shook a sheet of cream-colored paper at them. "And he ran."

Winnie inched around Renee and crossed to the edge of the bed where her view of Bridget and the piece of paper was better. "What are you talking about? And what is that?"

"Blackmail, exhibit A. I found it between the box spring and the mattress." Bridget lifted her gaze to the ceiling and muttered something under her breath.

"What was that you just said?" Winnie asked.

"I called Mr. Masterson a bloody fool."

"Because . . ."

"Because anybody who has ever written in a diary knows about that hiding place."

Renee plopped on the edge of the bed closest to the door, nodding as she did. "She's right. It's where I kept my diary when I was a kid."

Bridget waved the paper at Winnie. "See? It's as I said—he's a bloody fool."

"Can I see it?" Winnie asked.

"It's why I called you in here, dear." Bridget handed the paper to Winnie and then removed her glasses from her nose for a quick eye rub. "Read it out loud, so Renee can hear, too."

"Okay, sure." She took a moment to soak in the details—the standard-looking, albeit cream-colored printer paper, the standard type font, the crease marks left behind by its initial trifolded status—and then began to read aloud.

"Eh, eh, eh, not so fast, Hit-and-Run Man. Your nightmare isn't over yet. Same terms, same consequence still apply. So if you want to keep running from what you did to Caleb Norton all those years ago—"

Winnie returned to the name, read it aloud again, and then looked up to find Bridget's forehead scrunched in thought. "Caleb *Norton*? Do you think that's a coincidence?"

"I don't know, but I'm sure we can find out."

Renee placed her hands above the bed and then pointed their attention back to the letter in Winnie's hands. "Don't stop reading."

"Uh, okay . . ." Pushing the name from the forefront of her thoughts, Winnie searched for her veer-off point and continued reading. *"Put the cash in this envelope and place it inside the third book from the right on the middle shelf of the Quiet Room. Make sure it's there by midnight. If you do, your secret will be safe. If you don't . . ."*

The bed squeaked as Renee leaned forward, eyes wide. "Don't stop! Don't stop! It's getting really good!"

"That's all there is."

Renee turned to Bridget. "But she didn't finish the sentence. I want to know what's gonna happen if he doesn't put the money in the . . ." Raising her hands in surrender, Renee shook her head. "Okay, I'm an idiot. She left it that way to make him squirm."

Winnie looked again at the letter, the first three sentences confirming her gut reaction in a most unsettling way. *"Eh, eh, eh, not so fast, Hit-and-Run Man. Your nightmare isn't over yet. Same terms, same consequence still apply . . .* Sally didn't write this. Someone else did."

"What do you mean, some—"

"You're right!" Bridget snatched the letter from Winnie's trembling hands and read it aloud again. When she reached the end, she looked up at Winnie. "Someone took over where Sally left off, continuing the blackmail she started."

Renee pushed off the bed and came to stand beside Winnie. "Okay, but who?"

"Her *killer*," Winnie and Bridget said in unison.

Chapter 29

"Well, it looks like our poet isn't versed in diary stashing the way Ned . . ." Winnie stopped, narrowed her eyes on the open refrigerator, and cleared her throat loud enough to halt the verbal inventory being conducted by her stiletto-wearing friend. "What on earth do you think you're doing?"

Clearly startled, Renee stumbled backward, the clicking of her shoes against the linoleum floor dulled only by the slam of the refrigerator door. "Um, searching? Like we're supposed to be?"

Winnie folded her arms across her chest. "In the refrigerator?"

Some hemming and hawing ensued before Renee regained her composure. "Are you going to tell me you never hid anything in the crisper drawer when you were a little kid?"

"The crisper drawer?" She pulled out her phone, checked

her empty message box, and then shoved it back into her pocket. "C'mon, fess up. What were you really doing in there, Renee?"

Another, more amusing round of hemming and hawing quickly culminated in a wounded exhale and a defeated slump to the woman's bare shoulders. "Okay, okay, I was checking in the utensil drawer when I heard a funny sound."

Her smile exited her face. "What kind of funny sound?"

"My stomach. So I thought I'd just check and see if maybe there was something I could snack on before we head back to your place."

"No!"

Renee pulled her hand off the refrigerator door and let it drop to her side. "You know, you can be a real spoilsport sometimes, Winnie Johnson."

"I know. It's a gift," she said while scanning the limited counter to the left and right of the microwave. "So nothing in here, either?"

"Nope. All clear." The click-clack of Renee's shoes grew louder as the gap between the two friends lessened. When she reached the table where Winnie was standing, Renee pulled out a chair and sat down. "So you really think this person the comedian hit is related to the guy staying here?"

"They share the same last name . . ."

"That doesn't necessarily mean anything." Renee ran her hand along the top of the table, stopping every few inches to add a beat to whatever song was suddenly playing in her head. "I'm sure there are lots of Nortons running around the country."

"True. But if they *are* related and Colin somehow over-heard whatever went down between Sally and Ned, we may have just found a motive for Blackmailer Number Two. Although, it seems that if he's the killer, he'd have killed Ned instead of Sally." Winnie turned and made her way into the parlor. To her left was the single armchair Lovey had hid under just days earlier—a maneuver that had earned the tabby a can of tuna fish later that evening. To her right, atop the simple yet adequate desk, was the same stack of fan mail that had intrigued her earlier in the week. "While I wouldn't trade what I do for anything, it's gotta be awfully cool to get fan mail, you know? I mean, what better validation can there be?"

"Okay, so you don't get letters in the mailbox," Renee said during a break in her mental song. "But you do get numbers."

She paused her hand on the top envelope. "*Numbers*? *What* numbers?"

"The ones on the scales. Of your satisfied customers."

"Oh, so you're saying I make people fat?"

"You make people *happy*," Renee corrected.

"Happy. I can live with that." Winnie checked her watch and then her phone but there was still no word from Bridget. "Renee? Would you mind heading over to the magician's cabin and checking on Bridget? I still think it was smart that we split these last two cabins after how much time we spent in the other one, but she hasn't sent so much as one text in the last fifteen minutes and I'm getting a little worried. All we have left in here is this parlor and I think I can handle that myself."

Renee stopped tapping, shrugged, and stood. "Yeah. Sure. No problem. Meet you outside in ten minutes?"

"Sure. Sounds good. And, Renee?"

Renee stopped, her hand on the door. "Yeah?"

"Stay out of the refrigerator, will you?"

"Spoilsport."

And then Renee was gone, the click of the door in her wake barely noticeable over the sound of Winnie's own laughter. She allowed herself another chuckle or two and then turned her attention to the stack of letters she was powerless to resist.

Intrigued, she lifted the top envelope from the stack, flipped it over, and removed the yellowed paper from inside. With careful fingers, she unfolded the paper and began to read, her mouth draining of all moisture as the letter she'd expected to read turned into a heartfelt, beautifully written poem about a scarred woman who lived her life behind a mask. At the bottom of the page, with the same pencil that had been used on the rest of the poem, was a single name—*Caleb.*

She set the poem to the side and reached for the next envelope on the stack. This one, too, showed signs of age—yellowing around the edges, turned-up corners, even a smudge of dirt on the left side. The paper inside was also yellowed with age, the penciled writing faded. She switched on the desk lamp and began to read, the vivid, rhythmic description of the mountainous journey it shared leaving her breathless.

When she reached the last line, she skipped her gaze down to the single name written exactly as it had been on the first poem.

Caleb.

Winnie dropped the mountain-themed poem onto the desk and pulled her phone from her pocket. Maybe Renee was right. Maybe Norton wasn't a terribly uncommon surname. But the likelihood the name Caleb would just so

happen to show up on two poems in Colin Norton's possession couldn't be a coincidence, could it?

There's only one way to find out . . .

Tapping her phone to life, she punched in her password
and then clicked on her favorite search engine. With fingers
that were suddenly far more clumsy than normal, she typed
in the words *Caleb Norton* and *hit-and-run* and pressed
Enter.

Less than a second later, a half-dozen links popped up.

Charlton School of the Arts alum victim of hit-and-run.

Caleb Norton, 22, in a coma after hit-and-run.

No witnesses in hit-and-run of Charlton alum.

Slowly she scrolled through the remaining links tied to
the initial details of the tragedy. When she reached the end,
she went back to the top and clicked on the first link.

"Charlton School of the Arts alumnus, Caleb Norton,
was the victim of a hit-and-run on Piney Street Friday night.
Caleb was in town visiting his brother, Colin, a current
Charlton student."

According to the article, the incident was not witnessed
and the driver had not stepped forward as of the date the
article was written.

She read all the way to the bottom and was rewarded for
her efforts with an update posted nearly a year after the
initial incident.

"**Update: Caleb Norton remains in a comma with no
brain function. The hit-and-run driver remains at large."

"Actually, he's here . . . in Silver Lake," she whispered.
She closed out of the link and clicked on the next, the basics
of the tragedy the same. Only here, Caleb Norton's name
was highlighted in blue, indicating a link. She clicked.

Like magic, the Charlton School of the Arts website appeared on her screen with "In Memoriam" displayed across the top of the page in quiet, tasteful letters. She took a moment to really soak up the young face peering out at her from her screen—the quiet smile and inquisitive eyes a perfect match for someone who could write like he had and like his brother—

"I was going back and forth between a piece about a mountain and another about a mask, but now that the audition is no longer at play, I will turn my efforts toward submitting both for publication."

The words ricocheted inside her head with such force, she grabbed the corner of the desk for support.

"A *mask*?" she whispered. "A *mountain*?"

No . . .

Shaking the ludicrous thought from her head, she found her way back to the alumni page and the bio on Colin Norton she'd first read while bleary-eyed from lack of sleep. Somehow, she'd managed to retain most of it—the awards, the publications, et cetera. But the part about his gift for poetry not revealing itself until after graduation? That part she'd missed.

She scrolled back up to Colin's picture, his face exhibiting none of the qualities his brother's had. In fact, where Caleb had exuded quiet wonder, Colin exuded an edge that could best be described as angry . . .

Her phone vibrated in her hand, alerting her to a new message from Renee.

We found something. Meet you outside.

She typed back a reply.

So did I. Be there in 2.

Once she was sure the message had been sent, she deposited her phone back into her pocket and turned her attention to Caleb's poems. She hated placing them back inside their envelopes, but for now that's where they needed to be. Still, as she returned them to the pile, she couldn't resist the urge to soak up one more.

Confident in her ability to read quickly, Winnie reached deeper into the pile and pulled, the cream-colored page that followed wiping any remaining thoughts of poetry from her head once and for all.

Chapter 30

There was no mistaking the utter silence in the car as they passed the retreat center's van, or the subsequent sigh of relief as Renee turned onto the outer road and pushed down on the gas pedal.

"Oh! My! Gosh! That was so close."

Winnie took one last look in her side-view mirror and then sank back against the passenger seat. "That was *too* close, Renee. Much, *much* too close."

"You said you'd be out in two. What happened?"

She tried to gather her thoughts enough to answer but was thwarted by heavy breathing from the backseat. Alarmed, she pivoted her upper body until she had a clear view of her elderly neighbor. "Bridget? Are you okay?"

"I'm fine, dear. Just a little winded is all."

"Is your chest hurting?" Winnie asked.

"No."

"Your knees from having to run like that?"

"No."

"Your back?"

"No, I'm fine." Then, after smoothing her carefully selected sleuthing attire (her words), the eighty-year-old broke out in a face-splitting grin. "I haven't had that much fun in years, dear."

Renee laughed. "I think I have to agree."

"You guys are nuts." Winnie looked from Bridget to Renee and back again before joining in the laughter. "I don't know how you can run in stilettos, Renee, I really don't."

"That, my friend, is *my* gift." Renee hit the buttons associated with their respective windows and lowered them enough to let air flow through. "Well, that and *eating*, unfortunately."

"You were pretty adept at identifying that green stuff I found in Todd's top hat."

Winnie shifted her gaze off Renee and back on to Bridget. "Green stuff?"

"Our magician appears to dabble in far more than just bunny rabbits, Winnie." Renee slowed at the entrance to the lake, pulled into the public lot, and claimed a parking spot beneath a large shady tree. When the car was in park and the engine shut off, she turned herself sideways in her seat. "Bridget found drugs in this guy's top hat."

Winnie released her seat belt and turned sideways in her seat, as well. "Did you find anything else?"

"Anything else?" Bridget lowered her chin to allow a clear view of Winnie across the upper rim of her glasses. "Don't you think a stash of drugs is enough? Perhaps it's his secret."

"It *is* his secret."

When Winnie became aware that Renee was staring at

her as well, she held up her hands in surrender. "Okay, okay, I guess I forgot to mention that our magician dabbles in a little drug dealing on the side."

"Yes . . . yes, you did indeed forget to mention that, dear." Bridget slipped her hand inside her tote bag and pulled out her favorite notebook. "When did you find this out?"

"Yesterday. When I picked up Mr. Nelson from his magic lesson."

"Did Mr. Nelson see it while he was there?" Renee asked.

A group of hikers making their way across the parking lot to their car distracted Winnie for a moment, but with a little prodding from Renee, she got back on track. "No, George told me. He overheard bits and pieces of Sally's blackmailing session with Todd."

"He could go to jail for that."

She nodded at Renee. "And Sally, of course, knew that."

"So why did we waste time going through his cabin if you already knew his secret?" Bridget asked, her voice a touch huffy.

"In case George was wrong, I guess." Slipping her hand behind her back, she fixed her fingers on the sheet of paper sticking out of her back pocket—a sheet of paper, in hindsight, she probably shouldn't have taken. "Did you happen to find anything else?"

"Such as?"

Winnie pulled the paper out of her pocket and brandished it high enough for Bridget to see. "One of these."

"What is—"

Bridget leaned forward, her hushed gasp cutting off Renee. "I thought you put that back under Mr. Masterson's mattress!"

"I did."

"Is that why your two minutes turned into ten? Because you went back to the comedian's cabin?" Renee asked.

Winnie shook the paper in time with her head. "This isn't *his*. It's Colin's."

Bridget's eyes widened as the meaning behind Winnie's words hit their mark. "The blackmailer?"

"Listen." Slowly, she unfolded the cream-colored paper across her lap and began to read, the words as they left her mouth sending a fresh new chill down her spine. *"Eh, eh, eh, not so fast, Mr. Plagiarizer."*

"Plagiarizer?" Bridget echoed.

Winnie held up her finger and continued reading. *"Your nightmare isn't over yet. Same terms, same consequence still apply. So if you want to keep hiding behind Caleb's talent—"*

"There's that name again . . ."

Bridged shushed Renee and then motioned for Winnie to keep going.

"Put the cash in this envelope and place it under the printer in the Business Center. Make sure it's there by midnight. If you do, your secret will be safe. If you don't . . ." She refolded the paper and looked up.

"That's *it*?" At Winnie's answering nod, Renee groaned in frustration. "Enough with the cliff-hangers, already."

Bridget mumbled something about blondes under her breath and then brought the focus back to the letter's earlier content. "What do you think that plagiarizing comment meant?"

"Caleb Norton is Colin's brother. According to what I found on my phone, he was critically injured in a hit-and-run accident while visiting Colin during his time at Charlton. He's been in a vegetative state ever since."

"Oh, how awful!"

Bridget stalled all further commentary from Renee with a raised index finger. "And Ned Masterson, the comedian, was that driver, wasn't he?"

"Based on what we found under Ned's mattress, it sure looks that way. Anyway, near as I can figure, the poems that have earned Colin such recognition were actually written by his brother before the accident."

It was Bridget's turn to retract in horror. "He's been prospering off his brain-dead brother?"

"Again"—she said, lifting the letter into the air—"it sure looks that way."

"Wow." Bridget looked down at the still-unopened notebook in her lap and then returned it to her purse, clucking softly to herself as she did. "I wish I could say for certain that Todd didn't have one of those, but the moment I found those drugs in his top hat, I stopped searching."

Winnie leaned her head against the partially open window, her own groan not much different from Renee's. "I probably would have stopped, too."

"We still have the master key, don't we?" Renee asked.

Bridget tapped her finger to her chin. "She has a point, dear."

"I don't know, you guys. We came awfully close to getting caught just now."

"True. But we know what we're looking for now," Bridget insisted. "And if we make sure Renee is fed before we leave that should move things along even faster"

Winnie willed her lips to keep from twitching as Renee's cheeks reddened. "I thought I told you to stay out of Todd's refrigerator."

"I was *hungry*." Renee gestured toward her stomach and

the gurgle of agreement it unleashed in the car. "And now, because of you and your silly rules, I'm *ravenous*."

R enee reached into the bag of pretzels, made a face, and then shoved it across the table toward Winnie. "This is empty."

"It wasn't when you found it in my pantry." Winnie swung her legs over the bench and returned to the assortment of snacks she'd spread across the island. "We still have some chips. You want those?"

"Want? Yes. Need? No. Besides, you're still planning on making those special donuts for Mr. Nelson's show tonight, aren't you?"

"I am, which reminds me I probably should start on those now."

"You do realize, dear, what this encouragement of yours is going to do, don't you?" Bridget tossed her notebook onto the coffee table and inched her way forward on the couch. "It'll be like it was after you bought him that book of pranks. Suddenly there were whoopee cushions on my rocking chair, fake rodents on your stairs, and toothpaste in my Oreos."

Renee let loose a half laugh/half snort. "Mr. Nelson put toothpaste in your Oreos?"

"He did, indeed." Bridget sniffed, then pointed her finger into the kitchen. "Thanks to Winnie."

"What? I bought him a prank book . . . He *loved* it." Winnie, in turn, pointed at the open snack bags and, at the answering shake of Renee's head, attached chip clips where needed and returned everything to the pantry. "And, you've gotta admit, he got a lot of mileage out of that book."

"Too much mileage, if you ask me," Bridget groused. "And now you're encouraging him with this magic stuff?"

Winnie crossed to the baking cabinet and quickly located the various ingredients she needed for Mr. Nelson's surprise. "If it makes him happy, Bridget, what difference does it make? Besides, he's only had two lessons. I don't think he's going to be trying to saw anyone in half just yet."

"I wouldn't be so sure about that, dear."

Chapter 31

Winnie lowered herself onto her folding chair and pointed at the RESERVED sign stretched across the pair of seats on the opposite side of Renee's. "Since when do a magician and his assistant sit down during the show?" she whispered.

"They don't." Renee double- and triple-checked the settings on her point-and-shoot camera and then smiled up at the makeshift stage (aka Winnie's front porch) and the table Mr. Nelson had cleared of his latest chess game in preparation for his first performance. "I wasn't supposed to peek, but I couldn't help it. Mr. Nelson has Ty in a cape and top hat. I have no idea where he got it, but it looks positively adorable on him."

Winnie leaned around Renee to get a better look at the sign, but other than the one word—RESERVED—there was nothing. "Okay, weird . . ."

"I don't know why you're so surprised, dear." Bridget

crossed and uncrossed her ankles only to cross them once again. "We are talking about Parker, are we not? When does he do anything exactly the way you expect?"

Winnie stopped herself mid-nod out of respect to Mr. Nelson while trying hard not to anger her next-door neighbor in the process. It was a tightrope act for sure, but she'd gotten fairly good at it over the past two years. "I just don't understand where those two chairs came from. I put out three—one for me, one for you, and one for proud mamma over here."

The slam of a car door stole her focus from the pair of empty chairs and shifted it, instead, to two male figures headed in their direction. "Who on earth is—"

"Oooh, Master Sergeant Hottie is here." Bridget dug her elbow into Winnie's side and followed it up with a Lovey-like hiss in her ear. "Quick, dear! Move one of those chairs next to me!"

She guided the woman's elbow away from her rib cage and stood. "Greg, hi! I didn't know Mr. Nelson . . ." The words floated away like the last of the day's natural light and she steadied herself against the edge of her chair. "Y-you're Todd, aren't you? From the retreat center. The magician."

"I am." Todd extended his hand to hers and then did the same with first Renee, and then Bridget. "Parker invited me to come check out his show, and Greg here was nice enough to play chauffeur so I could come. I hope you don't mind."

Winnie was pretty sure she responded with something appropriate to the conversation, but she wasn't entirely sure. Because try as she could to envision the man standing in front of her as a drug dealer, something just didn't mesh. Then again, when your world was primarily made up of baked goods and people over seventy, how would she know one way or the other?

"Winnie?"

The sound of her name snapped her back to the moment and the handsome, yet familiar face studying her as Bridget's voice yammered on to her left. "Parker was very specific about where he wanted Winnie to sit for his show. And as the chairs are arranged right now, Renee is front and center, not Winnie. However, if you move your chair over here to my other side, Gregory, Winnie will be where she promised to be."

"You good with that, Winnie?" Greg asked, eyeing her curiously.

"Uh, yeah, sure . . ."

She tried to shake the fog that seemed to roll in the moment she saw Todd, but when she wasn't sure what was causing it, she wasn't sure how to make it stop.

Fortunately for her, the moment Greg's chair touched down in its new location, Ty appeared on the porch with his hands stretched wide. "Ladies and gentleman and"—his smile widened—"Mom . . . I'm proud to present the amazing *Mr. Nelson*!"

Ty waited for their applause to die down and then, with a grin eerily similar to his mother's when a bag of chips was opened, pointed toward the front door and the top hat–wearing man now caning his way onto the porch with an even bigger smile on his face.

And, just like that, whatever fog Todd had ushered in with his arrival faded as Winnie focused on her special friend.

"Tonight, I will surprise you, amaze you, and leave you

wondering what's real, and what's not," Mr. Nelson said. "So sit back and enjoy."

Stepping behind the table, he took off his hat, handed it to Ty, and asked the boy to inspect it closely. Ty obliged and then, at Todd's silent prompting, showed it to the audience before placing it back atop the tablecloth.

Then, placing a black cloth across the top of the hat, Mr. Nelson stepped back and accepted his wand from Ty. "Abracadabra, alakazam!"

"*Abracadabra?*" Bridget whispered. "Oh, please . . ."

"Shhh . . ." Winnie and Greg whispered in unison.

After a moment, Mr. Nelson placed a hand over his mouth and whispered (not so quietly) to Ty to remove the cloth. When the cloth was gone, Mr. Nelson reached into the hat and pulled out . . . an egg.

Winnie looked from Mr. Nelson, to the egg, and back again, the surprise she felt mirrored on the elderly man's face.

"It worked," he whispered (not so quietly) to Ty.

A soft laugh from two chairs over pulled her attention off the duo on the porch and fixed it, instead, on Todd, the man's smile reigniting her own as she joined in the applause.

With each subsequent drape of the cloth and each new flick of the wand, new things appeared inside the hat—a rook from Mr. Nelson's chessboard, a crumpled napkin, and even a grape. Each new trick was met with applause from the audience and stunned surprise from Mr. Nelson and his assistant.

After the sixth or seventh time, Mr. Nelson whispered (for real, this time) something in Ty's ear. Then, while Ty inched his way closer to the table, Mr. Nelson clapped his hands together. "If you think you have seen it all, you haven't." Draping the black square across the top of the hat once again, Mr. Nelson shielded his eyes from the glare of the porch light and looked out at the chairs. "Winnie Girl? This one is for you."

He held the wand over the cloth-draped hat and, once again, said his magic words. "Abracadabra, alakazam. Who needs a bunny when you can have a . . . *Lovey!*"

With a flick of his wrist, off came the black cloth. Only instead of a smile, Mr. Nelson's shoulders sank.

"Try it again, Mr. Nelson," Ty urged.

Shrugging, the man covered the hat a second time, waved his wand, and said the magic words. "Abracadabra, alakazam. Who needs a bunny when you can have—"

"Meow . . ."

Lovey ran out from underneath the tablecloth and then stopped to lick her hindquarters.

Ty broke the ensuing silence by gesturing toward the floor and yelling, "Ta-da!"

Again Todd's soft laugh peppered the air just before he led the latest round of applause. Mr. Nelson blinked, looked from Lovey to the hat and back again, and then placed the hat back on his head and held it in place as he bowed.

When the applause subsided, Mr. Nelson pointed to a clear plastic cup on the left side of his table and asked Renee to join him on the porch. Renee, in turn, shoved the camera into Winnie's hand and ran up the steps.

Ty handed his mother the cup and asked her to tell the audience what was inside.

"It appears to be water."

"It *is* water, Mom," Ty said, covering his mouth with his hand. "You can even take a sip if you want."

Renee just smiled.

"You can take a sip, Mom," Ty whispered.

"Oh. Good. I'm a little thirsty." Renee lifted the glass to her mouth and took a quick sip.

"Now, tell the audience what your very favorite color is."

Renee smiled out at Winnie. "Yellow."

"Yellow?" Ty echoed. "I thought it was pink. All girls like pink."

"I like yellow."

Ty's face fell. "Can you just say it's pink for now?"

"Oh. Sure. My favorite color is pink."

"Pink it is!" With one hand on his cane and the other in his pocket, Mr. Nelson caned his way over to Renee. Pulling his hand from his pocket, he placed it on her shoulder, while directing her gaze toward a passing car. When all eyes returned to Renee, she was staring down at her cup, a look of wonder on her face. "It's—*it's pink*! My water is pink! H-how did you do that? I was holding it the whole time!"

"Magic, Ms. Ballentine."

Magic . . .

"Wait. Magic?" Winnie heard Greg's distinctive applause peppered by a slightly more reluctant version from Bridget, but it paled against the sudden, yet equally distinctive thumping in her ears.

"I was holding it the whole time."

Yet, somehow, someway, when no one was paying attention, Mr. Nelson had managed to slip something into Renee's drink that altered its color . . .

A trick he learned from—

"It was *you*!" Bridget struggled to her feet and pointed at the man staring up at Mr. Nelson from the other end of the row. "*You* killed her!"

Winnie stood up so fast, her chair toppled over backward against the trunk of the pin oak. "Greg, call the cops. Tell them we have Sally Dearfield's killer."

"Sally Dearfield's killer?" Mr. Nelson looked left and then right, confusion guiding his attention back to Winnie and Bridget. "Where?"

"Right there." She pointed at Todd, who was now staring back at her in stunned confusion. "That trick he taught you . . . that's how he poisoned Sally's tea!"

Greg handed his phone to Bridget, crossed in front of Winnie, and pulled Todd up and out of his seat. "You, my friend, are in a whole lot of trouble."

"Stop right there!" Mr. Nelson stamped the porch floor with the end of his cane and, when all eyes were firmly on his, he stamped it again. "Todd didn't teach me that trick! The mime did!"

Somehow, Winnie managed to convince Greg to hold off calling the cops until they were on the retreat grounds. And she'd managed to pull that off only by allowing him to come along. The occupants in Greg's backseat, however, were another story all on their own.

Bridget, of course, had made the case that she'd been part of the investigation from the start—a claim Winnie had been unable to refute.

Mr. Nelson had chosen to go the sympathy route, pointing to all the times he'd wanted to help only to be pushed off to the side like unwanted trash (his words). The fact that he identified the killer (accidentally, of course) and made sure to reference that time and time again, didn't hurt his cause. It also didn't hurt that Greg had taken a shine toward the former (and somewhat crusty) navy man.

Lovey, too, had made the cut because, well, she wasn't about giving Winnie choices.

And Todd, well, he needed a ride back to the retreat center . . .

It was ludicrous really. But then again, so was the guilt she felt over having to leave Renee behind on account of it being a school night for Ty.

"Renee just texted," Bridget announced from her spot behind Greg. "She wants to know if you might consider putting her on something called FaceTime so she can be part of this?"

"Uh, no. I plan to be a little too busy for that."

"*I* can do it, dear."

Winnie met Greg's eye across the center console and then looked back at the road, the turn for the retreat center now no more than fifty feet ahead. "No, Bridget. You're going to wait in the car with Greg and everyone else."

Greg stopped in the middle of the road.

"The turn is up there," Winnie said, pointing just ahead and to the left.

"I know where it is, Winnie. I also know I'm not waiting in the car while you accuse this dude of killing someone. That wasn't part of the deal when I agreed to bring you out here, remember?"

"Okay, okay." The car lurched forward as Winnie addressed the man seated next to Bridget. "I have to admit I'm a little surprised that you're as gung ho about George's impending arrest as you seem to be, Todd. Surely you have to know your secret is going to come out."

Todd exhaled against his palm and then let it drift back down to his lap. "If it does, it does. I just can't sit idly by while someone uses magic for evil."

"But you're looking at jail time, too."

"Jail time?" he echoed. "Where'd you get that?"

"Selling drugs is illegal, Mr. Ritter."

He stared at Bridget. "Selling *drugs*? I'm not selling drugs!"

"I saw a bag of it in your top hat earlier today," Bridget insisted.

The horror on Todd's face was undeniable. "That's impossible!"

And then she knew. George had planted the drugs. To cover his own tracks. Assuming she was right, though, Todd still had to have a secret he didn't want getting out . . .

"So what did Sally have on you?" she asked as Greg's car made its way around the last of the known ruts and headed toward the line of cabins.

"I sold a trick that belonged to another magician."

Mr. Nelson shook himself out of his late-evening fog. "But you said that's against the magician's code."

"Because it is," Todd said.

"You said that could get you ousted from the world of magic."

"Because it can, and it likely will. But this—what George did with magic . . . it can't go unchecked, Parker. Not now, not ever."

Silence fell over the backseat as Winnie pointed to George's cabin. "It's the last one, over there."

Greg pulled alongside the curb, shifted the car into park, and dialed the Silver Lake Police Department. When the phone began to ring, he relayed the necessary details to the dispatcher as the pieces of the puzzle that had been there all along returned for an encore.

"If she'd known how little I'd been making before I got here, she could have saved herself the postage stamp she used to entice me up here in the first place . . ."

"Shock, fear, relief, opportunity. Take your pick. They all applied . . ."

"Sally's death put me back in the driver's seat . . ."

"I can't believe I was so blind. So quick to believe he'd been forthright because he had nothing to hide," Winnie said aloud. "But in reality, he'd been forthright because he had everything to hide. And I bought into it."

"We have him now, dear. That's all that matters."

Bridget was right. Still, she couldn't help but feel as if she should have figured it out sooner. Maybe even when he first told her about his—

"According to the note they found next to her body, she simply couldn't bear to live without him . . ."

She sucked in a breath as her heart began to race. "Greg? If Sally had been alone and a suicide note had been left by her body, would it have automatically been ruled as that? Especially if she were going through all sorts of family problems?"

"If we saw no reason to think otherwise, sure. Why?"

"Because I'm not so sure Sally is the only person George Watkins killed." Winnie shook her head and then turned again to Greg, the phone now back in his pocket. "Are we good to go?"

"We're good to go."

She met him on the walkway leading up to George's cabin as the whir of sirens kicked up in the distance. When they reached the door, she knocked, the sound of his footsteps, juxtaposed against the strengthening wails of the approaching police cars, impossible to miss.

The door swung open and George stepped out, his smile at the sight of Winnie slipping behind an emotionless mask as Greg stepped into view.

"Do you hear that, George?" She pointed toward the road and the comeuppance that was no more than a half mile away. "They're coming for you."

Chapter 32

Renee perused the selection of chocolate-covered strawberries, helped herself to the one with the best strawberry-to-chocolate ratio, and then pointed it at Winnie. "You do realize my son is even more in love with you than ever now, right?"

"*Ty*? In love with *me*?" Winnie arranged the donuts across the center of the platter and then stepped back to inspect her creation. "Why?"

"Not only do you make the"—Renee widened her eyes in a near-perfect mimic of her son—"coolest desserts ever . . . and have the coolest cat ever . . . and live on the coolest street ever, now you're apparently a real-life superhero, too."

"Wait. Ty thinks *Serenity Lane* is the coolest street ever?"

At Renee's nod, Winnie pumped her hand in the air in celebration. "Yes, my work here is done." She dropped her hand back down to the counter, rearranged the cinnamon sugar donuts against the white powdered donuts and then reached for the napkins she'd bought specifically for the occasion—even if it was a day late. "Though, between you and me, I don't get his fascination with me."

"I do."

Jay's arms snaked around her midsection and pulled her close, his breath against the back of her head sending shivers of excitement along every nerve ending in her body.

"Does he know yet?" Jay asked. "About the donuts?"

"He's about to." She snuck a peek toward the living room and smiled at the sight of Mr. Nelson on the couch with Lovey in his lap and Caroline at his side. Her housemate was trying desperately to make the teenager smile, and thanks to his newfound ability in magic and the coin he'd managed to locate behind her ear, he was actually succeeding a little.

"I'm sorry about the interview. I can only imagine how much that must have hurt Caroline."

"So you saw it, then?" he asked.

Renee polished off her carefully selected strawberry and then started another search. "I pulled it up on the computer between rescues today. It was painful to watch. I mean, not only did the Hollywood Hag neglect to mention she *has* a daughter, she made it sound as if the very notion of children is something almost beneath her."

"Because it is." Jay reached around Winnie for a strawberry and, when Winnie waved his find away from her mouth, he popped it in his own. "In hindsight, everything Didi did with Caroline when we were there happened behind the scenes where no one could see—they ate in private dining rooms, did in-home manicures, watched movies in Didi's house, shopped from selections Didi had delivered to the hotel, et cetera, et cetera. All tucked away where no one would see. I should have realized what was going on and I should have called her out on it right then and there."

"Then *you* would have been the bad guy," Renee said. "This way, as painful as it was—and likely still is—for Caroline, it's all on Didi. Where it *belongs*."

Winnie glanced back at the couch and the even wider smile that was now on Caroline's face. "I really love that man, you know? He's got a light that has a way of touching everyone."

"Sounds like someone else I know."

"If only that were true," she whispered.

"Caroline *asked* if she could come with me tonight." Jay kissed her on the temple and then released his hold on Winnie. "Maybe Mr. Nelson is right. Maybe she will come around in time."

Winnie took a moment to steady her breath and then lifted the platter of donuts off the table.

"You want me to record this?" he asked.

She started to say no but stopped herself. As much as she enjoyed living in the moment and cherishing it for what it was, there was going to come a time when memories were all she had of some of the most important people in her life. "Sure. Thanks."

As they approached the couch, Ty, who was seated on Caroline's other side, popped his head up and smiled at Winnie. She winked back at him and stopped in front of Mr. Nelson. "Mr. Nelson? Last night I made a special treat to coincide with your magic show. Unfortunately, things didn't go quite the way I'd planned. So . . . I made a new batch this afternoon. For us to eat after your second magic show."

"*Second* magic show?" Mr. Nelson asked.

"The one *we*"—she guided his eyes around the room with her chin—"want you to put on for all of us, this evening. Assuming, of course, you wouldn't mind."

"Mind?" With loving, gentle hands, he scooped Lovey off his lap and deposited her onto Caroline's. Then, grabbing hold of his cane, he scooted forward on the couch. "Why, I think I can pull together a show if Ty, here, is willing to help . . ."

"Yes! Yes!" Ty jumped off the couch and headed for the door.

Mr. Nelson followed at a slightly slower, but no less determined clip. When he got to the door, however, he turned and retraced his steps all the way back to his starting point.

"So what are you calling these, Winnie Girl?" he asked, helping himself to a handful of donuts.

"Now You See 'Em, Now You Don-uts."

Recipes

Your Jokes Make Me
Snicker-Doodle (Cookies)

1 cup shortening
1½ cups sugar
2 eggs
2¾ cups sifted flour (all-purpose)
1 teaspoon baking soda
2 teaspoons cream of tartar
½ teaspoon salt
2 tablespoons sugar
2 teaspoons ground cinnamon

Preheat oven to 375 degrees. Grease cookie pans.

1. In a medium-sized bowl, cream together the shortening
   and sugar. Add each egg, mixing after each one.

2. In a separate bowl, sift together flour, baking soda, cream of tartar, and salt. Stir into creamed mixture.

3. In a smaller bowl, stir together the 2 tablespoons of sugar with the cinnamon.

4. Roll the dough into balls, then roll in bowl with sugar mixture.

5. Place cookies on prepared cookie pan, about 2 inches apart.

6. Bake for 8–10 minutes. Cool on wire racks.

Now You See 'Em, Now You Don-Uts (Maple Glazed)

For donuts:
2 cups all-purpose baking mix
¼ cup sugar
⅔ cup milk
1 egg (beat lightly)
1 tablespoon vanilla extract

For maple glaze:
¼ cup butter
½ cup brown sugar
3 tablespoons milk
1 tablespoon corn syrup
2 teaspoons maple extract
2 cups powdered sugar

Preheat oven to 325 degrees.

1. Spray mini donut pan with nonstick cooking spray.

2. Mix all donut (not glaze) ingredients in medium bowl until well blended. Spoon approximately 1 tablespoon of batter for each donut into prepared pan.

3. Bake 10–12 minutes.

4. Meanwhile, it's time to make your maple glaze. In a small pan, combine butter and brown sugar. Whisk in milk and cook for about 5 minutes (medium heat). Continue stirring until butter is melted and sugar is dissolved.

5. Remove from heat and add in corn syrup and maple extract. Add in powdered sugar a little at a time—whisking smooth after each addition. You can add another teaspoon or two of milk if needed. Once all powdered sugar has been added, keep the glaze warm on the stove (whisk on occasion).

6. When donuts are done (toothpick inserted in center should come out clean), remove from pan and immediately coat in glaze. Let cool on a wire rack. Be aware the glazed donuts may drip as they cool, so place rack on a sheet of waxed paper to minimize mess.

Ready to find
your next great read?

Let us help.

Visit prh.com/nextread